THE SAGEBRUSH REBELLION

PASSPORT TO DANGER

◆

The Secret of the Mezuzah

The Sagebrush Rebellion

THE
SAGEBRUSH
REBELLION

MARY
REEVES
BELL

BETHANY HOUSE PUBLISHERS
MINNEAPOLIS, MINNESOTA 55438

The Sagebrush Rebellion
Copyright © 1999
Mary Reeves Bell

Cover illustration by Cheri Bladholm
Cover design by Lookout Design Group, Inc.

This book is a work of fiction. Although many of the landmarks described do exist in the Wind River Canyon area of Wyoming, the Walker Ranch itself is fictional. All characters, organizations, and events are the product of the author's imagination, and any resemblance to people living or dead is coincidental.

Published by Bethany House Publishers
A Ministry of Bethany Fellowship International
11400 Hampshire Avenue South
Minneapolis, Minnesota 55438
www.bethanyhouse.com

Printed in the United States of America by
Bethany Press International, Minneapolis, Minnesota 55438

Library of Congress Cataloging-in-Publication Data

Bell, Mary Reeves, 1946–
    The sagebrush rebellion / by Mary Reeves Bell.
      p. cm. — (Passport to danger ; bk. 2)
    SUMMARY: Con flies from his home in Austria to his grandparents' ranch in Wyoming where he spends the summer trying to save the family's old home from unknown saboteurs.
    ISBN 1–55661–550–7
    [1. Grandparents Fiction. 2. Ranch life—Wyoming Fiction.
3. Wyoming Fiction.] I. Title. II. Series: Bell, Mary Reeves, 1946–
Passport to danger ; bk. 2.
PZ7.B41155 Sag   1999
—dc21   99–6554
                                             CIP

For my parents, Harold and Violet Reeves,
who blessed me with their faithful lives
and kept for us our own "perpetual place."

And for Mary, Alisa, Kristen, Anna, Theresa,
Catherine, Gabrielle, Eugene, Robert, and Wesley—
the cousins—who gave to it "custom and ceremony."

Special thanks to Robert and Wesley,
my sons and in-house editors;
to Alisa Engnell and Deb Perry
for their early suggestions on the text;
and to Gabrielle Reeves for allowing me
to include her poem "Crackle."

MARY REEVES BELL grew up on a cattle ranch in Wyoming. As an adult, she spent several years in Austria, where she studied Hebrew and Holocaust literature at the University of Vienna. Mary frequently travels to Romania, where she works with abandoned children. She and her husband, David, have three sons and four grandchildren and currently live in Virginia.

CONTENTS

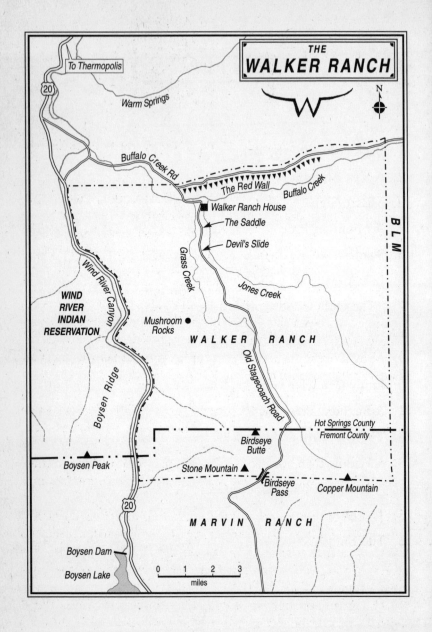

THE
WALKER RANCH

N

To Thermopolis

20

Warm Springs

Buffalo Creek Rd

The Red Wall

Buffalo Creek

■ Walker Ranch House

← The Saddle

← Devil's Slide

Grass Creek

Jones Creek

WIND
RIVER
INDIAN
RESERVATION

Wind River Canyon

Mushroom ●
Rocks

W A L K E R   R A N C H

Old Stagecoach Road

Boysen Ridge

Hot Springs County
Fremont County

▲ Birdseye
Butte

Boysen Peak ▲

Stone Mountain ▲

Birdseye
Pass

Copper Mountain ▲

20

M A R V I N   R A N C H

Boysen Dam

Boysen Lake

0   1   2   3
miles

B
L
M

BACK HOME ON THE RANGE

"ARE YOU LISTENING TO ME, CON?" MOM ASKED, HER VOICE rising with impatience. "Please pay attention."

Actually, I wasn't exactly paying attention because I had stopped breathing. There in front of my eyes, on the front page of the June 1 early edition of the *Vienna Zeitung*, was a picture of my old friend Hans Grunwald—aka "Dirty Harry"—under the bold headline "Neo-Nazi Terrorists Convicted." Stunned, I dropped my backpack—heavy with things I had packed for my long plane trip—and picked up the newspaper. Noisy crowds of people heading for their early morning flights at Schwechat Airport went on around me, but I ceased to see or hear them. I stared openmouthed at the headline.

"Stop murdering the flies, boy," my stepfather, Nigel, said as he reached over and closed my mouth with a tap under the chin.

"Breathe, Con. You're turning white," Mom added in that offhanded way she has about really important things—like my health.

"Look at this," I said, finally inhaling and thrusting the newspaper at Mom. Nigel and Hannah leaned close to see. It was their turn to stare at the picture of Dirty Harry and the one of Hannah and me taken last October as we came out of the police station in Zürich.

The picture brought it all back: the bombing of Simon Wiesenthal's office, the day in court when Hannah and I had testified against the terrorists who had kidnapped us . . .

For a moment it was as if we were back in that boat, tied and gagged, with Dirty Harry spitting out his hatred at me for outsmarting him in front of his fellow thugs, promising to come back and kill me—and he would have if Nigel hadn't helped the police find us first.

" 'Three terrorists were convicted yesterday for last fall's attempted murder of local Nazi hunter Simon Wiesenthal and the kidnapping of two American teenagers in Zürich,' " Mom read aloud while we looked over her shoulder. " 'The three men will be transferred next month to the maximum security prison in Berlin. Each will serve fifteen-year sentences, which some are already calling too severe.' "

"Too severe?" I shouted. "For bombing, for attempted murder, for kidnapping? It should've been life."

Hannah kept staring at the paper after Mom finished reading. Her face was pale, and her beautiful dark eyes looked scared. Hannah was my best friend, and my silly scheme to chase spies last year had nearly gotten us both killed. Now the whole story was plastered on the front page of the newspaper, bringing it all back with a thud. And I felt guilty again about how those thugs had treated her. How they had hated her for being Jewish.

"I'm sorry, Hannah," I mumbled, knowing I couldn't erase the memory of what they had done to her. "At least they'll be in a *maximum* security prison," I went on, trying to reassure her and myself. "Which hopefully means the kind of prison that's hard to get out of. . . . I mean, I wonder how often people *do* escape from a maximum security prison."

"Not often," Nigel said, his face clouded. "But that isn't what worries me—"

"What do you mean?" I interrupted.

"It's the transfer to Berlin that I'm concerned about. There are plenty of places along the way for their well-trained fellow neo-Nazis to attempt a rescue."

"Nigel!" Mom exclaimed. "How can you say that?"

"Sorry, Roberta," he said, looking sheepish. "Just thinking out loud. I'm sure nothing will happen. Anyway, Con is going to be out of Austria for three months. And by then these men will be safely imprisoned—with the key thrown away."

Good for me, I thought. *But what about Hannah?*

She was still staring at the picture. "Hannah . . ." I tried again. "Say something. Are you okay? What are you thinking?"

"I'm thinking," she finally said, tossing her curly black hair back from her face and blowing off her concern, "that in fifteen years when they get out of prison, we will be thirty and too old to care. I'm also thinking you *really* need a haircut. Con, your grandparents will confuse you with one of the other cousins. And if we don't hurry up, you are going to miss your plane."

"Very funny," I said. "No one has ever mistaken *me* for a girl."

It broke the tension, and Mom offered a tiny little laugh. Nigel picked up my bag, and we resumed our way to the ticket counter.

A chime meant to get your attention before an important announcement echoed in the cavernous Schwechat Airport terminal.

"Austrian Airlines flight 324 nonstop to New York is now ready for boarding at gate area C." The disembodied voice repeated this announcement in German and French, followed by more chimes.

Crowds of people pushing, pulling, and carrying luggage made their way toward the door marked C. A perky attendant in a dark red suit was steering a mother with two small, crying children around to the front of a growing crush of people eager to board.

"Oh brother, I hope I'm not sitting next to crying babies," I said miserably. Too excited to sleep last night, I was hoping to catch up on the long flight across the Atlantic. I had spent every summer of my whole fifteen years of life in Wyoming with my six girl cousins on my grandparents' cattle ranch. I couldn't wait to get there. And best of all, I was traveling alone. Mom and my new dad, Nigel, would follow in August.

The only downside was that I wouldn't see Hannah again

for three months. We had been through a lot this year, and I was going to miss her.

I kept remembering things I needed to tell her, but Mom was interrupting me with the same set of instructions she had given me last night, on the way to the airport, and a dozen other times.

"Yo, Con. Your mom's talking to you."

Mom smiled appreciatively at Hannah and kept talking as she handed me my ticket, which I put safely in the inner pocket of my worn leather flight jacket. Even that small reach set my muscles off again. My whole upper body was sore from lifting weights last night. I had been planning on getting fit for the ranch and putting on some weight so people would stop saying how "tall and thin Con is getting" every time they see me. Except I had started the body building a little late, and working out last night had only made me miserable, not huge.

"I'm counting on you, Con," Mom continued to give me directions. "You have to help your grandfather this summer. I'm worried about him. He has never regained strength since his heart attack last winter, and now stupid Yeats falls down on him and your grandfather breaks his leg."

"It's not Yeats' fault," I protested.

"Yeats?" Hannah asked, totally confused.

"Yeats," I explained, "is Grandpa's horse. He stepped in a prairie-dog hole a month ago, and Grandpa went flying over his head, breaking several bones and puncturing his lungs. But my grandpa is tough as nails. He'll get over it. Don't worry so much, Mom. It's not like you."

"But he's *not* getting over it," she continued to worry. "And there are so many things going wrong right now. It's not natural. Problems seem to be multiplying faster than the cattle at the moment."

"Like what?" Hannah asked.

"Well, like too many cattle dying and disappearing, fences cut, mix-ups with the cow trader, the bank . . . all kinds of things. I think someone may be trying to take advantage of the fact that he is weak and unable to look after the ranch right now.

There are people who would like to destroy Whit Walker and the old Walker Ranch."

I had heard this stuff before, and I thought Mom was really exaggerating. In fact, I thought she had gone a little off her rails on this one. But Hannah was either interested or being polite.

"Who would want to ruin them?" she asked.

Encouraged by Hannah's interest, Mom continued. "Chief Running Wolf might. He's the old, practically ancient, leader of the Shoshoni and Arapaho tribes. Walker Ranch shares a border with the Wind River Reservation, and there have been . . . well, disputes over the years."

"Whoa. Hold it," Hannah, who was from New York City and unfamiliar with Western life, stopped her. "This sounds like movie stuff, cowboys and Indians battling over old feuds."

"Yeah, it does a little," Mom said sheepishly. "But it may be partially true. Chief Running Wolf is not a bad guy—in fact, he is a legend around there for being a wise leader. He's been fighting for the rights of his people for decades. Quite a colorful character, Hannah. I wish you could see him. He has these long, snow white braids that come down to his waist. He used to be friends with the Walkers, but years ago something happened. He had some differences with my father. Now some of the younger men of the tribe might still want revenge."

"Oh, please, Mom," I said, adding my expert opinion. "If anyone is out to get Grandpa, it would be those weird neighbors, Fred and Lilly Marvin."

"Well, they would love to get their hands on his BLM grazing leases, that's for sure," Mom agreed. "But would they actually use force to try to ruin him? I just don't know. I can't see Fred Marvin out in the dead of night cutting fences and killing cattle."

"What's a BLM lease?" Hannah asked.

Mom seemed glad for the chance to talk about it and explained how the BLM, the Bureau of Land Management, administers land owned by the federal government. In 1936 the Taylor Grazing Act gave ranchers and farmers the right to lease for life any government land adjoining their own property.

"So the Walker Ranch has the right to run their cattle on all those thousands of acres of wilderness land as long as they pay up and do not misuse the land?" Nigel asked.

"Right," Mom said. "And BLM leases can make or break a big ranch. Including ours."

"Fred Marvin couldn't push Grandpa or Gran around," I said upon reflection. "Not for all the BLM leases in Wyoming. I've seen Fred and his silly wife, Lilly. Come on, Mom. They aren't a threat to anyone but themselves. It couldn't be them. And why would Chief Running Wolf want to hurt us? I never heard about any problem between the tribes and Grandpa."

"Well . . ." Mom hesitated. "It's a long story. I don't know all of it. Something happened a long time ago. I do know that the tribal leaders, and the old chief in particular, probably wouldn't be unhappy to see the ranch fail."

"Oh, Roberta," Nigel said, "that sounds a little farfetched, don't you think? The Indians out to get the cowboys? As Hannah said, rather like an old John Wayne movie."

Mom smiled weakly at him. "I know it sounds silly, Nigel, but I really am worried. Maybe I should go now with Con, and you can come in August."

I couldn't believe my ears, and Nigel didn't look too happy, either. My own father had been killed before I was born, and Mom and I had lived alone until she married Nigel last year. In fact, we had spent every summer together at the ranch. But I liked the idea of traveling alone this time and didn't want her changing her mind now.

"Oh, please, Mom. The plane leaves in half an hour. Get over it. Everything will be fine! You're imagining things."

Actually, my Mom wasn't a worrier, and it wasn't like her to be so melodramatic, imagining bogeymen out to get the Walker Ranch.

The chimes went off again, followed by another announcement. This time it was a final boarding call. I glanced at the door and through the glass wall toward the mammoth 747. Most people heading for New York with me had already left the terminal and were making their way across the tarmac and up the steps of the plane. I looked back at Hannah's dark, watchful eyes and hoped they looked misty.

She was wearing a hooded white sweat shirt with a tiny emblem of our American International School. Her hair fell to her shoulders and into the hood.

"I am counting on you, Con," Mom went on. "On the other hand, don't do anything stupid. Oh, I wish I were going with you—"

"Chill, Mom," I interrupted the worried flow. "Besides, you and Dad will be there by August, and everything will probably be back to normal at the ranch by then." I removed my hand from her too-tight grip and picked up my backpack. "I'll be careful. I'll be good. And I'll be helpful, I promise."

Mom hugged me good-bye and smiled for the first time all morning. "I'll be glad for two out of the three," she said, more like her usual sarcastic self. "Have fun. Be careful. And be your grandfather's eyes and ears until he gets better."

Nigel gave me a pat on the back and reminded me I had promised him a good time when he arrived with Mom later in the summer. I was slowly getting used to calling Nigel Dad and was definitely looking forward to introducing him to the cousins and showing him Wyoming.

"Tough as Wyoming winters" is how Mom usually referred to her parents, but her concern for them now was real. And contrary to what she might think, while I had been looking at Hannah, I had heard her.

Hannah had sensed the serious nature of Mom's instructions, too, and said, "Sounds like you're in for trouble again, Con. Sure you can manage without me this time?"

Her good-bye hug was brief, and before I could reply she slipped me a note. "Read it on the plane and look for me on the observation deck." Then she moved away through the crowd without looking back.

I slipped the note safely into my pocket, along with my ticket and the slim leatherbound book of poetry Mom was sending Grandpa, then boarded the plane. Fortunately, my seat had a window on the left-hand side of the plane, so I could see the terminal and Hannah. She was there on the observation deck in the cool morning mist, leaning over the railing and waving occasionally, her hair blowing around her face. I watched while we took off as Hannah became a smaller and smaller white speck fading finally into the blur of runways, buildings, and then the airport itself, which receded into a small gray patch among the sea of spring green in the woods and farms below. As the plane banked over Vienna, I could see the cathedral spires of St. Stephens lit by the morning light, and a rabbit warren of building rooftops in the old city that stretched up toward the Vienna Woods from the Danube River.

"Whoopeee!" I exclaimed—fairly quietly for me—and ignored the stares of my fellow travelers. I was glad to be leaving the boring old city for the Wild West. In my mind's eye, I could see the miles of sagebrush-covered prairie, the red rock cliffs that rimmed the canyon where our ranch house has stood since 1875, and Grandpa's beautiful black Angus cattle grazing everywhere. I could almost smell the earthy odor of hundreds of cattle moving together over the land, kicking up dust mixed with the smell of crushed sagebrush. The vast empty space of Wyoming, peaceful and unchanged. I was going home for the summer. Home with my grandparents and all the aunts, uncles, and cousins. It seemed too good to be true, except that Hannah wouldn't be there. Remembering her note, I took it out.

The small folded piece of paper looked as if it had been written in a hurry. It was on Austrian Airlines paper—probably mooched off an attendant while I had checked in.

Dear Con:

Wish I could go with you. You have made the ranch sound like the most wonderful place in the world. Enjoy your wild places where the deer and antelope play and terrorists are not seen all day. Wish I could have joined you on the flight. We would have had fun playing cards and bothering the flight attendant for food and Cokes. I will call you someday if my mom lets me. Vienna will be really boring and lonely for the next three months without you—no spies to chase, no bad guys to escape from, no stupid schemes of yours to get us into trou-

ble. Don't do anything silly without me there to rescue you. Ha. Just kidding. Have fun. See you in September. Email me. Oops, I forgot to ask. Do you have email at the ranch? Well, send smoke signals or something.

Hannah

Email at the ranch. She must be kidding, I thought, smiling. Gran was still getting used to the answering machine. But I rather liked the part about her being lonely.

And despite being unable to shake off a little nagging sense that Mom might know or have guessed something she hadn't told me about troubles at the ranch, I ran my finger over the "Flying W" brand I had burned into the leather on my backpack strap and fell asleep dreaming of the welcome-home chocolate cake Gran would have waiting for me on the other side of the Atlantic.

◆

"Thermopolis will be the first stop on our flight number 917 to Cody, Wyoming, this afternoon. You folks just buckle up and enjoy the flight. We'll be arriving in Thermopolis at about five P.M. Expect some turbulence as we turn north and west across the mountains . . . nothin' much to worry about. Hang on, and thanks for flying Rocky Mountain Express."

It was twelve hours and several cultural zones since I had said good-bye in Vienna. The neat landscape of Europe had given way to the jagged Rocky Mountains below. The pilot's Western drawl and the line of cowboy hats in front of me on the small prop job meant I was nearing the end of my trip. Some kids only have to go across the street to get to their grandma's house. For me it was a little more complicated and a whole lot longer.

"Did he say 'hang on'?"

The question came from across the aisle. I turned to see a boy slightly older than me. Despite his marine haircut and muscular frame bulging through a Utah State sweat shirt, there was fear in his eyes not disguised by a very tight smile. I looked at him and hoped my feeble efforts at beefing up and a summer of work on the ranch would turn my tall, thin frame into such an imposing hulk.

"You betcha. It gets mighty rough up here," I answered in my best Westernese.

"How rough?"

"Well . . ." I toyed with the idea of scaring someone who could clearly clean my clock if he chose, but in the end I decided against it. "Don't worry . . . it usually isn't much," I assured him in a calming sort of way.

The expected turbulence hit about thirty minutes later. I noticed "Muscles" wasn't enjoying the bucking ride. In fact, he looked like he might be sick any minute. I decided to take pity.

"Hi." I reached my hand across the aisle. "I'm Con, and don't worry . . . I've been on this thing lots of times. It always does this on late-afternoon flights about here. Something about the hot air rising over the mountains and forming thunderheads."

"I know what causes turbulence," he snapped testily, ignoring my offer of a handshake.

"Okay, man. Just trying to help," I said, noticing that his hand continued to grip the armrest as if it were a life vest.

The small plane rolled in the rough air. Six single seats lined each side of the pencil-shaped airplane. A real no-frills flight, no snacks, no rest rooms, no flight attendant. No place to be sick.

Thud. The plane hit a big air pocket and took a particularly nasty drop. I bumped my head on the roof of the plane and let out a small shout of glee.

"You actually like this, don't you?" the stranger inquired through clenched teeth.

I nodded. The poor guy was looking more pale with each jolt, but in an effort to be cool he managed to pry one of his hands loose and offer it to me.

"I'm Jed, and I *don't* like it. You must be crazy."

"People have suggested the possibility." I grinned, shaking his hand. "And yes, I do like it. It's kind of like riding a horse that hasn't been broken. Only you're much less apt to get hurt in this thing." Not that I had actually broken any horses, but I had certainly watched Grandpa and his hired men do it.

Jed didn't question my credentials or look convinced about the safety of the aircraft.

"Do you live in Wyoming?" I asked him, not because I cared much but to pass the time.

"Nope. Never been here before, and I don't like it already. You don't sound like you're from around here, either."

I couldn't understand what he meant by that. I didn't think I had an accent at all—despite the teasing of my cousins to the contrary.

Jed was talkative now that he'd gotten started. "I have a summer job in Thermopolis," he went on. "I'm half Native American, but I've never been on the reservation where my father grew up. So I've decided it's time for me to do the 'roots' thing and experience the land. I hadn't counted on experiencing the air, though."

I laughed. The ride was smoothing out, and I noticed Jed relaxing and beginning to look more comfortable.

"I know some Native Americans," I said. "In fact, my grandfather's ranch foreman, Benjamin Big Bear, is a Shoshoni Indian. I've know him for years. He's really great."

"Oh, isn't that nice," Jed said sarcastically, dropping the smile, instantly angry. "Your grandfather, the great white employer of the poor Indian laborer who can't run anything on his own." His face was clouded, and he leaned his bulky body toward me across the aisle, aggressively filling the tiny space between us.

"It's not like that," I snapped with equal testiness. "Running Horse is *not* a hired hand. As a matter of fact, he is practically running the place now that my grandfather is sick—and it's out of friendship and because they've been *partners* for years. Big Bear has his own ranch on the reservation." I was struggling to make him understand.

"He and my grandfather have been running cattle together for years," I went on. "And right now he is probably making more money than the Walker Ranch, so back off."

"Okay, okay." Jed raised his hands in mock fear like I was going to hit him. But he didn't look convinced and didn't bother to conceal his anger. Like Wyoming history was my fault.

I should have left it alone, but keeping quiet wasn't one of my strong points. And I figured Jed was in for a surprise with his overrated Native-pride thing. Poverty and alcoholism were rampant on the Wind River Reservation, which borders the town of Thermopolis on one side and the Walker Ranch on the other. I figured the Utah State boy had more in common with me, whether he liked it or not, than he would with his "roots" on the reservation. And the big chip on his shoulder wouldn't make his life very easy in Thermopolis, either, I thought, so I decided to set him straight.

"My grandpa's ranch has been in the family for generations. It has nothing to do with the Indian thing, so get over it."

"Get over it?" Jed asked, his attitude still hanging out there in my face. "Get over it? Con, maybe you need to do some checking on your own roots this summer. Whose land do you think it was before your generations and generations of Walkers? Who made and broke promises with Native Americans, then shoved them onto useless reservations, taking away their dignity with their way of life?"

"Not my grandfather," I shot back. "All that happened years ago." But despite my tone, I was uncomfortable with the truth of what he had said about broken treaties and unfair laws. And I wondered very briefly why Chief Running Wolf *didn't* like the Walkers, and was glad my new acquaintance didn't happen to know that bit of family history.

"It's not that simple!" I protested in a quieter voice, as I noticed our conversation was attracting the attention of the men in cowboy hats sitting around us.

"No, it's not," he agreed, his tension level lowered several notches. "So let's drop it."

At 5:01 exactly, the wheels of the little aircraft touched down in a nice, smooth three-point landing. The pilot taxied up to a terminal that was smaller than most houses.

Leaning down to exit through the small doorway, I paused

at the top to take a deep breath of Wyoming air, and before I could exhale I was shoved from behind, causing me to stumble none too gracefully down the metal steps of the plane and sprawl on all fours across Wyoming soil.

"Get out of my way, kid. I don't have all day to stand around this dump," a man's slightly high-pitched voice said as he brushed past me on the tarmac, hitting me as he did so with his soft leather designer carry-on bag. The man went striding off through the other passengers, looking totally out of place among the cowboy hats and boots.

"Do you always kiss the ground upon arrival?" Jed asked, laughing as he gave me a hand up.

"Always," I replied.

And then we both saw Alisa.

Alisa—sweet sixteen and my favorite cousin—was waiting for me behind the "security barrier," which was nothing more than a three-plank wooden fence. Alisa seemed to have added inches to her already tall, thin runner's frame. Her long blond hair was pulled back away from her face, and she was wearing a long-sleeved white cotton shirt loose over Levi's. One boot rested on the bottom board of the fence, and she was holding a sign that had *Welcome Home* artistically burned into old gray wood.

"WOW!" Jed exclaimed.

"Yeah. Great sign, huh? They love me out here."

"Umm . . . I was referring to the *girl*, not the sign," he replied, eyes fixed on my devoted cousin, who appeared not to be looking our way at all.

"Look, Con!" she called, waving her arms and pointing to a spot on the tarmac behind me.

There, walking down the steps from his own private Learjet, flashing that famous grin, was Robin Blackford. My favorite movie star—and the best actor in the world—was right there in Thermopolis, arriving practically at the same moment as I was. "Now, that's cool," I said to myself, forgetting for the moment about the jerk who had pushed me aside. "What could go wrong with this holiday after such a great start?" I said, hugging Alisa hello.

"Plenty," she replied. But before I could ask her what she meant, Robin Blackford and his entourage had reached the security barrier and were greeted by the local press. All three of them. The mayor and a representative from the reservation arrived at the same time, and the mayor rushed up to shake the hand of the famous man.

"What brings you to our little town?" the breathless voice of a young woman reporter from the *Thermopolis Tribune* asked as she leaned as close as she dared to the movie star, holding a small black tape recorder up to his face. Blackford was wearing ostrich-skin cowboy boots, Levi's, and a Western shirt. I couldn't believe I was actually seeing him in real life. He was huge. Those stories about him doing his own stunts seemed true enough just by looking at him. He was surrounded by men in business suits and one very large Native American.

"I've come," he said in that very deep, smooth voice I knew so well from listening to it in dark movie theaters, "to buy a ranch. And help save the West."

A VAST AMOUNT OF TROUBLE

"COOL," I SAID, MY VOICE CARRYING OVER THE CROWD. I couldn't believe that my favorite movie star was standing right here in middle-of-nowhere Wyoming, live and in the flesh.

"Hush." Alisa poked me. "And listen up."

"I have come to start what will be known as the Sagebrush Rebellion," Robin Blackford announced dramatically, pausing for applause. There were a few scattered giggles, the mayor's enthusiastic clapping, and blank stares from the rest of us.

"And," he went on, draping his arm around one of the suits next to him, "I have brought some officials from the Department of the Interior. These men came with me today—all the way from Washington, D.C.—because they care about the West and your little town of Thermopolis. These men are from the BLM—I'm sure everyone around here is familiar with the good work of the Bureau of Land Management."

The men from Washington looked pale and pathetic next to the tanned Californian, and no one except the mayor cheered for the BLM bureaucrats.

"We are going to meet with your fine mayor today," the actor explained, "to help him find ways to bring in more tourist dollars to this upstanding little town."

The mention of money finally brought a cheer from the crowd, but a grizzled old farmer next to us shouted, "Why do *you* care about our little town?"

"Good question," Alisa whispered.

"Who cares?" I whispered back. "Robin Blackford is here, in person, and I'm going to get an autograph to prove it to Hannah."

"Good question," Blackford responded. "And the answer is that I care about the West because the West belongs to all of us. We just want to help preserve it for future generations."

The men from the BLM beamed their concern.

"And we will be meeting with the true Americans, the Native Americans from the Shoshoni and Arapaho tribes who live on the beautiful Wind River Reservation. I want to learn from men like Mr. Yellowdog." He nodded to the tribal elder standing next to the mayor. "They can show us how to achieve harmony with the earth—the sun, the soil, and the water. They can show us the way to preserving the wilderness."

I looked at Jed, who like most people on our flight had stayed to check out Blackford. Jed looked pleased at Blackford's words praising his people. Maybe finding his roots would turn out better than I had thought.

"That's all very interesting, Mr. Blackford," the unimpressed farmer said. "But how does preserving the wilderness bring in more tourist dollars?"

The mayor looked displeased at the ungrateful citizen. Mayor Richards was not a native; he had moved in a few years ago and run for mayor, promising to help Thermopolis grow. When he smiled, his eyes nearly disappeared into his face, his head bobbing up and down in excitement over this very big fish come to his town. He certainly didn't want some local yokel spoiling it with difficult questions.

The Airport Café had emptied now, and diners joined the growing little group crowded around to get in on the excitement. A waitress held a cup of coffee she had probably been taking to a customer. Only the guy who had shoved me down the steps seemed to have left this "dump"—taken his designer bag and gold jewelry and disappeared.

"Tourism. That's the answer," Blackford was explaining. "People will pay to fish in the Wind River with Native American guides. Or pay to hike in the wilderness. Tourism gives the common citizen of this country access to their own lands. Government land that is now being exploited by . . . well, let's be honest . . . sometimes the truth hurts—exploited by greedy farmers and ranchers."

That got a rise out of the crowd. And except for the men from Washington and the overeager mayor, it wasn't a friendly reaction.

"Who is he calling greedy?" I asked Alisa, getting a little annoyed.

"Exactly," she replied.

"Which ranch are you interested in buying, Mr. Blackford?" the young woman from the *Thermopolis Tribune* asked, ignoring all the stuff about saving the West.

Taking off his sunglasses, Blackford leaned a shade closer to the already rattled blond reporter, charming her with his deep blue eyes.

"I have no idea which ranch. There are so many beautiful spots in this fine country. But I do know I would like to live in a community of people as nice as you folks—and help preserve this land for others."

"Oh" was all the stunned reporter could manage in the face of such charm.

"That's not true," Alisa said, mostly to me—and in a shocked voice.

"Are you going to give up acting and become a rancher, then?" the reporter followed up. "And live here full time?"

Blackford leaned back on his heels a bit, put his sunglasses back on, and seemed to hesitate before answering.

"I certainly do *want* to live here," he explained. "But I believe, as did the French philosopher Rousseau, that the fruits of the earth belong to us all, the earth, and no one. Greed should not get in the way of our responsibility to preserve the earth. In fact, I believe that if we do not act now to save the West for the next generation, then we'll lose it. . . ." He paused for effect. "I don't want to buy a ranch to run cattle on it or to make money, but to make sure we don't lose the West."

I was beginning to think Robin Blackford should go back to making movies.

"That's easy for you to say. You're already rich," I shouted out without thinking. "And besides, it would be kind of hard to *lose* something as big as the West, wouldn't it?"

My smart-aleck remark brought laughter from the crowd but probably cost me the autograph. It wiped the smile right off Blackford's face.

"Way to go, Con," Alisa said. "It's nice to see you haven't changed."

Mayor Richards' face fell, the layers of flesh dropping back into place and exposing unfriendly eyes directed at me as he saw his moment in the sun ending prematurely. Clearly miffed, Blackford briefly thanked everyone for coming out, ended the interview, and, followed by his entourage, headed toward a row of shiny black Broncos waiting at the edge of the small airfield.

"Way to go, Con," Alisa said again, laughing at me. "Way to run him off. He may be cute, but he doesn't have much of a sense of humor, does he? And speaking of cute, who was that guy who got off the plane with you?"

I looked around, but Jed had gone.

"Aren't you glad you came to pick me up?" I said. "And if you hadn't come to pick me up, you'd have spent your whole life without ever seeing Robin Blackford! You can thank me."

"That's what you think. Go pick up your bag, and I'll bring the truck to the door." She looked at her watch. "It's getting late—Gran and Grandpa will be worried. Hurry up. I have lots to tell you."

On the way through the tiny terminal, I stopped to buy a postcard for Hannah. It had a picture of our Walker Ranch with the setting sun hitting the famous Red Canyon Wall behind the house. *Visit Wonderful Wyoming* was written along the border of the card. I hoped Hannah would take it as a personal invitation.

"Where are the others? I expected more than one cousin to welcome me," I said, throwing my bags into the back of Grandpa's very used Ford pickup truck. I ran my hand lovingly over the familiar dents and scratches—more than a few of which I was responsible for.

"None of the others are here yet," Alisa explained. "But with Blackford in town, they might come sooner than planned."

"You mean I'm not enough?" I collapsed against the hot, dusty pickup seat—totally happy. Totally glad to be back.

"Here to save the West? Yeah, right. Can you believe that guy?" Alisa put the truck in gear and headed for Main Street.

"No," I replied. "He's huge. What muscles! He's a little pompous, but hey—who would have ever thought we would see someone famous in Thermopolis. The last famous person to visit was probably Butch Cassidy, here to rob the place. Blackford says he's here to help it. Except for a rather weak sense of humor and all that dribble about saving the West, he's pretty cool, huh?"

"Con, get a grip. He may be huge and in my estimation rather gorgeous, *and* we may love his movies . . . but that man was lying." She pounded the steering wheel for effect. "Lying through his teeth to the good citizens of Thermopolis."

"What are you talking about? And how on earth would you know?" I looked at my cousin, whom I had always thought of as a little flaky around the edges and slightly bossy, but otherwise a completely normal person.

"Because, dear Con, last week an agent for Mr. Robin Blackford came out to the ranch and offered our grandparents a very large sum of money to sell the place to him. So he was definitely lying when he said he didn't know which ranch he wanted to buy. He wants ours."

I was speechless. Briefly.

"No way! Boy, will Hannah be impressed," I exclaimed.

"CON! Are you crazy? This isn't a *good* thing."

"Why not? I'm sure Grandpa told him no. So Blackford goes on and finds another ranch, even though he liked the Walker Ranch best. That's very cool."

There was a small worry line on Alisa's forehead. "Things are not quite so simple this summer, Con."

She then began to explain about Grandpa's health and some of the trouble that had been going on. I listened as we drove through the little town I knew so well and got that same weird feeling I always did coming here from Austria. Like I was in a time warp kind of thing, traveling from the Old World to the Old West.

Thermopolis was just a dusty little cow town with a few hundred people when it got its start in the mid–1800s; by then Vienna was already the political and cultural capital of the Hapsburg Empire.

A century and a half later, Thermopolis is still just a dusty little cow town with a few hundred people. Main Street looks much the same as it has for a hundred years with brick, false-front buildings lining the short stretch known as downtown. *World's Largest Mineral Hot Springs* is written in white rocks on the face of a bare, knobby hill overlooking the town. The sign stops a few tourists who swim in the hot spring pools on their way to Yellowstone Park, but otherwise the town sleeps on, content to be what it's always been—a remote ranching town without so much as a shopping center to mess it up.

The afternoon sun was in our eyes as we stopped at the only traffic light on Main. The greasy spoon known as the Broken Spoke was on our left.

"Hey, isn't that the guy who got off the plane with you?" Alisa said, shielding her eyes from the glare and looking across the street. "He is kinda cute."

"That's what he said about you," I replied and saw her smile. She honked and I waved, but Jed had already opened the door and was being welcomed into a neat, new office building on the corner. *MOTHER EARTH!* was lettered into a topographical globe made of wood and mounted on a pole outside the front door. *Ecosystems Management Consulting* was printed on a bronze plaque on the door.

"That's odd," Alisa said. "The man greeting him looks like that man who pushed you down the stairs of the plane."

She was right. I recognized the slick shiny suit and gold jewelry.

"Weird. Jed never talked to that guy on the plane," I said. "And what is Mother Earth, anyway?"

There was no breeze blowing through the truck, despite the

open windows. Alisa wiped the sweat off her forehead with the back of her hand as the truck idled at the stop light. The door shut behind Jed, and I figured that was the last I would ever see of him.

"Mother Earth is a new 'environmental' organization that Grandpa and Gran happen to think is full of a bunch of crazy radicals who wouldn't know the real environmental movement from a hole in the wall."

"Grandpa and Gran are probably right."

"Con, our dear grandparents are a generation behind, and I don't think they understand people have to be taught how to take care of the earth," she explained in her slightly annoying I-am-older-and-wiser-than-you-are voice.

Alisa shifted down into first and pulled left when the light turned green.

"I read in the newspaper," she went on, chugging slowly across the intersection, "that Mother Earth is working with all the tribal leaders from the reservation. In fact, Chief Running Wolf was at the dedication of their new office building. And that makes Gran even more suspicious since she thinks Chief Running Wolf has it in for Grandpa."

"Does he?" I asked. "Mom said the same thing."

"I don't know. Something happened in the past between Grandpa and the chief, I guess, but they don't talk about it. Look, Con, as much as we love our grandparents, they do sort of live in another time zone—environmentally speaking, ya know?"

"Oh, please, Alisa don't give me that environmental junk again. I feel as if I've been flying for days, so tell me something interesting and not your half-baked eco-nonsense."

She took that rather well, I thought, throwing back her head and laughing at me. "Nice to have you back, Con. I can see all those adventures in Europe last year haven't changed you as much as we had hoped. In fact, the proverb 'The wise are so uncertain; the ignorant so self-assured' still applies, little cousin."

"Ha! I may be a year younger than you, but I am definitely not little." I flexed my new muscles to impress her. "And I see you'll still be boring us with your silly proverbs." We both laughed, because we had had this same conversation so many times before. Like every year. That settled, life as I knew it in Wyoming took on its usual, comfortable air. Nothing, I thought, had changed after all.

Alisa proceeded to catch me up on news of the cousins while I savored the rich, thick chocolate shake we picked up at the A & W drive-in on the edge of town.

"It's the year of the cousins," she announced as we turned off Highway 20. "None of the aunts and uncles are arriving till mid-August. We're on our own with Grandpa and Gran until then. Lindy, Claire, and Abby will arrive on the Fourth of July. But Kate joined the Casper Troopers Drum and Bugle Corps and is traveling with them. She's only fourteen, but they made an exception because she's pretty good and they needed more flag bearers."

"So much for the Casper cousins," I said, disappointed. There were seven Walker cousins in all—six girls and me. Sisters Lindy, Claire, Kate, and Abby lived in Casper, over the Owl Creek Mountains about two hours away. Then there were the Oregon girls, Alisa and Jess. Grandpa and Gran had three daughters and no sons, so none of us carried the Walker name, but all of us showed the genes.

"What about Jess? Why isn't she here yet?"

"She has to work. College coming up next year and all that, so she's stuck in Oregon until the first week in August."

"Oh well," I said, hiding my disappointment. "More food for us until they get here."

"Yeah, like there's ever any shortage."

I breathed deeply, enjoying the familiar smells of the country. Hot, dusty air filled the pickup as we barreled down Buffalo Creek Road with the windows wide open. The narrow gravel road was bumpy, making the twenty miles to the ranch hard on my already tired backside. I hated being driven around by my girl cousins. *Life would be different*, I thought for the hundredth time, *if I had been born first and been the oldest as well as the only boy cousin.*

"We can't wait to meet Nigel," Alisa broke into my daydream.

I smiled at the thought of my new dad, the very British Nigel. I couldn't wait for him to visit the ranch. In fact, it brought to mind some very interesting and entertaining ways I had planned to introduce him to the West. Like a drive up Devil's Slide with me at the wheel.

"What're you thinking?" Alisa must have seen the gleam in my eye.

I caught my first glimpse of home as the setting sun hit the old logs of the three-story house and lit up the windows in shades of gold. Rising in the distance behind the barn was the Red Wall—as the rock cliffs that made the Walker Ranch famous were called. Between the Wall and the house, Buffalo Creek ran its winding course.

"I'm home," I sighed, so happy to be back. "I might live in Austria, but this place . . . this is home."

Gran greeted me with her usual loving hug, then guided me past the three-layer chocolate cake on the oak kitchen table and up the stairs to see Grandpa.

"His heart is weak, and the broken leg isn't healing like it should," she explained. "He can't wait to see you, but you must not tire him out, okay?"

Nervously, I pushed open the door.

Grandpa was asleep, propped up almost in a sitting position in the four-poster bed, which had been in that very bedroom for 120 years. His rough hands were lying on top of a colorful quilt that Alisa's mom had made. Aunt Leigh had put our family story in the quilt, each block representing some part of the family history and life at the ranch. I ran my finger over my name and birthday, which were stitched into the family-tree block right in the center of the quilt under a neatly sewn replica of the ranch's brand—the Flying W. Other cross-stitched representations included Grandpa's horse Yeats, the cattle, the cousins' summer theater productions, the big black family Bible, and the old piano, which came to the ranch by rail the year the house was built.

My eyes began to sting, and my throat felt as if it was closing up as I looked at Grandpa's strong hands, leathery and gnarled from years of hard work. My tower of strength was now old and weak. I fought back the tears.

I looked around the familiar room. It was airy and bright with a stone fireplace on the west wall, left over from the days before central heat. Built-in bookshelves covered two walls. Tall, skinny windows let in the afternoon light, and I looked out across a sloping lawn and beyond to see cattle grazing down by the river. I took a seat in a worn but comfortable overstuffed blue-and-white striped chair next to his bed.

"Grandpa," I whispered finally, taking his hand, "are you awake?"

He opened his eyes. His smile was the same. It welcomed me home.

"I brought you a book of poetry—William Butler Yeats. Mom found it in London." I laid the old, rare edition on the oak washstand beside the bed. "And she sends her love."

That brought an even bigger smile, but he reached for my hand, not the book. There was plenty of strength still in his grip.

"Son," he said, "I'm glad you're here. I've been waiting for you. I hear you've done some growing up since last summer."

"Yes, sir. I hope so."

"Tell me about it." Grandfather rested his eyes as I talked, but listened to every word, frowning, nodding, smiling in response.

"And," I concluded my story about what had happened last year with Hannah, "the terrorists have been convicted and sentenced to fifteen years. We read it the newspaper at the airport this morning."

"You were very brave, Con," my grandfather responded. "And I expect you've learned a lot about people, haven't you? About hatred and prejudice."

"You wouldn't believe what it's like in Europe, Grandpa."

"We have plenty of prejudice here, too, son."

Grandpa, you don't have a clue, I thought. *You've never even seen skinheads and neo-Nazis.*

"Nazis, I'm afraid, are not the only racists, Con. They come in many forms."

Gran stuck her head in the door then with a message from Big Bear about the cattle.

"Con," she added, "dinner is nearly ready. Be down at half past."

Wonderful smells from the kitchen had permeated the house, and I couldn't wait to eat. There would be homemade bread tonight, grass-fed beefsteak grown on the ranch, and the traditional welcome-home chocolate cake topped with fresh fruit and Coke to chase it down. Finally, real food . . . Grandma style. Fortunately, she didn't worry much about current health-food fads.

"Anyway," Grandpa went on, obviously not obsessing on the thought of dinner like I was. "I'm glad you are here, Con. I need your help."

I gulped.

"Don't know when I'll get out of this bed," he went on. "And things aren't going too well on the ranch in my absence. I need you to watch things for me, see who's stirring up this trouble. You'll be my secret weapon—someone I can trust to blend in at all the usual places like the Broken Spoke Café and the sale barn and let me know what's going on. How do you like that idea?"

"Wow." I didn't know what else to say. I waited for Grandpa to go on.

"Coyote wait and watch a herd, then attack only the weak. Well, I'm weak now . . . and I tell you, Con, someone, some human predator, is out there attacking this ranch. If I don't soon find out who and why, it may be too late. I have until mid-August to sort this out or sell off the herd—which will mean bankruptcy—"

"No, don't say that," I interrupted, thinking he—like Mom—was exaggerating. But he waved his hand for me to listen.

"Let me finish, son. The trouble started in the winter, after I had my heart attack. Then I got back on my feet and back in the saddle. But then Yeats stumbled in that prairie-dog hole. Busted my leg bad and set me back again. Word gets around. Now the trouble is getting more serious. Big Bear found some fences cut up in Birdseye Pasture. Gates have been left open, cattle are disappearing and dying. Too many cattle. And the manner and number of their deaths . . . it doesn't feel right. One expects a certain amount of trouble, so I tried not to think too much about it at first. Then there were other things, like the trouble with the BLM. Walkers have been leasing BLM land for eighty years without any trouble. Then this spring they sent their new man from Washington, D.C., Raymond Rice, to tell me our grazing lease was going to be withdrawn due to 'gross environmental violations,' which is hogwash. He says we've overgrazed the land, killing the grass and letting the cattle ruin the banks of Jones Creek. Nonsense," he snapped. "We have never needed outsiders to tell us how to respect the land. But this Rice fellow has it in for us and has convinced the top people at BLM that we're guilty."

Grandpa paused at that, the angry look on his face softening with his quiet laughter.

"That's terrible," I said. "What's funny about that?"

"Well, Mr. Rice was sitting right there where you are, and your grandmother was handing him a friendly cup of coffee when he started in about our 'environmental violations,' " Grandpa said, enjoying the memory.

"When your Gran heard that, she withdrew the cup of coffee—none to graciously—and invited Mr. Rice to return to his office and await word from our lawyer, who would explain gross *legal* violations for falsely accusing honest citizens. She went on a bit, but you get the point." He continued to chuckle. "Mr. Rice got the point, too, as a matter of fact. He left without coffee."

"Good ol' Gran," I laughed. "Never at a loss for words."

"I wonder who inherited that," he replied, the wrinkles around his eyes deepening with his smile.

"And then some movie star—who doesn't know a cow from a hole in the ground—sent an agent out here and made us an 'overly generous' offer to buy the ranch. Can't remember the actor fella's name."

Robin Blackford would probably be surprised to know that not only were my grandparents unimpressed by his offer, but they'd never even heard of him.

"Do you think this vast amount of trouble is all bad luck, Con?" Grandpa gazed intently at me.

My grandfather was known as someone who thought before he spoke. My grandmother, on the other hand, was someone who spoke before you had time to think. Before I could respond to his question, Grandpa answered it himself.

"I don't. I don't believe in luck. Good or bad. And this trouble has a design."

"How do you know? I mean, all of those things could have been coincidence."

"Maybe you're right. Maybe I'm going a little crazy cooped up in this room, but that's where you can help me, Con. Find out if all these things are, as you say, coincidence. I think someone is trying awfully hard to make me sell. I want you to help me find out who. And why. Before it's too late."

"Whoa!"

"Exactly," he said, leaning back onto the pillows. "I'm not going to let some movie star scavenger buy our home for a trophy. Or let some government agency ruin me with lies. This is our home—all of us—and it's not for sale."

He sounded like himself when he said that. But the sight of his sick, weak body helplessly confined to the bed made me afraid for the first time. *If his fears are real, so is our trouble.*

"Can you follow instructions, Con, while you're using that clever brain of yours to think things through? And"—he looked at me with something like humor in his eyes—"be humble enough to remain quiet about it?"

I wondered if he was still talking about me. It all sounded pretty crazy. I didn't want to say the wrong thing and disappoint him, or say the right thing and then mess up.

Grandpa had always been an imposing man—even out of the saddle. He stood six foot three in his socks and was strong enough to brand cattle with a broken leg, or throw a small steer if need be, which I had seen him do. I knew he'd once stood up to a drunken Fred Marvin, who had gone after Big Bear with a loaded shotgun.

Whit Walker was a legend; people loved him or feared him.

35

I didn't want to disappoint him. He was asking me to stand in for him and help save his ranch. I wondered if maybe Mom had exaggerated my experience with the Nazis.

"What about Gran?" I finally stammered. "She could take on the whole county without much trouble and no help from me."

"You're right," he said, smiling. "And she does so occasionally. Right now she's banned from the BLM office in Thermopolis for disturbing their peace."

"Oh no," I groaned in mock horror. "They may wish they had chosen to accuse someone else of environmental violations. She'll sort it out, Grandpa."

"Yes, but your grandmother can't do it all. She may be busy with . . . well . . . I'm not getting well, and we must face the possibility that—"

"No," I interrupted him, jumping up and striding about the room. "Don't say that. Don't even talk about dying. You can't just give up."

"Hush, Con. Come sit down and listen. Death isn't something to fear. It's a culmination of God's grace at the end of a long life. I'm not afraid to die and be with God."

I shook my head, mumbling for him to stop. I hated hearing him talk about it.

"The thing is," he went on despite my protests, "before I die, I need to know that the ranch is going to be financially sound for your grandmother, that it will go on being a place for all of you to come home to. Our 'dear perpetual place,' as Yeats says."

His voice took on that special tone and cadence I knew so well as he began to quote his favorite poet:

"Like a bridegroom
I brought her to this house
Where all's accustomed, ceremonious;
For arrogance and hatred are the wares
Peddled in the thoroughfares.
How but in custom and in ceremony
Are innocence and beauty born?
Ceremony's a name for the rich horn,
And custom for the spreading laurel tree."

As usual, I didn't understand the poetry, but I loved the sound of his voice and sat there content to let the words roll over me. Custom and ceremony—it brought back all the images of summers past and our times together at the ranch. Images of the plays we cousins worked on for weeks every summer, then performed for the family . . . of cakes and cousins and long summer hikes to secret places in the big pasture . . . of long talks with aunts and uncles about the wonders of the world, far into the night while sitting on the porch and watching falling stars.

And someone wanted to take it all away.

"It's going to take all of us together, Con," Grandpa said. "But I need you, my only grandson, to help me. You fooled those Nazi thugs because they underestimated you. That's exactly what I'm counting on now. Everyone will see you as they always have, as my grandson—just a kid on vacation having fun with his cousins. But you will be listening and watching for me, Con. Look for anything that is out of place, anyone or anything out of the ordinary. Bring everything you see back to this room every night. Together, we'll fool 'em."

He seemed positively cheerful at the idea, and I was beginning to like the sound of it, too.

"This friend of yours, Hannah—she sounds like a fine young lady. Tell me more about her." He surprised me with the change of subject.

I told him how hard it had been to leave my friends in Grossgmain and move to Vienna, where all the kids in the school were so different from me. Then I told him how I got to know Hannah when I was assigned to tutor her in algebra.

"I was nervous at first about having a girl for a best friend. But Hannah told me, 'Don't think of me as a girl, Con. Think of me as the only other normal person here.' "

Grandpa chuckled.

"She would fit in great with the cousins."

"Sounds like she would at that," he said. "Wish I could meet her."

"Maybe you can. Maybe we'll need her help. Remember another Yeats poem you taught me: 'It's plain the Bible means that

Solomon grew wise while talking with his queens.' "

Grandpa's eyes twinkled, as bright blue and clear as ever, even if sunk in a weary face. "Sorry, Con, good try—but I don't think so. We'll have more girls than we know what to do with around here before summer is over."

Actually, he adored all his granddaughters, and they didn't get coddled around the ranch any more than I did. Still, there was some kind of a male thing between us. Especially strong, maybe, because my own father had died before I was born. Grandpa had been the closest thing I'd ever had to a dad until Mom married Nigel, and I hated seeing him suddenly so old and sick.

"I'll help you, Grandpa," I promised as he drifted off to sleep. "I promise."

◆

After eating all the thick, juicy steak I could put away and more cake than I should have, I thanked Gran and went outside to stretch my legs and see the horses. It was nearly morning Vienna time, and tiredness was creeping into my limbs, but I wasn't ready yet to sleep.

The stillness of the evening was broken only by the occasional nighthawk cutting through the cool air, diving at incredible speeds after mosquitoes hovering above the damp lawn. Moonlight alone lit my way. The Red Wall loomed behind the house like a dark, giant barrier to the rest of the world.

I stopped in the tack shop to get some corn to entice the horses to the corral fence. As I opened the door, I was greeted by the familiar smell of oiled leather and sweaty horse blankets.

This was not a building often used at night, so the little light that came on when I pulled the toggle chain cast a weak glow that didn't even reach the corners of the room. Remembering that rattlesnakes sometimes crept in there in search of mice, I put my hand very carefully into the bucket of corn—and quickly back out again with three big, hard ears.

Grandpa's faded yellow oiled-canvas slicker hung on the wall beside his quirt—his special riding crop—and a longer whip used for sorting cattle. Beside them, dangling from a hook in the low ceiling, were his riding boots, spurs attached. They were covered with layers of dust and cobwebs.

I suddenly felt angry with Grandpa for "hanging up his boots." *They should be polished at his bedside waiting for the day he can ride again*, I thought as I went in search of his favorite horse—W. B. Yeats.

Yeats, a big sorrel quarter horse, getting along in years, looked gentle enough standing there with his head stretched through the fence, nuzzling the kernels out of my hand. But I knew the old beast and wasn't fooled. Grandpa had never let me ride him.

"He's still too much horse for you, Con," Grandpa had said last summer.

It's true Yeats wasn't exactly a kid's horse. I had watched him work lots of times. Brilliant at moving and sorting cattle. Many a cow had felt Yeats' strong teeth nip their hindquarters for not moving quickly enough. I was longing to ride him and figured I was old enough this year. I hoped Grandpa would agree.

I leaned my head against the corral fence and closed my eyes.

Memories of Grandpa filled my head . . . riding Yeats, working the cattle, teaching me to ride, drive, brand, and shoot, and even like poetry a little.

Yeats continued to cheerfully scrounge his flexible snout into my palm in order to get the last kernel, his bristly nose hair tickling my hand. Even when the corn was gone, the big horse didn't walk away but let me go on petting his bony head, reminiscing, and he didn't seem to mind as warm, salty tears began to splash upon his nose.

3

MISSED SIGNS

"Asparagus? And wild flowers? You've got to be kid-ding!" I gasped. "Gran, I didn't come all the way from Austria to pick flowers," I complained sleepily, stumbling into the kitchen after being awakened too early the next morning.

Gran's response was a loving hug and directions to Grass Creek. "The asparagus grows wild along the creek bed. Cut only small, tender shoots. Alisa will show you how."

"But I thought I was supposed to be helping Grandpa," I complained. "I'm sure he has something more important for me to do today than look for terrible-tasting vegetables."

The sun had only recently come up, lighting but not yet warming the early morning air.

My grandmother was wearing a down vest over her long plaid bathrobe and binoculars around her neck. She shepherded me out the door onto the broad front porch of the house. A permanent stand for Gran's telescope was turned toward the hills.

In the evening she used the telescope to see the stars. And she liked to start her day there, too, looking for deer darting out of the hay and gracefully leaping over fences as they re-turned to hide in the hills. Or a fox heading for his hole, or even the odd badger hurrying for cover before the sun got hot. Most of all Gran loved her birds. She knew them all and kept a record of their yearly pilgrimages back and forth through Wyoming. Unlike my grandparents, few of the birds were hardy enough to spend the winter.

Gran shooed me off the porch and said, "When you get back, your grandfather will be awake, and he'll want a report, I imagine. So keep your eyes open, Con. My word, how you've grown! You'll be six foot before the summer's over. Tall and handsome like your grandfather."

I ignored the flattery and grudgingly took the five-gallon bucket Gran handed me and sincerely hoped I wasn't supposed to fill the thing up. I thought with irritation that I wished people would stop telling me to keep my eyes open and start explaining what I was supposed to be looking for.

Alisa was waiting for me in the pickup and making annoying little toots on the horn. She looked her usual disgustingly bright and happy self, not even fazed to be up at such an hour.

"Hurry up, Con, let's get going."

"Okay, okay. I'm coming. Stop honking already."

Alisa, who usually managed to spend more time at the ranch than the other cousins, had inherited Grandma's optimistic nature and her love of nature and bird-watching. She had binoculars around her neck, too.

Ben Big Bear came around the corner of the corral carrying two pink blocks of salt for us to take to the cattle up in the pasture.

"Hey, Con, good to see you back where you belong, in wonderful Wyoming," he said as he tossed the heavy blocks of salt up into the bed of the pickup.

"Hey, yourself," I replied as he gave me a powerful bear hug. The man was like a rock.

"How're things across the big pond?" He always kidded me about living in Europe—like it was another planet. "I hear you had a little trouble last year. Wish I had been there when those men grabbed you."

"Yeah, me too. You would have made mincemeat of those guys. Where were you when I needed you?"

His friendly pat on my back nearly sent me sprawling.

"Just try to stay out of trouble, you hear? And be careful driving up Devil's Slide," he added to Alisa as I pulled myself up in the cab.

41

"Put one block of salt at the windmill on Birdseye Pass," he explained, "and one at the watering hole on Grass Creek. And give me a count of how many cattle you see, okay? Especially new calves. There should be several, and your grandfather needs some good news for a change."

"You bet," Alisa and I said in unison, picking up the local lingo where we had left off last summer.

"And be careful on Devil's Slide."

"Okay, you said that already."

He opened the tight barbed-wire fence gate and waved us through into the sagebrush-covered prairie where miles of pastureland stretched as far as the eye could see.

"Are we supposed to fill this thing up with asparagus?" I asked, kicking the bucket out of the way to make room for my long legs.

"No, dummy," Alisa said affectionately. "That's for the flowers. It rained all over the Copper Mountain area last week, and the ground along the creek beds is simply covered with the most magnificent Indian paintbrush, buttercups, snow lilies, and yellow daisies. And the rain brought up new tender asparagus shoots, so stop looking so crabby. It's Grandpa's favorite food. He usually cuts some when he rides Yeats to check the fences up there in the springtime. This year they haven't had any because he can't ride the fences."

We were both silent thinking about our grandfather—unable now to even ride his favorite horse and care for his ranch. Alisa drove slowly over the rough tracks that passed for a road. The smell of crushed sage drifted in my open window as we headed up toward the Saddle, a natural pass between sagebrush-covered hills.

"Look, a killdeer." Alisa slowed down and pointed out her window.

There was a little brown bird limping along, dragging her wing in the dirt, chirping pitifully.

"Silly mama bird, we're not going to hurt you," Alisa said as we passed the clever little bird still feigning injury as she limped through the grass trying to draw us away from her nest.

As I looked at the brave bird, I thought about my conversation with Grandpa last night, remembering what he had said about needing to be brave. Still thinking everyone was exaggerating, but hoping for some excitement that might call for bravery, I felt a renewed sense of commitment to not let him down.

"Why are you driving so slow? If Grandpa wants fresh asparagus, let's get it over with."

Alisa pressed down a little harder on the accelerator, and we bumped along at a faster pace. A straight barbed-wire fence made a line through the miles of pasture ahead of us, as far as we could see. Generations of Walkers and their cowboys had put their worn-out cowboy boots upside down over the fence posts.

"That one's about gone," I commented on an especially rotten boot hanging by the heel.

"This family tradition of putting old boots on fence posts is not very ecologically sound. I think Grandpa should put a stop to it and have the ones here removed."

"Oh, please, Alisa, don't give me that eco-garbage. We can do what we want. It's our land."

"That's not the point," she said, sure as always about the point.

We drove along Old Stagecoach Road. It ran for several miles, and Grandpa had lined the road with cattle guards—devices set in the ground that cars could cross but not cattle. So anyone brave enough to tackle Devil's Slide could still explore the historic road without worrying about opening or closing gates.

"And my boots are about ready for the fence," I added, looking at the worn-out ones I was wearing from last summer.

I took off my jacket and rested my arm out the window as we approached Devil's Slide. "You sure you know how to drive over this?" I asked. Alisa was concentrating now as we neared the steep, rocky portion of the road that narrowed to the width of the pickup. A deep precipice fell away on either side.

"No problem," she said, putting the truck into four-wheel drive. "It's coming down that's hard. And the key is to never,

never, never look over the edge."

"We're dead," I muttered, covering my eyes as the red gravel flew up behind the tires. But Alisa took that old pickup skillfully, steadily, grindingly up to the top and over what had once been the most dangerous part of the stagecoach route from Denver to Thermopolis.

"Well done, cuz," I admitted when we arrived safely on the flat surface of the red butte high above the river and ranch house below.

Alisa smiled in reply, her Walker blue eyes sparkling at the thrill of the drive and beauty of the morning.

We sat there for a moment, enjoying the view. The ranch house was hidden in the cottonwood trees, but the river was visible as it wound its way around the bend behind the large red barn and nearly empty corrals.

Somehow it felt very grown-up to be here without an adult. I could remember when I was little riding in the back of the pickup looking over the edge of Devil's Slide—terrified of falling into the rocky creek below. But even then excitement had outweighed the fear. Late at night, in the tents where the cousins slept, we would scare each other with tales true and imaginary about that fateful date in 1891 when a stagecoach had gone over the edge. The stagecoach had been escaping from Butch Cassidy and his gang. The driver pushed the horses too fast, and all six passengers and two drivers were killed when the coach crashed into the ravine thousands of feet below.

Furious about what the outlaws had done, our great-great-grandfather, the first Whit Walker, started the first "vigilance committee" with townspeople and other ranchers. They chased Butch and his gang back to the Hole-in-the-Wall hideout, and Thermopolis was safe for some time from their kind. From that time on, the Flying W brand had been a symbol of honesty and integrity. Sometimes I looked at the portrait of that first Whit Walker, which hung in the old parlor next to the one of his Swedish wife, Lindgren, and thought that maybe I looked a little like him. I wondered what he would think if he knew the

Walkers were in danger of losing the ranch he had carved out of the wilderness in 1875.

"Look, Con," Alisa interrupted my thoughts. "That's a mature bald eagle. See his white head?" She excitedly reached for the binoculars, coasting the truck to a halt while she stared at the soaring bird. Not quite as thrilled as my cousin about every bird that flew past, I turned my attention instead to a light plane flying toward us, still some distance off.

As it came closer, I could see it was a dark blue high wing—Cessna probably, a two-seater job. It circled low over us, dipping the pilot's side toward us.

"See who's in the plane," I suggested, and Alisa grudgingly turned the binoculars off one bird onto the other.

"Um . . . it's hard to say. He looks familiar, but I can't say for sure." Standing in the open door of the pickup, Alisa followed with the binoculars as the plane turned slowly in the sky overhead, offering her a great view of the pilot. Then with a jerking motion it banked sharply right.

"Oops . . . I lost it. Whoever it was, he's gone. I was looking right in his eyes before he turned."

"Maybe he didn't want you to see him."

"Don't be overly dramatic, Con. But still . . ." She hesitated, thinking it over. "It is odd. What was it doing flying so low over our land? Maybe it was Robin Blackford looking at what he hopes to buy," she surmised.

"Nah. He wouldn't be caught dead in such a cheap little plane. Besides, he's probably out looking for a different ranch to buy," I said. "Maybe it was that BLM guy—what's his name? Mr. Rice. You know they're probably still looking for ecological violations."

"I don't know. I've never seen Mr. Rice. But this isn't BLM land. It's Walker land."

We watched the plane gain altitude and increase its speed as it headed due east . . . toward our leased BLM land.

Off in the distance, to the south, we could see the outcropping of rock called Birdseye Pass. The old stagecoach station ruins were at its base, right inside the Walker Ranch property.

On the other side was the Marvin ranch. We were planning to eat the homemade cinnamon rolls Gran had sent with us while picking the silly flowers in the ruins of the old stagecoach stop.

"Maybe the Marvins are causing the problems," Alisa said as we resumed our journey. "They have always been jealous of Grandpa's success. And they stand to gain the most if he loses his grazing rights."

"Why? Can't they get some other BLM land to lease?"

"Because, as Grandpa just explained to me, a ranch has the first option to all BLM land that borders it. And in our case, since Walkers have held those grazing rights since they were originally granted in 1935, they can only lose the right to lease that land *if* they misuse the land *or* if the ranch is sold. Then anyone can bid on it. That's why the charges by Raymond Rice at the BLM office are so dangerous, and why the Marvins would be jolly glad if Grandpa and Gran have to sell or the BLM kicks them off."

"Wow."

"Exactly. Either way, the Marvins stand to gain a lot."

"And they can't afford to buy our ranch themselves, right?"

"Right."

"So," I reasoned, "they have motive—greed and jealousy. And they have means—their land borders ours. And they know where and how to get to the cattle, cut fences, and stuff like that. They could also spread rumors to the BLM guy about the so-called environmental damage."

I was quite excited that I had figured it all out already.

"Piece of cake. Case closed."

Alisa laughed. "You never change, Con. Things are not so simple, I'm afraid. Even if it is true—and we don't know that—where's the proof? And Gran doesn't think it's Fred and Lilly Marvin causing all the problems anyway. She assures me old man Marvin can't be carrying out all these things because—and here I quote her—'he doesn't have the gumption or the brains to carry out much more than the trash.'"

I wasn't convinced, but hunger was gnawing away at my empty stomach, making it hard to concentrate.

"Whatever," I replied. "Let's discuss it over the cinnamon rolls." But instead of speeding up, Alisa braked suddenly, nearly throwing me through the windshield.

"Look at the cute little horny toad!" she exclaimed.

We waited patiently until the reptile scurried out of the way of the huge truck wheels and disappeared into a burrow beneath a prickly cactus.

"Oh, please, Alisa, let's get on with it. I've seen enough horny toads in my life."

"They're an important part of the ecosystem, too," she explained and started driving again. Before we knew it, the cool morning had totally slipped away. We came across a "baby-sitter cow" and about twenty calves. That meant we should be getting close to the water tank and windmill at Birdseye Butte. Cows put their young calves down and—as our parents were always eager to point out—*they* never moved until Mom returned. One cow, the baby-sitter, always remained grazing close by to protect them from coyotes and other predators.

"How *do* the cows decide which cow has to stay with the calves?" I wondered out loud about one of the mysteries of range cattle.

"It's not easy," Alisa said. "Probably causes lots of bickering—'It's not my turn, I stayed with the kids last week.'"

There were a hundred head of cattle, by my count, milling around the windmill when we finally pulled to a stop near the aluminum water tank at its base. The cattle had obviously had their drink of water and were resting before moving off to graze for the day.

Short-legged, broad-backed black cows with the familiar Flying W on their right hip were peacefully chewing their cud. Some older calves romped about chasing one another. They all looked fat and healthy to me.

"Drop the salt block over there." Alisa directed me to a spot about fifty yards from the watering tank itself.

The blocks were not as easy to lift as Big Bear had made it look when he loaded them, and I nearly dropped the heavy chunk of salt on my toe. I stumbled to the appointed spot.

There, to my surprise, I saw a brand-new salt lick. Unlike the pink one I was carrying, this one was white and sunk partially into the soft earth as if it had been dropped. Hard. The surface was cracked but still smooth and flat, untouched by the rough tongues of cattle.

"Hey, I thought the cattle were supposed to be out of salt," I yelled back to Alisa. "There's a new one here already. Should I leave this one, too?"

Alisa waved a yes to me, and I walked back through the dust to where she waited. Stomping cattle hooves had killed the grass, sagebrush, and even cacti for a short distance around the water tank, leaving the ground bare.

"Are you sure we were supposed to leave that salt block here?" I asked again.

"You heard Big Bear. He said to put one by the windmill. There is only one windmill in this pasture, so this must be the spot."

I shrugged, losing interest. By now I was *really* looking forward to eating our cinnamon rolls, and so when we resumed our journey, I had my sights set on the stagecoach ruins. But before we got very far, Alisa stopped the pickup once again.

"Oh no, let's get on with it. I'm hungry."

"Con, look, that cow's in trouble. Come on," she said, leaping out of the pickup without shutting the door.

Sure enough, the cow in question was lying down, breathing hard, thrashing in pain, her big belly bulging and heaving. It wasn't too hard to guess what was wrong. Most of the cows had already calved, but there were always a few late births and sometimes a young heifer would die giving birth to a large calf.

Grandpa would never have allowed a heifer to be out in the prairie before calving. *He really is losing control of things*, I thought, frustrated again by his weakness.

The cow was a dusty white color, the only Charlois in the otherwise all black herd.

Alisa got to the cow ahead of me and crouched down beside the suffering animal, who rolled her eyes at us in fear.

"We should go back and get someone to help," I suggested.

"Big Bear will know what to do."

Nervously chewing on a piece of grass she had picked, Alisa went through our options. "We don't have time to go get him. It would take us an hour there and another back—minimum. The cow looks so weak. I don't think she'll live that long, Con. They'll both die if we go back to get help."

The cow was moaning but no longer struggling so much. Alisa was right—she was weak, and there was no sign of the calf's forelegs, which should be coming out first, followed by a little pink nose.

Panicked, I paced back and forth, crunching cacti and sage beneath my heavy cowboy boots.

"Alisa, they can't afford to lose any more cattle. What're we going to do? And look at her eyes. She's suffering. Grandpa wouldn't let her suffer like that. We've got to *do* something."

"Is the rifle in the truck?" she asked, knowing it was.

We both knew very well that Grandpa kept the twenty-two rifle in a rack behind the seat of the pickup, for rattlesnakes and other emergencies. I had been thinking the same thing but couldn't bear the thought. And what if we were wrong? It would not be a good idea to shoot a cow about to give birth to a healthy calf just because it *looked* like she was in trouble.

Neither one of us made any move to get the rifle.

"Con, do you remember the big red cow that hung around the corral last year—the one we called Education?"

"Yeah." I crouched down beside my cousin, careful to avoid a cactus. "So what?"

"Well, a couple years ago when Education was a heifer, she had trouble having her first calf. She was about to die, and Grandpa and all the hired men were gone. Jess and I helped Gran pull the calf, so Gran named her Education. I was there. I helped! I know what to do."

"Oh, good." For some stupid reason I thought about that scene in *Gone With the Wind* where the maid Prissy says, "I knows all 'bout birthin' babies, Miss Scarlet."

"You know all about birthin' calves, then, Alisa. That's a relief. Go ahead. I'll hand you things."

Alisa hit me with a rope she had pulled from the bed of the truck. "Good try, Con. Come on, let's do it."

She stood up with resolve. "Go get extra gloves, those big scissors, binder twine, and anything else that looks useful from the toolbox. Then go up to the water tank, fill the bucket with water, and pick up an extra rope if you see one. Hurry, Con." Sounding much less sure of herself, she added, "And . . . bring the gun. Just in case."

Exceedingly glad for my practical cousin, I scrambled to get the things she'd asked for without silly questions about what they were for. I had seen calves born before, but I hadn't paid attention to the particulars. This was one job I was glad to leave to the "expert."

I started off at a run with the bucket, but Alisa shouted after me, "Don't run, Con. We're in a hurry. Drive the truck, dummy."

All of the cousins had been allowed to drive around the farm long before we were old enough to get a license. Hoping I hadn't forgotten how over the year in Austria, where you have to be eighteen to drive, I climbed in the pickup and found some gear—which jerked a bit but got me the short distance to the tank and back with the water.

Alisa already had a rope tied to the calf's forelegs, which were just beginning to come through.

"Quick, Con, it's coming! The hooves look right. Oh, thank goodness it's not backward. Help me pull. . . ."

I positioned myself to the side of Alisa, with my back against a big sagebrush. Looking the other way, I began to tug on the rope, hoping desperately Alisa knew what she was doing and we weren't in fact killing the poor thing.

"Not too hard, Con . . . gently. When the cow strains, pull hard. That's it, we can do it. Good, there's the nose. It's going to be okay."

Alisa's hair was wet with sweat around her face, and her braided ponytail fell forward over her shoulder and onto the rope when she pulled.

The cow was hot, too. We didn't know how long she had

been in labor or how long she could last in the midday heat.

We rested when the cow did, and now that the calf was actually moving, the cow seemed to renew her efforts to push it out.

After what seemed forever, and with a last burst of strength, the cow struggled to her feet, knocking us both over backward, and dropped a wet, messy little calf none too gently to the ground.

"Yipeeee! We did it! We did it!"

We danced and shouted in the dust, hugging each other at the wonder of it all.

I managed to untie the rope from the two spindly forelegs, and minutes after his birth, the little guy struggled to get up. The cow licked the birth sack off the calf's baby nose so he could breathe, then continued licking him with her rough tongue until the calf was dry all over. His hair curled as it dried.

"Check him out. Is he cute or what?" I said, amazed.

The cow was wary of us but too weak to drive us off, so we sat quietly and watched the little creature begin to wobble around on his legs looking for lunch.

He was a little bull calf the color of its mother, off-white with patches of darker hair forming little circles around each eye.

"You're cool, Shades," I said.

"Shades?" Alisa asked.

"Yeah, looks like he's wearing sunglasses."

Alisa was grinning from the sweet success of our efforts. But she was getting worried at his lack of success in finding food.

"If he doesn't drink soon, he'll dehydrate in this heat," Alisa said as we continued to watch him teeter to the wrong end of his mom, who was grazing contentedly on the scarce but nutritious prairie grass. The cow gently licked her baby and nudged him back in the right direction.

The unused rifle lay nearby, a reminder of our panic.

"I understand the rope and the rifle, but could you explain the bucket of water?" I asked my efficient cousin.

"Men," she replied, shoving her arms up to her elbows into

the cold water, "are apt to miss the obvious."

"Yeah, right," I laughed, joining her in washing my much less dirty hands. "Like you thought of washing up before."

We watched them until the calf had managed to drink and was lying down resting.

"Bye, Shades. You're a cool calf," I said, petting his unbelievably soft, wet nose. He didn't move as I stroked the still-damp curly hair between his eyes. It was amazing to think he would have died without us—the cow, too.

"Yipeee!" I shouted. "What a morning. Let's go eat."

While I stowed the gun carefully back in its case, I asked my clever cousin why she had wanted the scissors and binder twine.

"Maybe to cut an umbilical cord? And what do cows usually do, wait for the midwife cow to cut the cord?"

"Very funny, Con. I was . . . well . . . being prepared, that's all. And don't look like that."

"Like what?" I asked innocently, tossing the bucket in the back and climbing in the driver's side again.

"Like you're dying to tell someone. I know that look of yours, but I will simply deny it. Scissors? I don't know what Con's talking about. I never mentioned them."

I started the engine and jerked forward before she could realize what I was doing.

"See ya!" I waved, holding up the package of cinnamon rolls. "On my way back."

Sprinting in cowboy boots wasn't easy, even for a runner like Alisa. But she grabbed the endgate before I got away and leaped in the back like Indiana Jones in braids.

Hours later, glowing with the success of our morning and with a bucket of wild flowers and more asparagus than Grandpa could eat in a week, we arrived back to trouble of a very different kind.

A MIDNIGHT RIDE

THE MIDDAY HEAT HAD TURNED THE MORE DISTANT, STILL snow-capped peaks of the Absaroka Mountains to the north and the closer Owl Creek range in the west into a shimmering blue haze as heat rose up from the desert.

"What's that?" I asked, my stomach knotting as I saw flashing lights at the end of the lane up by the summer porch.

"Oh no, not Grandpa," Alisa said, pouring on the gas until we came to a screeching halt beside an ambulance. Its motor was idling, its lights flashing.

Simultaneously the pickup doors flew open as we rushed to see what had happened. In her haste Alisa knocked over the bucket containing her precious wild flowers. Flowers and water spilled over the seat. A trickle of water ran out the door and made a puddle of mud beside the truck.

"Gran," we shouted, rushing toward her as she followed, pale and trembling, beside Grandpa, who was being carried out of the house on a stretcher. His eyes were closed, and his stillness scared me. The family doctor was beside the stretcher. His face was calm.

Gran hugged us close as the men gently slid the stretcher through the door.

"He's going to be okay," she said, comforting us. "Your grandfather started having chest pains right after you two left. I called the doctor, and he came in the ambulance. He's given him some medication now. A setback but not serious. Right?" She looked at the doctor, their old family friend, for reassurance.

He nodded, smiling kindly.

"I'll need to keep him overnight, do some tests, adjust his medication."

It all seemed so sudden, and I wondered if Gran and the doctor were telling us the whole story.

A bad-tempered speckled cat we called Tragedy—because she was getting old and still hadn't had kittens—sat perched on a fence post glaring crossly at the commotion that had disrupted her nap.

"Who is that?" I said, motioning to a stranger standing on the porch behind us. He didn't look like one of the paramedics. He was a funny-looking, antsy little man, nervously shifting from one foot to the other.

"Con, Alisa, this is Mr. Raymond Rice." Gran bit off his name like it was his head. "He came to talk to us about the BLM lease. I shall stay here and discuss it with him. Con, will you go with your grandfather to the hospital? I'll be in later after I finish with Mr. Rice."

I panicked. The last thing in the world I wanted to do was ride in that thing to the hospital with Grandpa in his condition.

I looked at Alisa hopefully.

"Sorry," Gran said. "I need her to go to Casper for me and get some legal papers from Uncle Ted."

Gathering up his nerve, Mr. Rice interrupted her. "Please, you go with your husband. My business . . . can wait . . . until later," he stammered. "I . . . I am only concerned about Mr. Walker's health."

Raymond Rice was of medium build. His eyes were set too wide apart for the size of his nose, and his hair had been combed from one side of his head to the other and plastered down with hairspray to cover a bald zone. The wind was lifting the wisp of stiff hair off his head, standing it straight up so it looked like a single punk spike. The Western clothes and boots he wore clearly were not natural to him and made him look a kid dressing up in someone else's things.

Gran looked as crabby as the cat, and they both stared at the intruder.

"And you needn't look at me like that, Mrs. Walker," he went on nervously. "I am very sorry about your husband's condition, but I am . . . I am only doing my job. It's not my fault Mr. Walker collapsed with chest pains. . . ." His voice trailed off lamely as it dawned on him that that was exactly what she was thinking.

"Don't whine, Mr. Rice. I haven't accused you of anything . . . yet." My grandmother froze the man in his insincere tracks.

"The Bureau of Land Management may be able to wait to discuss this business, but we cannot. We have a ranch to run and a major disaster to face if you succeed in withdrawing grazing rights that are lawfully ours. So save the sappy sentiment you clearly don't mean, and let's get to business. Con is perfectly capable of accompanying his grandfather to the hospital."

Raymond was not in friendly territory, and he knew it. Turning red from anger—or embarrassment—he looked like he would rather be on the moon than left to face my grandmother.

"Don't worry, Gran. I'm glad to go." I climbed into the ambulance, trying to make my voice sound calm. She closed the door behind me and waved a feeble good-bye.

They stood there together, Alisa and Gran. Very still. Eyes on the ambulance.

I didn't envy Mr. Rice.

Grandpa was pale, and an oxygen tube had been strung from behind his ears and tucked under his nostrils. *I hate this*, I thought miserably. *I hate this so much.* Forcing down my rising panic and desire to leap out of the ambulance, I took hold of Grandpa's rough old hand.

"Grandpa . . . you knothead," I said softly, using his kidding endearment for me. "Why'd ya have to go and do this?"

"What did you see up in the pasture this morning?" was his only reply.

◆

Cooling my heels in the hallway of Hot Springs Hospital outside the emergency room hours later, I tried to take my mind off Grandpa's condition by concentrating on the question.

What I had seen was all he'd wanted to know before drifting off in medicated sleep.

I saw sagebrush and fat cattle and more asparagus and wild flowers than I ever hoped to see again.

I saw a lot and I saw nothing.

I talked to him all the way to town—in case he could hear me and because I couldn't stop. I talked while I watched his slow, labored breathing, praying he wouldn't die. I told him about Alisa insisting—even after we had a bucketful of flowers—that we simply had to find one special white flower Gran likes, the butterfly lily or some silly thing. And how she made me cut only the most tender asparagus shoots for him, and that I hoped he would get well soon to eat the stuff so I wouldn't have to. I talked about how good the grass looked and how fat and content the cattle seemed to me. I told him about Shades—but left out the stuff about our panic, which I would save for later when I could make him laugh. Even as I talked, I found myself thinking it would be better for him to die than live like this, like some weak, helpless old man.

Sitting in the corridor, my head buried in my hands, I asked God to forgive me for such terrible thoughts. "Please, God," I whispered, "heal his heart. Let him live no matter what."

Helplessly I waited on, sitting on the floor with my back against the wall right outside the wide swinging doors of the emergency room. The clock above the doors read 3:59. I was getting hungry, too. I wondered why Gran hadn't arrived yet.

I smiled a little, remembering poor Mr. Rice and his attempt to shrink off the porch and escape my grandmother's wrath. I knew she had called my uncle Ted in Casper—father of Lindy, Claire, Kate, and Abby and one of the best lawyers in the state. He had given Gran advice on how to handle the BLM's false accusations. I bet Mr. Raymond Rice hadn't counted on my Gran having a lawyer in the family when he decided to make up allegations about the Walker Ranch. Too bad Uncle Ted was in the middle of a big case in Casper at the moment and couldn't come to help right now.

I closed my eyes to the hospital sights around me, putting

my sleeve over my nose to avoid the smell of disinfectant, dirty laundry, and uneaten food that filled the corridor. I breathed deeply through my sleeve, hoping for the scent of sage from the morning, but instead I got only my own sweat mingled nicely with the hospital odors I was trying to avoid.

"Yuk! Yuk! Yuk!" I complained, wanting to be anywhere but there.

"Watch for things out of place," Grandpa had said. What had I seen out there this morning, he had asked. Nothing.

There wasn't anything to see, I thought with frustration. Fences were tight. Water in the tank. Gates closed. There was nothing wrong today in Birdseye Pasture. I was sure of it. I had kept my eyes open. There had been nothing to see.

"Tush getting tired?" a friendly voice inquired, interrupting my unhappy thoughts.

I looked up to see a starched white nursing uniform on an old lady with a smile so kind it was out of place in such a stiff outfit. Her comfortable wrinkled face was all friendliness. She looked fifty at least. I expected nurses to be younger. Sterner. Or prettier.

"Yes," I answered, accepting her hand up. "As a matter of fact, it is."

"Well, why don't you wait in the waiting room, where they have nice soft things called sofas designed to eliminate tired tush. I promise to come and get you when the doctors are finished examining your grandfather."

Stiff from sitting on the hard floor, I stretched and followed her.

"You look like him, you know," she said, walking along beside me. "You're going to be as tall *and* as handsome as he is!"

I didn't think so, but it was a nice thought. "Do you know my grandfather?"

"Do I? Everybody around here knows Whit Walker. It's a small town. My name's Mrs. Evans, by the way, and my guess is you are Roberta's boy. It's the accent, you know, gives you away," she rambled on as we walked. "Why on earth a Walker would live off in some foreign place like Australia, I can't imagine."

"It's Austria, not Australia," I corrected her. "And I don't have an accent."

"Whatever. Why not live right here on the most beautiful ranch in Wyoming?"

The waiting room was empty. A sign on the door said, *Children Under Twelve Not Allowed in Waiting Room Unless Having Surgery.*

"Whoa!" I said, stepping back in mock horror. "They operate on kids in the waiting room? Where do they operate on adults, the coffee shop?"

To my surprise, Mrs. Evans let out a cackling laugh that pealed like a bell in that dismal place. "You might look like your grandfather, but you sound like your grandmother." She went away still laughing, leaving me there comforted somehow.

I watched the occasional nurse come and go across my line of vision through the open door. About the time my patience with waiting had run out, I heard a low, mournful chant with a faint rhythmical jingling coming toward the room. A different smell, incense maybe, drifted into the waiting room as the sounds got nearer.

A group of Native American men carrying a homemade litter had stopped in the corridor right outside the waiting room door. Four men, one on each corner, carried the unusual stretcher, while the other men lined it with their bodies like an honor guard. A white blanket with bright red and turquoise designs woven into it was tucked around the body of an old, old man. He was wrapped like a mummy, arms inside, and only his long, snow-white braids lay over the traditional Indian blanket. I recognized Chief Running Wolf by his famous trademark— those long white braids.

Interesting, I thought. The old cattle rancher and the old chief. Two strong men now at the mercy of nurses. I wondered again what the trouble was between the two of them.

A hospital administrator was desperately trying to take charge and restore order.

"You can't bring the patient in here until all the paper work is signed," she said in a high-pitched voice, looking down her nose at the men. "And get that incense pot out of here at once. This is a hospital, not a powwow."

The mournful chant in an ancient Indian tongue went on despite her, but one man stepped forward.

"My name is Yellowdog," a cold, hard voice said. "Chief Running Wolf is very ill. You have kept us waiting long enough. You will see that he gets a doctor now."

Some force of dignity or power in his voice stopped the woman in her tracks. When Yellowdog moved I saw, to my complete surprise, who was beside him.

There in the middle of those tribal leaders was Jed, my surly companion on the flight into Thermopolis, standing ramrod straight beside the chief like the other older men. Unlike them, he was wearing a Mother Earth T-shirt with the green globe logo.

This was the same Jed who said he had never been to Wyoming before and had come to *find* his roots.

Unknown summer visitors looking for their roots did not stand with tribal elders at the bedside of a dying chief. Yet there he was in his short marine haircut and summer job T-shirt, looking totally out of place. But his eyes, fixed on the old man, seemed to hold real grief. I shrank back in the doorway, not wanting to intrude.

All the men but Jed continued their mournful song as they waited for the doctor and a room to put the old man in.

Pushy nurses bustled about in the corridor, still complaining. But despite the unorthodox behavior of the men, when the doctor finally came he had the old man rushed into the emergency room. I watched from the doorway of the waiting room as Jed and all the others were stopped at the sliding doors of the ER. Modern medicine had taken charge.

I stepped back so Jed wouldn't see me and wondered again how he came to be at the bedside of the most important man on the reservation. Chief Running Wolf had been around forever, and his ancestor Chief Washakie had signed the peace treaty with President Ulysses S. Grant. Jed, it seemed, had found some very interesting roots after all.

---◆---

It was eight o'clock and the sun was getting low behind the Owl Creek Mountains when Gran and I emerged from the hospital many hours later. Alisa had driven to Casper to pick up some legal papers from Uncle Ted's law office. Gran had finally arrived at the hospital about five in the afternoon and was ready now to take me home. It had been a very long day. I felt shot.

Grandpa was out of danger for now, the doctor assured us. His heart was stabilized on medication. He needed lots of rest and no stress.

The long day had taken a toll on Gran, too. She walked slowly through the parking lot, her limp from an old horseback riding injury showing up.

"Sorry, Gran," I said, laying my hand on her shoulder. "You okay?"

I was taller by several inches, and she had to look up to smile at me. It was a thin, weak smile, but not a defeated one. Years of working and living outside had left deep lines in her face and given her a permanent dark tan. Her short, dark hair, which had never turned gray, made her look much younger than Grandpa.

Walking along beside her, I filled my lungs with the sweet scent of light rain, which had dampened the dust.

"Hey, look at that," I said. "Jed is driving nice wheels." A white Chevrolet pickup with the green Mother Earth topographical globe logo painted on the door was parked near Gran's car.

"Nice," I whistled. "A four-by-four extended cab Silverado 1500 series."

"Crazy radicals," Gran sputtered. "Look at those bumper stickers. Ridiculous!"

She wasn't kidding: *The Only Good Cow Is a Dead Cow*, *Real Men Don't Raise Cows*, and *Feed the Wolves—Your Baby Calves*.

"Come on, Con," she said, disgusted. "I'm tired."

I glanced in the back as we passed and saw several salt blocks in an otherwise clean truck bed. They were white. . . . I paused for a second, small warning bells going off faintly in my tired brain.

"Why would a so-called environmental group violently opposed to ranching be hauling around cattle salt?" I asked.

"I can't imagine, Con. And frankly, I have more important things on my mind." Gran motioned for me to follow her to their maroon Lincoln Town Car.

I had given up trying to talk my grandparents into buying European. But even though the Lincoln couldn't compare to Nigel's BMW, it was comfortable, and I rested my head on the plush headrest as we drove.

I kept thinking about Jed showing up at the bedside of Chief Running Wolf. I wanted to tell Gran about it and ask her what Chief Running Wolf had against Grandpa. But she was worried about other things, and I didn't want to bother her with some ancient—and maybe not so pleasant—family history.

"Are you sure you will be all right here alone for a few hours?" Gran asked me thirty minutes later while standing in the quiet kitchen preparing to go back to town to spend the night at the hospital with Grandpa. "I'm sure Alisa will be back soon. I've never spent a night away from your grandfather since our wedding, and I hate to start now. Will you be okay alone until she comes?"

A vase of Alisa's wild flowers stood on the counter, reminding me of the wonderful start to this long day.

"Sure, whatever—" I said, not really hearing her question because the elevator finally got to the top floor in my brain and exploded with a thought so scary it drove out everything else.

"Gran," I said, my mouth feeling dry, "do you happen to know if Grandpa always buys *pink* salt blocks for the cattle?"

She gave me a where-did-that-question-come-from look but answered, "Yes, as a matter of fact, he does."

"Are you absolutely certain? I mean, what if white ones were cheaper?" My voice was trembling. I could see in my mind's eye the white salt block half buried in the soft mud at the Birdseye watering hole. "Could Big Bear possibly have put out white salt blocks for the cattle?" I pushed her.

"No, he couldn't have! Con, what on earth are you talking about? I don't know what difference it makes, but yes, I am certain. And it doesn't have anything to do with price. There is extra mineral in the pink salt. Your grandfather always uses it, and I don't even think the farmer's co-op sells the white salt blocks. But why on earth does the color of cow salt interest you, especially at a time like this? Really, Con, sometimes I wonder about you."

Yeah, me too, I thought, trying desperately to think of a logical explanation why a brand-new block of salt had been in our pasture where Big Bear had said no salt should be. And a *white* one just like what Jed happened to be carrying around for the anti–cattle ranching Mother Earth organization.

Cattle dying, Grandpa had said. Too many unexplained cattle deaths.

I couldn't bring myself to add to Gran's worries, and since Grandpa was counting on *me*, I decided I had to go back up to the pasture and get rid of the other salt block before it was too late.

Way to go, Con, I said to myself. *Way to blow it on the first day.*

The cattle would all come in for water at first light in the morning. And they would follow up with a lick of salt. What if it was more than salt?

"Never mind, Gran," I said, gulping down my alarm and giving Gran a kiss on the check. "Don't worry, I'll be fine. And tell Grandpa I'm taking care of things for him."

After Gran left, I headed for the corral, glad Alisa wasn't there to stop me. This was my chance to ride the best horse on the ranch.

The moon was full, and I could see the buttes in the distance as I nervously led Yeats through the barbed-wire gate and out into the vast pasture.

I could feel the big horse pulling away as soon as I placed myself in the saddle. Knowing I couldn't stop him if he chose to take charge, which he promptly did, I held on for dear life.

Keeping my head low over his neck, I pulled with all my might on the reins as Yeats got his head unchecked by my efforts to control him. *So much for weight lifting*, I thought. *I have all the strength of a girl.*

Sagebrush came rushing toward me in a blur. Yeats was running fast and loving it. Ears laid back, he attacked each gully like it was a steeplechase and sidestepped cacti with weaving motions meant to lose me or miss them, I couldn't tell.

"Whoopeee!" I shouted into the wind when I realized I was staying on after all. What stupid urge had caused me to saddle Yeats instead of a more reasonable horse, I couldn't imagine, but I was glad. And glad Grandpa didn't know.

When the horse finally tired and slowed down to a more manageable speed, I patted his sweaty neck. "Okay, William Butler Yeats! A horse with an attitude. And Grandpa thought you were too much horse for me."

The horse relaxed against the bit, giving me at least an illusion of control. That first mad gallop had brought us through the Saddle and up on top of the buttes, a long way toward the rock outcropping where, hopefully, I would find my imagination had once again run away with me. Then I would return home and never tell a soul about my crazy midnight ride.

"Good boy," I said, feeling more in charge, rather proud to discover I could handle Grandpa's horse after all.

I held him tight and to the center of Devil's Slide. His hooves dug into the loose gravel as he pulled up the steep climb. Eerie shadows hid the bottom of the deep canyons on either side, where the moonlight couldn't reach. *Just as well*, I decided, keeping my eyes straight ahead.

Driving up Devil's Slide would be scary. I was glad to be on a horse.

Yeats seemed to be content to travel at my pace after that first burst of independence, and we stayed on the cattle trail. Cattle have a habit of following one another single file along certain paths to water. These paths tend to be narrow and crooked but usually the shortest distance between two water holes, so I stuck to it, hoping it led to the right water hole.

The night air was cold, and I was glad for my leather jacket and heavy sweat shirt underneath. Except for the crunching of horseshoes against the occasional rock and Yeats' legs brushing against the sagebrush, the night was quiet. Even the nighthawks were asleep.

Vast empty space stretched unbroken to the horizon, where it met the starry sky. The possibility of getting lost had not occurred to me when I set out. But then, I had never been in the wilderness alone at night. Some of the cousins could have navigated by the stars—or at least figured out general direction. I wished desperately I had paid attention to the nighttime stargazing sessions we always had, with Claire lecturing us on the constellations.

Lost. I didn't like the sound of it.

I shivered in the increasingly cold night.

I thought about Hannah. She would have loved this crazy ride. But she also would have probably complained about it the whole time.

I smiled in the darkness, missing my best friend and wondering what she was doing so far away in Europe.

As I came over a small rise, the path dipped into a valley and I saw a group of large scary shapes looming like stone tombs in front of me. Yeats didn't flinch, and I quickly realized Yeats and I had followed the wrong trail and veered west. The "tombs" were only the sandstone rock formations we called the Mushroom Rocks. Large bulbous tops sat on narrow stems about four or five feet high and made them look like gigantic mushrooms.

Yeats' shoes struck the sandstone as he carefully picked his way over the rocky surface, unbothered by the familiar terrain. Grandpa had taken him over this country hundreds of times, day and night. I had been here plenty of times, too. Hiking to the Mushroom Rocks was a favorite cousin pastime. Our very own cousin theater troupe had once performed an act of *A Midsummer Night's Dream* here, although we usually held our summer plays, organized and directed by the girls, under the shade of the old cottonwood trees near the house. Casting had always been a problem for our troupe, with only me to fill the male parts.

I stopped at the Mushroom Rocks and rested Yeats, remembering past summers. I had sometimes complained about the summer plays, but our "Shakespeare in the Rocks" had been fun. Even our audience—Grandpa and Gran, Uncle Ted and Aunt Sharon, Uncle Richard and Aunt Leigh, and my mom—hadn't complained much about being dragged up there to watch our production, especially when we served them tea cakes, coffee, and sandwiches afterward on the tailgate of the pickup.

The food had been Kate's idea. *Kate, the louse. Off somewhere with the Casper Troopers Drum and Bugle Corps instead of here with us.*

Water was standing in a tiny pool formed in the top of the rock. I dipped my finger in it. *It must have rained up here this afternoon,* I thought. Such an afternoon summer squall usually did nothing more than settle the dust. I licked my finger. Sweet summer rain—and I had missed it sitting in that stinking hospital.

"Giddyup, Yeats. We have 'miles to go before we sleep,' to quote Robert Frost, another of Grandpa's favorite poets. 'Miles to go and promises to keep.' " I corrected our course and resumed my mission.

Finally in the distance, with the moon still on the rise behind them, the tall outline of the uneven pinnacles of rock came into view.

"Yes, Birdseye Butte!" I shouted into the quiet. Now to find that stupid block of salt. I urged the horse on with a gentle nudge of my boots.

Through the moonlight I could see the windmill and water tank. There were more sandstone formations, small roundish ones.

Oh no! I gasped, my heart pounding. There were no mushroom rocks anywhere near the windmill.

The still shapes outlined by the moon were not rocks, of course, but dead cattle.

5

SHADES

"No . . . no . . . no . . ." I said over and over again.

I wandered around numbly from one dead body to the next, leading Yeats with me, thinking the same thing each time I stumbled across more of Grandpa's beautiful cattle, now cold and terribly dead.

I've failed him. He told me to keep my eyes open, to look for things where they shouldn't be, and I totally missed it.

I felt lost and stupid and hopeless. Grandpa had trusted me, and on the first day, I failed. Big time.

I counted over a hundred dead cattle before I collapsed against the water tank while Yeats calmly took a long drink. I was sure things couldn't get any worse.

And then they did.

There in the middle of all those black bodies, I was startled to see a ghostly glow as moonlight fell on the only light-colored cow in the herd—her Flying W brand a grim reminder of why she died.

A Charlois. Shades' mom, like all the rest, was dead of poison left by someone out to ruin the Walker Ranch.

"Not you, too," I moaned, kneeling down beside the once beautiful cow. I looked at the now lifeless eyes and remembered the terror in them this morning as she struggled for life. Desperately, I looked nearby for Shades. But he wasn't there. Neither were any other small calves, I realized.

I remembered the baby-sitter cow Alisa and I had noticed

on our way through the pasture—about three miles back. Those calves should be safe enough if found before they died of thirst. But Shades wouldn't be with them. He was too small to travel that far. In fact, his mother would not have moved him far from the spot where he'd been born.

Anger overcame my guilt for the moment and gave me something to do. I went in search of Shades. I had to find him, before he died, too. And I had to find the white salt block that must have carried poison powerful enough to bring down thousand-pound animals dead in their tracks.

Mother Earth . . . I could testify to seeing white salt blocks in their truck parked outside the hospital. I wondered if they had given similar ones to Fred Marvin and he had crossed over from his land last night to deposit the tempting salt right by the water tank, where the cows were sure to find it. Or it could have been dropped from the sky, from the light blue Cessna Alisa and I had observed flying low over the pasture—and ignored while looking at the eagle.

Of course. I kicked the dirt with my boot. How could we have been so blind? And dumb. Picking flowers and watching birds while someone was poisoning Walker cattle practically in front of us.

Well, I would find the poisoned salt block. If we could prove Mother Earth had killed the cattle, maybe we could make them pay. Before August. Before it was too late to save the ranch.

Anger and frustration drove me on as I crashed about through the sagebrush, forgetting to watch for snakes, determined to find the evidence—and Shades.

Finding the block of salt didn't prove to be too hard. In my hurry, I tripped and fell over it, banging my shin in the process and landing face down in the dirt.

Yeats, who had been faithfully plodding along behind me, now put down his head, nudged my arm, and gave a little snort.

"I'm okay, if you're asking," I said to the big horse. "And at least I've found it."

As I sprawled there on the ground, I ran my hand over the rough surface of the salt. Without thinking, I licked my finger.

"Yuk," I sputtered, leaping to my feet and madly wiping my tongue on my sleeve—grabbing the canteen out of the saddlebag and realizing, too late, that I had just repeated the same action that had dropped the big cows dead in their tracks. I guzzled the stale water, spitting it out and sputtering, expecting any moment to keel over like the cows.

I didn't keel over—or even feel sick.

"That's odd," I said aloud, and then I figured out why I wasn't dead.

I had stumbled over the *pink* block of salt, the one I had put out. Nothing but nice safe salt.

Relieved, I continued my search.

Crawling around on my hands and knees, feeling in the dirt, I searched for the evidence.

"It's here. It's got to be right here, Yeats. Stop eating and help me," I said stupidly to the poor horse, who ignored me and went on grazing. Unable to find it, I stopped thrashing about and moved in a systematic circle round and round where I knew it must be. Farther out with each pass.

What I found didn't exactly cheer me up. As I ran my hands over the flat surface of the ground, I found a shallow hole—where the salt block *had* been.

Whoever put it there had been back again.

I put my head between my hands and shook with anger and frustration.

The cold night air began to seep through my seat and into my bones. Miserable and shivering, I lay flat on my back and looked up at the stars.

Yeats was getting restless, pulling a little on the reins, so I tightened my grip.

"We'll find a way," Grandpa had said. *"People won't expect you to be able to help, Con. But we'll surprise them, won't we, son?"*

Actually, we had surprised only me so far. With my own stupidity.

I picked out Jupiter—and maybe one of its moons. A satellite moved across the sky. I wondered what message it was beaming back to earth. And then I used the oldest communication known to man, which did not require technology, only a humble heart. I prayed.

It cleared my head.

I had blown it. And I couldn't afford to do it again. Tonight might not be the end for the ranch, but it did bring the end a little nearer, especially if I didn't kick in and start thinking. Random thoughts began to come together.

First things first. Proof. I really needed proof. Maybe the cracked piece of salt broke off. Maybe it was left behind.

Maybe I had given up too soon.

Maybe was better than nothing.

Moving more slowly this time, I ran my hand carefully around the place were it had been, sifting the dirt through my fingers like I was panning for gold. Over and over. All around.

Finally I was rewarded with a small sliver of salt. A chip off the old block.

"Yes, yes, yes!" I shouted, pumping my fist in the air. "Whoever you are out there, you left something behind, and I have it." I squeezed the small sliver tightly in my fingers.

"The only good cow is a dead cow." That's what the bumper sticker on the Mother Earth pickup had said. Well, I wondered if whoever that organization sent to retrieve the poisoned salt block laughed at the sight of all our dead cows, if it made them glad.

Well, we'll see who laughs last. Clutching the precious evidence in my left hand, I reached inside my jacket and removed Hannah's note with my other. I carefully folded the Austrian Airline notepaper into a tight little envelope and put the sliver of salt inside. Hannah would be pleased when I told her how I used her note. I put the envelope safely back into my inner pocket, along with my Swiss Army knife.

Now to find Shades.

If he was still alive, he couldn't last much longer, I figured. Not without his mother. Encouraged by the little piece of evidence in my pocket, I was more determined than ever to find the baby calf.

With Yeats following along behind on a loose rein, I retraced our path to where the cow had lain.

There was a thicket of willows and chokecherry bushes nearby. Shade and protection, I reasoned. The cow might have left her newborn calf there when she went to water.

I crouched down at the edge of the willows and listened for any movement, any sound of breathing. The quiet was deadly; even the crickets and—hopefully—the rattlesnakes were all asleep.

Only the gentle jingle of Yeats' bridle broke the silence. Loosening my hand on the reins, I moved farther into the prickly bushes, hoping and praying I'd find a living, breathing calf and nearly giving up when a howl pierced the air. Yeats reared back, nearly pulling his reins through my fingers and dragging me a few feet through the sagebrush.

"Whoa, it's just coyotes, you silly horse." I struggled back to my feet, wiping off bits of sage and grass and cactus prickles, glad for the protection of my leather jacket.

Another howl, followed by another. It sounded like a pack.

Coyotes would never attack a calf with the mother cow standing watch. But they would have a weak, helpless newborn for lunch. I looked deeper in the willows and found Shades curled up in the undergrowth. My heart surged with relief. The coyotes had smelled him and were circling, but I got there first. I felt his body and wanted to shout with relief to find it still warm.

"Shades," I said, tracing the circles around his eyes with my finger. I touched his nose. It was way too dry. His mouth hung open a little, and his breathing was shallow and raspy.

"Shades, you poor little guy. I'm sorry."

I wondered how long it had been since he had eaten and if those first drinks we saw him take moments after he was born had been his only. Those wobbly steps would be his last if I left him here alone.

But saving Shades was going to be harder than finding him had been.

While I pondered my options, I took the canteen out of the saddlebags. Bracing him between my legs and tilting his head slightly back, I tried to pour what water was left down his throat. The stale water ran out of his mouth onto my Levi's.

The calf was too weak to even swallow. Big Bear could save him, but only if I got him home. Fast.

I had seen Grandpa pick up calves much bigger than Shades, throw them over the saddlehorn, and let the horse do the carrying.

It was a nice idea. Except one, I wasn't strong enough, and two, I wasn't strong enough.

I couldn't carry him back with me. And I couldn't leave him unprotected from the coyotes. A few hours could make the difference. I did the math. I could tie Yeats to the thicket to keep the coyotes away, then run back to the ranch and get Alisa to drive the pickup back. It would take approximately three hours. I pondered it as an option. Not perfect, but my only one.

In the end, I tied Grandpa's favorite horse securely to the willow tree nearest Shades and left him—praying he would still be there when I got back. A good cow horse wouldn't step on a calf, and coyotes wouldn't dare come near the big horse.

At least it isn't hot, I thought, setting off down Old Stagecoach Road and pacing myself with a fast jog.

I was trying not to think about how I was going to get back if Alisa hadn't returned from Casper. Driving up Devil's Slide at night by myself was not part of my plan.

It was nearly two A.M. when I reached the house. The ranch was quiet as a churchyard. Alisa had driven the second vehicle—a very used Jeep—to Casper. It was not in the garage. She was not in her bed. I was still alone.

I collapsed into the quiet kitchen in despair. Drinking directly from a liter bottle of Coke, I checked the answering machine. Sure enough, there was Alisa's cheerful voice explaining that she hadn't finished getting what Gran needed in Casper and was going to spend the night with the cousins. She'd be back midmorning.

"Have fun, Con. You've always wanted the place to yourself. Here's your chance." I could hear the giggles of Lindy, Claire, and Abby in the background of the recorded message.

Tired and sore, I felt a little sorry for myself. But in addition to Shades, I had left Grandpa's favorite horse tied up in the pasture. I had to go back.

I have no choice, I kept telling myself as I downed the whole bottle of Coke. *If Alisa can drive up that dangerous, narrow, steep pass, so can I.* I grabbed a couple extra Cokes out of the refrigerator. One for me and one for Shades. Maybe the caffeine would revive him.

The old grandfather clock struck two times as I walked out the front door. With a sinking heart, I remembered something Grandpa once said: *"Good judgment comes from experience, and experience comes from bad judgment."* I was not comforted by the old proverb because I didn't know which side of that circle I was on—except I had the distinct impression I was about to exercise some very bad judgment.

Clutching the pickup keys in my sweaty hands, I set out to face Devil's Slide alone. Twice.

6

LIFE AFTER DEVIL'S SLIDE

FEAR HAD TURNED TO TIREDNESS. JET LAG, LOSS OF SLEEP, and nothing to eat had worn me out. I felt my head slipping farther and farther down until I found myself staring blurry eyed *between* the steering wheel and the dashboard at the streaks of light on the road in front of me.

After the terror of driving up Devil's Slide by myself and living through it, exhaustion was putting me to sleep on the long, flat, empty road.

"Come on, get a grip," I told myself, smacking my forehead with the palm of my hand.

As I neared Birdseye Butte, I kept my eyes away from the devastation by the water tank, hoping desperately that Yeats was where I had left him. It had occurred to me on the long walk back to the ranch that whoever came back to retrieve the salt block might not have been far away and glad for a chance to kill Grandpa's favorite horse, also.

I heard Yeats' stomping before I saw him.

He wasn't happy about being tied up in the pasture for hours, but he was there. The coyotes had given up and gone away, it seemed, and to my great relief, Shades was still alive.

I breathed a prayer of thanks and loaded the horse into the pickup first, tying him securely to the front of the stock racks behind the cab. It was going to be a bumpy ride back, and after all I had gone through to save Shades, I didn't want Yeats accidentally stepping on him. The calf was getting weaker, and he didn't resist as I picked him up. Which wasn't easy. Shades was a big calf, and I stumbled under his weight, then as gently as possible pushed and shoved until I had him in the back of the pickup, well away from Yeats.

The sun was emerging now, lighting the eastern horizon and threatening to break day as I closed the endgate on the stock racks and headed for home.

Fast.

I didn't particularly welcome the day. I kept remembering Alisa's advice about driving Devil's Slide. *"Going up is easy. It's getting back down that's tough. And never, never, never look over the side."* I didn't trust myself not to look, so I preferred the dark.

Going up *had* been easy. A piece of cake, in fact.

Beginner's luck, Hannah would have called it.

I had made my approach exactly as Alisa had done, gearing down in four-wheel drive and holding her steady, careful not to spin out. Darkness had hidden the dreadful precipice on either side.

I had made it up alive and desperately wanted to stay that way.

I drove to beat the light, not slowing at cattle guards, even though the metal bars, which were set several inches apart over shallow pits to keep cattle from walking over them, rattled my teeth as I charged across.

Maybe Yeats felt my nervousness. His wild eyes stared at me through the cab window, and his high-pitched whinny made prickles of fear run down my back.

Tossing his mane and stamping his feet, Yeats pulled against the reins that tied him. The stock racks formed a pen in the bed of the truck; they also towered over the cab, making the pickup top-heavy. I felt it sway as I pulled around each bend in the road. And the stomping horse didn't help. I hoped he would forgive me for tonight, tying him up, leaving him in the pasture, driving too fast. But I had to beat the dawn to Devil's Slide. And I had to get Shades back before it was too late.

Sliding the cab window open, I tried to calm Yeats. If

Grandpa talked to him to calm him down, I could, too.

I reasoned wrong. His whinnying became wilder, and his hooves continued to slide on the slick bed of the pickup as he thrashed about. Twelve hundred pounds of tense horse.

I arrived at Devil's Slide too late. Morning had broken, and the red granite buttes I had to drive between were clearly visible as the sun rose behind me, lighting the way I *didn't* want to see.

The steep gravel track was only slightly wider than the axles of the truck. Shallow ruts lined the way. The key was not to swerve, skid, or slide. And tipping would, of course, be followed by tumbling, which I definitely didn't want to do. I tried not to think about the old stagecoach remains at the bottom of the gulch.

"It's now or never," I muttered to myself. I slowed way down but didn't hesitate on my approach—afraid I'd lose my nerve.

In first gear and standing on the brake, I dropped the nose of the pickup over the edge and held on tight, eyes in the center of the road.

The tires scrunched noisily over the loose gravel, but they held in the ruts as I made my descent, afraid to exhale.

The weight of the truck was forcing me faster than I wanted to go down that too-steep hill. Pumping gently on the brakes, I held the wheel as steady as I could, trying not to look left or right.

And then, when I thought I had it made, a nighthawk swooped in close over the top of the cab, darting at the nervous horse. He reared, broke the reins, and slid, shifting the balance of the truck. I felt the stock racks sway right and tilt toward the edge, so close I couldn't help but see the empty space reaching down to the valley floor thousands of feet below.

"No!" I yelled.

I pulled left in an effort to correct and felt the wheels slide out of the rut and toward the other side.

I think I screamed.

Yeats did, too. Struggling to his feet, he lunged back across the truck bed, balancing it enough for me to pull it right and hold it straight until somehow I reached the bottom of the Slide.

As the road broadened out onto the plain, I let the pickup coast to a stop, then collapsed over the wheel, thankful to be alive.

I sat there for a while, clammy from fear, determined never to drive that road again. Ever.

Not for anything.

◆

For three weeks things got worse. Long, hot summer days set in, and our problems grew faster than the hay in the meadow.

The sheriff had laughed at my "evidence" when I took it to him that very same morning. *"Cattle die all the time, sonny,"* he had said and sent me home to "play."

Grandpa came home from the hospital, but he mostly stayed in bed, too weak to do the physical therapy needed on his leg. I thought the loss of so many cattle was making him worse, and I knew that was my fault. I still went each evening and sat in the beautiful old room to talk to him, but there seemed very little for either one of us to say. I missed the grandpa I could count on and the lazy days of summers past.

Raymond Rice from the BLM office continued to press charges of "environmental abuse," giving Gran until August 15 to prove otherwise or lose their leases. According to Rice, a "government expert" had completed a study that showed "overgrazed range and severe riparian damage along Jones Creek."

"We never overgraze," Gran fumed. "And the banks of Jones Creek break a little every year—washed away by spring rain."

But we had no expert on our side, only experience, and it didn't look like it would be enough.

And to make matters worse, Hannah hadn't called.

Watching the now growing, healthy Shades run and play with the other orphaned calves kept me sane.

Then one afternoon while I was helping Big Bear haul some

hay, the Casper cousins drove in.

"What are you doing here?" Alisa said, throwing up her arms and racing across the yard to meet them. "We didn't expect you until the Fourth of July."

Gran and I were close behind.

Lindy was the first to step out of her little Honda Accord. At eighteen, she was the oldest Walker cousin and had just spent one year at the University of Wyoming. She didn't *look* any older for having gone to college. Her long blond hair was pulled back and stuffed in some kind of knot on her head—with curls sticking out all over. Her smile had always made me laugh.

"Con, Alisa, Gran, I'm so glad to see you," Lindy said, tears running down her cheeks as she hugged us all. She cried at everything. Lindy, "the Tenderhearted," we called her. I had seen her burst into tears at the sight of long-dead road kill.

There were hugs all around.

"Claire, you're getting shorter every year," I said to the only non-tall Walker, who hit me in reply. For a fifteen-year-old, she packed a pretty good punch.

Abby—nine years old and "the Cow's Tail," as Grandpa called her because she was the last of all his grandkids—crawled out of the backseat, where she'd been smushed between all the stuff the girls had brought. It looked like they were moving in. Unlike her big sister Lindy, Abby saved her emotion for the calves.

"Con, come on, show me Shades," she said, taking my arm and pulling me to the pen. It was love at first sight. Abby, who always spent her time outside with the animals, put a halter on the tame calf and led him back to the lawn to show her sisters.

"Does Grandpa really let you ride Yeats now?" she wanted to know.

"Yup," I said. "He thinks that if I stayed on during my midnight ride, I am certainly ready."

"Wow!" Abby was amazed. "I hope I can ride him someday, too."

"Keep that calf out of my flowers," Gran told Abby and then lamented the missing Kate. "Wish Kate could have come now, too. I miss her," she said. Kate, fourteen, was the quiet one who loved to help out in the kitchen with Gran. Chocolate chip cookies were her specialty. Kate was the most beautiful of all the girls. And good at every sport. She was always joining something, and this summer it was the Casper Troopers. I was still mad at her for abandoning us.

"You'll see her in August, Gran," Lindy said. "Kate will be at the head of the band when they march in the Thermopolis parade."

"August." Gran sighed and shook her head sadly. "Who knows what will happen by August."

There was an uncomfortable silence, no one wanting to actually talk about the troubles.

"Come on, Alisa," I said. "Let's get our tired, hot cousins something cold to drink. Sorry there are no welcome-home cookies or cake, but we didn't know you were coming."

But there was lemonade the way Gran made it. Fresh squeezed with slices of lemons floating in with the ice cubes. We brought out tall glasses for everyone but Shades.

Sitting there on the lawn with Alisa, Lindy, Claire, Abby, and Gran, listening to Buffalo Creek run its course in our backyard, things seemed better somehow.

"So what's the deal?" I asked, enjoying the moment. "What brings you here today?"

"Well," Claire answered, "we decided you and Alisa were not doing too well alone, so we've come to help."

"We've been so worried," Lindy added, tearing up again, "that we couldn't wait until the Fourth of July. I quit my job, and here we are."

"I don't know how you can help," I said. "I don't know how any of us can help."

"Con! That doesn't sound like you," Claire said. "There's lots we can do, like first of all figure out how to prove who poisoned the cattle and why that dummy Raymond Rice is lying about environmental violations. So we'll set up our own investigation center—in your room, by the way, since there isn't space upstairs. We've brought computer equipment from Dad's office, so we can get online and communicate with Jess in Oregon."

"Excuse me," I said, feeling defensive.

"Con," Lindy jumped in to smooth things over, "you and Alisa have done great; you just need some help. We can't stand to think about losing the ranch, either, you know."

Gran reached over and handed her a handkerchief.

"Claire is right, Con," Alisa declared. "We could use some help. Robin Blackford wanted a Sagebrush Rebellion. Well, now that you all are here, we'll start our own Sagebrush Rebellion to save our ranch from whoever thinks they can take it away."

And before I could respond, the phone rang. I took it in my room.

◆

"I lived," I said to Hannah, concluding my harrowing tale of navigating Devil's Slide and the story of the "Birdseye Massacre," as Alisa and I had dubbed it.

"You didn't," Hannah replied, her skepticism flowing over the phone lines from the other side of the Atlantic.

"Sure I did. That's why you can hear my voice now."

"No, dummy. I mean you *didn't* drive your grandfather's pickup up that dangerous road by yourself at night. You could have been killed."

"Uh-huh. But due to my great driving skill, I wasn't. And I rescued the baby calf from the coyotes and brought back Grandpa's favorite horse."

Hannah had listened, grudgingly impressed and then horrified. "Con," she gasped, "that's terrible. Did it really start to tip, or is this your usual exaggeration?"

"Would I exaggerate?"

"Yes, you *would* exaggerate." Hannah decided it probably wasn't as bad as I was making it out to be. "But the question is, Con, have you figured out who's doing all this stuff to your grandpa?"

None too eager to discuss my failures so far, I changed the

subject as I maneuvered the telephone cord over the head of Claire, who had started moving stuff in before I got off the phone.

Lindy's car had been packed with tons of girl stuff and the computer equipment borrowed from their dad's law office.

Claire was working on my desk at the moment, setting up our "investigation center."

Since Claire and I share the same age space in the cousin family tree, we have had our own adventures over the years and act more like siblings than cousins, according to our moms. Claire has a shorter, stocky frame, thick reddish brown hair, and green almond-shaped eyes, which come from her father's side of the family. Her cheeky personality she got from Gran.

"Excuse me, Claire. Could this wait? I'm trying to talk here," I said, wishing she would give me a little privacy.

"Sorry, Con. Priorities of our investigation and all that . . . Got to get this stuff set up." She didn't even bother to look up from her efforts to maneuver all their computer stuff onto my tiny desk.

Priorities, my foot. She was enjoying listening to my conversation with Hannah and wasn't about to move.

"Are you still lifting weights?" Hannah asked.

"Nah, I don't need to lift weights now. I'm lifting hay bales and baby calves instead," I bragged.

Claire giggled.

Cousins could be a pain.

I pulled the phone cord as far away as possible and listened as Hannah told me her big news.

She wasn't calling from Vienna but from Washington, D.C.

"We're going to spend the rest of the summer here," she explained. "My dad's working for a new company that makes a high-tech environmental testing device. He'll be showing it to different agencies in the U.S. government, then back in Europe—in time for me to start school with you in Vienna in September."

"Great. That means we're at least on the same side of the Atlantic. I wish I could join you for a weekend."

"I know," she said. "Think of all the spies we could find here in Washington, Con, what with the White House and foreign embassies and stuff. The place must be crawling with special agents." I could hear the teasing in her voice. She was never going to let me live down my bright idea to look for spies in Vienna last year.

"Hey, my plan turned out to be exciting, at least," I complained.

"A little too exciting," she agreed, a hint of reproach in her voice.

"What are you going to do in D.C.?" I asked. "Hang out with your dad while he sells this environmental testing thing?"

"As a matter of fact, yes, I am. And that's not bad, since the 'environmental testing thing' is really a very cool mass spectrometer called a SpectaTrak, which is a compact analytical laboratory, backed up by a phenomenally powerful computer, which can purge and trap gases, vapors, and solids. It's used in forensics and drug interdiction and—"

"Hellooo, Hannah," I interrupted her scientific flow. "You are not selling me a spec-ta-thingie-tra-meter. And in case you have forgotten, let me remind you I am missing the science lobe in my brain. So cut the technical jargon."

In stereo, over the phone and in the room, Claire and Hannah suggested pretty much in unison that wasn't the only brain lobe missing.

"Claire," I growled, "I thought you weren't listening to my conversation."

They both laughed, creating the stereo effect again.

"And," Hannah went on, stifling her laugher, "Dad is going to demonstrate the machine at the FBI for forensic testing purposes, and I get to go along. Too bad you can't come, too. Think how much fun we'd have sleuthing around the FBI!"

I thought it was too bad, too. Mr. Goldberg called to Hannah then. They were off to the Department of the Interior for his first demonstration, and Hannah was going with him—a "summer class in science and government," her Dad called it.

Feeling a little lonely after she hung up, I continued sitting on the bed, watching Claire organize the laptop computer, printer, and fax machine, thinking about something Hannah had said.

"Isn't the BLM part of the Department of the Interior?" I asked Claire.

"Beats me." Claire shrugged and went on hooking up all that stuff on *my* desk.

"Well, I think the BLM *is* part of the Department of the Interior, and I wonder if Hannah could have that obnoxious Raymond Rice fired while she's there with her dad today."

"It'd be nice." Claire smiled in agreement. It was good to have the other cousins at the ranch—even if it was a pain to put up with so many girls. The summer was beginning to feel like old times now that Lindy, Claire, and Abby had joined Alisa and me.

"You know, John Wayne didn't have all this high-tech stuff, and he did okay catching bad guys."

"Think what John Wayne could have done *with* all this high-tech stuff.

"Tell me more about what the sheriff said when you showed him the poisoned salt," Claire went on, leaning over the edge of the desk, trying to make room for the fax machine. "When I get the modem hooked up, I want to write down everything that's happened so far—just the basics—then email it to Jess."

"Why did she have to stay in Oregon and take that stupid job anyway? She should be here with us now. Who knows what will happen by August."

"Ever hear of money, Con? People need it to go to college, and Jess will be a high-school senior this fall, so she's saving up. Besides, she can research stuff for us and help out from Oregon."

I didn't see how, but I related the events of my trip to the sheriff for the benefit of Jess.

"There's not much I can add to what I told you already. I went to the sheriff's office that very day after being up all night. Alisa drove me to town and dropped me off while she went to see Grandpa in the hospital. I showed the sheriff my evidence and reported the scene of the crime. He said that cattle die all the time on the range, that it's bad news but hardly a crime. Then Sheriff Hays asked me if I had ever heard of larkspur."

I could still remember his smug attitude.

"Remember Robin Blackford," I asked Claire, "when he played the awesome sheriff in the movie *Western Justice*? Well, now picture the exact opposite and you have Sheriff Leslie Hays, the main lawman of Thermopolis."

The sheriff had worn a dirty Stetson, tipped brim-up on his head. He continued leaning back in a creaky wooden rocking chair—with snakeskin boots propped up on his desk—the whole time I was there, never even bothering to take a note. His desk was covered with loose papers, including computer printouts and an A & W hamburger wrapper. He was wearing a bolo tie made of clear plastic that covered a rattlesnake rattle, two fangs, and "snake eyes" dice.

Mimicking the sheriff's sneering voice, I repeated his conclusions for Claire:

" 'You've probably never heard of larkspur, sonny, living overseas and all. But it's a poison weed. Cattle eat it and die. Happens all the time. So why don't you leave things to those of us who understand the West, okay? You run along and play cowboy without bothering me.' "

Thinking about it made me furious—again.

"Can you believe that?" I asked Claire. "And how would he know I live overseas?"

And before Claire could respond, I added: "Don't say it, Claire. For the last time, I do *not* have an accent. I'm sick of everybody thinking I'm a foreigner—or a *kid*. 'Run along and don't get hurt, little boy.' That stupid sheriff wouldn't recognize a crime if it happened in his office."

"Yeah, sure, whatever, Con. Calm down. Get to the important part. Why wouldn't he test the piece of salt for poison?"

"How do I know? Because he's a moron and thinks I imagined the whole thing. Because he doesn't want to waste his valuable time—he was reading *Road and Track* when I came in. I don't know why he won't test it. He just won't."

"You didn't leave it with him, did you?" she asked, looking genuinely concerned.

"No, of course I didn't leave our one little piece of evidence with him. Do I look stupid as well as foreign?" I replied sarcastically. "Besides, he would probably have crushed it with the heel of his boot and used it on his lunch."

In fact, the small white sliver of salt I had risked so much to get was safely in a "Visit Wonderful Wyoming" tourist mug on my desk—for all the good it was going to do us. So much for that dead end. If the sheriff said we didn't have a case, we didn't have a case. I wanted to visit Jed and make him admit the organization he was working for had planted the poison. But I remembered how huge he was, and making him tell me anything seemed a little unlikely—even to me.

"And today," I explained to Claire, "Alisa and I went to the sale barn to check things out."

"Discover anything interesting?" Claire asked.

"That there are more earthy odors in a cattle auction barn than I remembered."

"Con."

"No, of course we didn't discover anything. Nobody is talking. At least not that we could hear. And Fred and Lilly Marvin weren't even there."

"Guilty conscience, maybe?" Claire asked hopefully.

"Listen to what's being talked about at the sale," Grandpa had said last night. *"See if the Marvins are there and what they're up to, whom they're talking to. Watch for anything and everything that seems out of place."*

Everyone met at the sale barn. News was spread there from ranch to ranch like a grass fire through a dry desert. Only all we'd heard this afternoon was a lot of hot air. And none of it was about the Walker Ranch. None of it was interesting, either.

Lindy, Alisa, and Abby joined us then after moving all their personal things into the third-floor attic bedrooms.

"I'm worried about Gran," Lindy said, plopping down on my bed to watch Claire fiddle with the computer. Abby curled up next to her big sister. Alisa sat cross-legged on the floor, making a sign of some sort with a large black magic marker.

"Gran seems too quiet to me," Lindy went on. "And she's limping a little from that old riding injury. Do you think she's okay?"

I had noticed it, too. Gran was looking less and less like her bouncy self and more and more defeated.

"I think she's worried about Grandpa," I answered. "And about the BLM August deadline. If they can't prove by then that Mr. Rice's charges of environmental violations on the BLM land are false, Rice wins and Grandpa will have to sell off the rest of the herd because he won't have any winter pasture. Without winter grazing he's done for. They lost lots of money last year when the cattle market fell out of bed. And now all the trouble this year . . . It will be the last straw. They'll have to sell the ranch or go bankrupt."

The possibility of losing the ranch hung heavy over the room. We sat in gloomy silence, each one thinking what it would mean to lose this place.

"Remind me why all this stuff needs to be in my room," I asked to break the tension.

"Because it's the only room with enough space. All of us girls get stuffed in the attic."

"Four girls and two bedrooms is hardly stuffed," I assured Claire. "And if you didn't bring so much junk, there would be enough room." I didn't really mind having the computer here since I figured I could find time for a few games and talk to Jess and maybe Hannah on email. But the fax was a bit much. Like we'd be faxing anyone.

"Do you think it hurts if the fax machine sticks out over the edge at the back of the desk like this, Con?" Claire asked.

"No, Claire," I said, observing her work. "I think crawling on your hands and knees between the wobbly legs on this old desk to pick up the fax copies is a *good* thing. It'll be especially convenient for Gran."

"Don't be a dope, Con," Claire said, satisfied with her efforts. "Gran isn't likely to be using any of this. She still isn't sure a phone is totally necessary."

Tragedy was perched on the desk and growled each time Claire moved her to rearrange things. Fascinated by the noise of the printer, the cat batted the paper as a test page printed out.

"Poor ol' Tragedy," Lindy said, stroking the fat cat. "I know what makes you crabby. Your biological clock's running out and still no kittens."

From my window, which faced south toward the dry sagebrush pasture, I could see a cloud of dust stirred up by a herd of young bulls in the distance. They were coming down toward the river for water. Those registered purebred bulls were the most expensive stock left on the ranch. Plodding single file along the cow path I had followed on Yeats, they broke into a trot as they got close enough to smell the water, bucking and jostling each other as they ran. I watched as they lined up along the riverbank, noses deep in the bubbling stream to drink their fill. Finally, full at last, the slick black animals wandered lazily over to the salt and contentedly licked the *pink* blocks with their big rough tongues.

I turned away and threw a pillow against the wall in frustration. It hit Tragedy, who let out her low, complaining yowl. Tired of crabby humans, she leaped out of the room with her tail up.

"Con," Abby complained, "don't take it out on the cat."

Finally Alisa stood up, and Claire helped her tack the sign to the door.

Sagebrush Rebellion Investigation Center

It cheered us up a little, even if we didn't yet have a clue.

◆

The very next day Lindy, going by her full name of Lindgren Larson, went to town to apply for a job at the local television station. She needed the job for college credit. If she didn't get it, she'd have to go back to Casper to work.

An air of gloom descended over all of us when the station didn't call back for more than a week. We feared the worst and couldn't stand to think of Lindy leaving. It appeared the Sagebrush Rebellion was pretty much flat before it got started.

Abby, who never said much, said even less, watching the orphaned animals for hours on end and muttering darkly about the murders on Birdseye Butte.

My talks with Grandpa provided him with no clues, and he provided me with no suggestions. I read in the newspaper that Chief Running Wolf had returned home to the reservation after an extended stay in the hospital. I ran that information past Grandpa to see if I could get a rise.

"Good" was all he replied.

But things were not good and getting worse.

And no one had made a chocolate cake for a whole week.

Then Jed turned up again.

"You're doing what?" I yelled at Alisa when she returned from town and told us her news.

"I'm going to the Fourth of July fireworks celebration tomorrow night with Jed," she repeated. "Are you having trouble hearing, Con?"

"No. I'm having trouble believing. Believing you would go out with that bum. How could you, after what he did? And why would he want to go out with a rancher's granddaughter anyway? You're not exactly the Mother Earth kind of girl."

"Con, we don't know he *did* anything, do we? He works for Mother Earth. They *might* have poisoned the cattle. That doesn't mean Jed knew about it. And besides, how better to find out what is going on in Mother Earth than to go out with Jed?"

Claire and I were sitting around the kitchen table after lunch. Lindy had gone off to take a phone call.

I thought Alisa looked a little too starry-eyed to be doing this for research, but in typical female solidarity, Claire agreed with her.

"Well, try to remember you're a Walker when you go out with the little weasel," I muttered.

"According to Alisa, he isn't little." Claire sniggered.

"And he doesn't look much like a weasel, either," Alisa giggled.

"Girls!" I said, disgusted, and started to storm out. Our lives were going down the tubes, and all they could think about was some cute guy.

"Goooood news," Lindy said excitedly, bursting into the room at that very moment. "I got the job. I'm officially working for KKOA Radio and TV." She was glowing.

"As what?" Claire and I more or less asked together.

"Excuse me," she said dramatically. "I'm a television personality now, and I don't have to bother with little people like you . . . unless I decide to interview you, of course."

Kicking off her sandals, shaking her curly hair loose, and dropping her grown-up-applying-for-a-job look, she sat down. Tucking her legs under her on the chair, Lindy explained:

"The KKOA guy said I will be assigned to some special projects covering local interest stories, which will be fun, and probably lots of pretty boring stuff, too. But it's perfect for my college requirement, and who knows? It might come in handy for us. At least it means I can stay here for the rest of the summer."

It was the first good news we'd had for a long time, and I was relieved to know Lindy would be sticking around.

"To Lindgren, our very own television personality." Claire and Alisa and I raised our Coke cans in salute.

"Lindgren Larson, strong of mind, mushy of heart," I said.

"Lindgren Larson, the new Barbara Walters," Alisa added her toast.

"Lindgren Larson, is that my top you have on?" Claire asked.

"Actually, I picture myself more as an investigative reporter," Lindy continued, ignoring her sister. "You know, influence peddling, corruption in City Hall, that kind of thing."

"Good idea, Lindy," I agreed sarcastically. "And you could call it *Sixty Seconds*—which is how much corruption you'll find in Thermopolis. This is *not* Washington, D.C., you know."

"I hope they don't ask you to cover any tragedies—you

know, like, 'Mother Antelope Shot by Hunters,' " Claire added helpfully.

"Ha! You two can laugh, but it's not a bad idea, you know. A little investigative reporting of Raymond Rice and the BLM office might be just what we need."

And in the middle of hearing about Lindy's good news, the phone rang again.

"Well, answer it, Claire, you're practically sitting on it," I said and soon wished I hadn't as it was Hannah again.

Claire managed to keep the phone away from me and engaged Hannah in several minutes of conversation before I got it away from her.

"Guess who I saw today at the Department of the Interior?" Hannah asked, more excited than was reasonable for a visit to a government agency—especially one that included the Bureau of Land Management!

"Uh . . . the Secretary of the Interior maybe?"

"No, really . . . who do you think?"

"The president of the United States."

"Better than that."

"The king of England."

"Con, get serious. There is no king of England at the moment. Really, guess who I just saw."

I waited, assuming she would end this silly game and tell me. And when she finally did, the coincidence made me gasp.

"No way. He's everywhere!"

"Who? Who's everywhere?" the girls wanted to know when I got off the phone.

"Robin Blackford. Hannah saw him today at the Department of the Interior. She even took a picture and said she'd send me one. Isn't that the most amazing thing? We have never seen a film star in our lives, and now all of a sudden our favorite actor turns up everywhere."

"THE ONLY GOOD COW IS A DEAD COW"

"LET'S GO FOR A RIDE," ABBY BEGGED ON THE AFTERNOON of July 5. "I want to go up to Birdseye Butte to see where Shades was born and climb the rocks to hunt for arrowheads—like we always do."

She was right. We needed one of our usual outings together to clear our brains. Help us think. It was Sunday, and we'd been home from church for about an hour. Now everyone wanted to pump Alisa for information about her date last night with Jed. A long ride together seemed like a good place to do it.

Claire and I saddled the horses with Abby's help while Lindy and Alisa put fresh water in the canteens and filled our saddle-bags with snacks.

The sounds of creaking leather and snapping brush were welcome, familiar sounds as all five of us swayed gently in com-fortable old saddles and let our horses pick their way between sagebrush and cacti at a steady but unhurried pace. We were quieter than usual, each one thinking our own thoughts about this ride, not completely comfortable with what we would find at its end, where the cattle had been killed. Even Alisa managed not to point out every bug, plant, and bird and comment upon them as we rode together back to the scene of the crime.

"What did you and Jed do last night?" Abby asked Alisa in-nocently.

We had planned to be more subtle.

"I met him at the Broken Spoke Café for a burger. Then we climbed the hill behind town, sat on the rocks that spell 'World's Largest Mineral Hot Springs,' and watched the fireworks. It was nice. End of story."

We were sure there was more to the story. But that was all we got.

"Race ya up the Slide," Claire said, easing her solid brown horse next to Yeats at the foot of Devil's Slide. With a kick in her horse's ribs, she burst past me.

Yeats, needing no encouragement from me, lunged forward with his ears laid back, pulling his massive frame into high gear as he charged up the rocky incline.

"See ya," I called back to Claire. The wind carried my words back to her as my faster horse surged past and beat everyone to the top by at least two lengths. Pleased with his victory, the sweaty horse stomped and snorted while first Claire, then Abby, Lindy, and Alisa joined us.

"Show-off," Claire said, but she was smiling. "I still can't believe you drove the truck up this thing at night."

"And back down again," Abby added proudly. "No big deal, right, Con?"

"Right," I replied. It was nice having one cousin still small enough to think I could do anything.

Resting our horses at the top, we gazed down the plunging precipice and off into the distance where the front range of the Wind River Mountains could be seen, and down at the ranch house tucked away in the big cottonwood trees. Behind it, the Red Wall, majestic, massive. There were no afternoon thunderclouds today. The clear, blue sky was swept clean by the wind.

"Has Mr. Big Bear had someone move all the dead cows away from the windmill?" Abby asked, moving her paint pony up next to me.

"Sure, Abby," I answered.

Lindy's eyes were getting red just thinking about it again. *Oh no*, I thought. *I hope for her sake, as well as Abby's, that I'm right and nothing is left behind, no physical reminder of that horrible night.* I knew Lindy shouldn't have come. "Ms. Marshmallow for a Heart" would fall apart if she saw so much as a salt block to remind her of the massacre—let alone any dead cows. But Lindgren Larson, the new television personality for KKOA, had promised us she wouldn't cry if we would let her come along.

Gusts of wind were turning the windmill wheel when we arrived, pumping cold, clear water from a well deep in the earth. Only, no cattle would be coming to drink in this pasture this summer, thanks to me, I thought, still miserable that I hadn't picked up that block of salt in the first place and saved the cows. Grandpa would have known. He wouldn't have left it there. I hadn't been very good eyes for him so far.

There might not be any cattle coming here to drink anymore, but Grandpa had told Big Bear to leave the windmill on for the deer and antelope to drink since the herds had become accustomed to coming there when the creeks dried up. And Grandpa believed he was to be a good steward over all the creatures that shared the land with them.

Unlike their human riders, the horses approached the tank without emotion and badly in need of a drink of water. All five horses put their noses deep in the water and drank deeply after the hot, dry ride.

Lindy got off first. She kicked the dried mud around the tank with her boot, failing to keep back the tears. Stoic Abby stared straight ahead with big, accusing eyes.

Alisa and I retraced our steps with Claire, remembering the morning that seemed so long ago now, explaining the whole thing to her as we walked. The sun-baked desert had no more wild flowers. We didn't see so much as a horny toad or a bird fly. overhead. The emptiness was eerie. There should have been hundreds of cattle with the Flying W brand peacefully grazing nearby.

"Let's go," Lindy finally said, getting back on her horse, Blacky. "I can't stand this place anymore."

"Wait, I want to climb the rocks first," Abby insisted. "Like we always do." In the end we all agreed but without much heart for the climb. We tied our horses to a wooden rail by the old stagecoach stop ruins at the foot of Birdseye Pass, the rocky outcropping from which Birdseye Butte got it name.

The hike was not long from where we tied our horses. Native Americans had camped at the top of the rocks once. You could see for miles in every direction from the top of the butte. It would have been a great spot to watch for approaching enemy tribes and, later, white settlers moving in. Over the years we had found lots of arrowheads and other stone implements made by the early Plains tribes.

"What if this is the last time we ever get to come here?" Claire asked as we sat and looked off into the vast valley at our feet and remembered all our wonderful times together hiking and camping in these rocks.

"Maybe this is how some Native American family felt as they sat and watched wagonload after wagonload of settlers moving into what had been their home," Alisa added.

"So what are you saying?" I asked, irritated that she wasn't focusing on our present pain instead of some ancient history. "You've been spending too much time with Jed. Is that what he's telling you, that this land should be the tribes' now instead of ours?"

"I'm not saying that. I'm merely pointing out the fact that time moves on and it may be our time to be displaced—like it was for other people who lived here not so very long ago."

"How can you even say that, Alisa?" Abby asked, shocked.

"I didn't mean I want it, too, Abby," she quickly explained to her little cousin. "Or that it will happen. Just that it has happened before and could again. Things are changing out West."

"It's not the same thing," I said stubbornly. "We didn't drive out the tribes. Neither did Grandpa or his parents or grandparents. They bought this land with hard-earned money and years of work. Besides, it's not going to go back to the Shoshoni or Arapaho people if someone like Robin Blackford buys it."

"Con's right, we can't do anything about history," Claire agreed. "But we can do something about our future!"

"Get real, Claire," Alisa said. "How? How can we prove who murdered the cattle? How can we stop the BLM and Raymond Rice from taking away the grazing leases? How can we help Grandpa get well so he can take care of things again? If

Grandpa and Gran go broke and Robin Blackford makes another offer, they will have to sell. And what can a bunch of kids do to stop it?"

No one disagreed. More depressed and discouraged than ever, we started down the rocks. Slogging silently through the brush back to the horses, we were all quietly facing the depressing reality that this might be our last time here together.

Until Abby's scream pierced the air.

"Nooo . . . oh no. . . ." Her voice changed to sobs.

Out front as usual, Abby had swung under a scrub cedar tree at the base of the butte and landed near the shrunken form of a small black calf.

I dropped to my knees beside her, and the pain of that moonlit night came back with a force as I looked at the dried-up remains of what had been a gentle little baby calf, dead of thirst. Unable to reach high enough to drink from the tank, and with his mother dead, he had wandered off to die alone.

Alisa and Claire joined me, kneeling in the dirt, staring silently at the baby calf. Abby continued to cry, big gulping sobs. She reached out her finger to touch the hardened black hide stretched over little bones.

"Watch out, Abby," Alisa yelled, grabbing her young cousin's hand back. "There's a spider on it. It's a black widow." Sure enough, a fat black spider sat on the web she'd made across what had been a soft little nose.

"Yuk," I said. "I hate spiders. Give me a rattlesnake any day."

"How do you know it's a black widow?" Claire asked, nervously keeping her distance. "You can't see her stomach with the red hourglass."

I backed away as Alisa broke a twig from the bush and touched the web; it pulled but didn't break. The spider moved aggressively toward the intrusion.

"The web is much stronger than most, almost like nylon, and it makes a rattling sound. You can hear it if you put your face down a little closer," Alisa explained.

Only Abby did so.

"Abby, do be careful." Lindy pulled her sister back. I shuddered at the sight of that horrible hairy thing, all legs and belly running over the dead calf's nose. I had always hated spiders, but this one was truly deadly.

"Let's go," I said, eager to get away from the spider and the depressing sight.

"A black widow bite is not as deadly as a rattlesnake's bite," Alisa went on. "But in extreme cases they can kill someone as small as you, Abby. So never, *never* take a chance around a spider that might even possibly be a black widow. They're more aggressive than most spiders and would certainly attack if you bothered them, especially if her egg sac is in danger."

Turning away, I noticed Lindy's face for the first time since Abby had screamed. The softness was gone. Her mouth was set, teeth clenched, and there was a cold anger in her *very dry eyes*.

"Whoever did this thing," she pointed without looking at the calf, "cannot drive us off. And for this little calf, they will pay."

I stared at my softhearted cousin. I knew how she felt. I had been feeling that way ever since that night when I saw the results of Mother Earth's handiwork.

"Good," I said as we walked back to the horses. "Now do you agree we have to confront Jed? Make him tell us what he knows about his employer's eco-terrorist activities and what he might be doing for Chief Running Wolf, whom he seems to be rather close to."

"It isn't that simple, Con," Lindy put in.

"That's what I've been trying to tell him." Alisa seemed happy to have Lindy on her side. "Everything is circumstantial. I just don't think Jed is capable of doing this stuff. Even if he *did* have a part in planting the poison, which I doubt, he was only following orders. He probably didn't know what was in the salt. I've spent some time with him, Con, and he's not the monster you seem to think he is."

"It may be circumstantial, Alisa, but it's all we've got. And I don't think you are capable of seeing him straight, either."

She didn't deny it.

"I did see someone interesting in town the other day," Alisa said as she tightened her saddle before remounting. "I was filling Lindy's Honda with gas, and this guy drove up to fill his tank. He was driving a Mother Earth pickup, and I think from Jed's description that he's the boss. Jed told me the guy's a little flaky. Well anyway, he was talking on his cell phone loud enough for me to hear."

"Yeah? Go on," I encouraged her when she hesitated.

"Well, it wasn't what he said exactly, except he called himself Charlie the Crow, like he's a Native American, which he's definitely not! He's as Anglo as we are. So he struts around in pseudo–Native American clothes, talking on his cell phone at the filling station in Thermopolis, acting more like he's in L.A. He was spouting about how they offer 'ecosystems management consulting' at a hundred dollars an hour and on and on."

"Eco-terrorist management consulting is more like it," I said bitterly. Mother Earth, and extremist groups like them, were against logging, ranching, even having children—since humans use up mother earth's resources. "They have to be in this up to their radical necks."

"Sounds like they're not really about teaching people how to take care of the environment," Claire said. "More like they want people to die off and leave the place to the wild animals."

"I like animals," Abby said. "But not that much."

"That's because you're not crazy," Claire said.

"I think I will write a poem about that poor little calf," Abby went on thoughtfully.

"So maybe Jed shows up for a summer job he doesn't know much about," Lindy suggested. "And they ask him to do things he doesn't like. He might have agreed to go in the plane and drop the salt and not know it would kill the cows."

"Maybe," I conceded. "But if Mother Earth wants to stop cattle ranching in general, why hit only Walker Ranch? We haven't heard about any other people losing cattle like that. And we would have heard talk about it at the sale barn."

"And Jed told me," Alisa offered, "that while he is still officially working for and getting paid by Mother Earth, he's spending all his time out on the reservation."

"Now, that is interesting," Lindy exclaimed.

"But what does that mean?" I wondered aloud. "Why would Mother Earth and the tribes work together to target us? And why did Jed lie to me from the beginning—before he knew who I was—about coming to Wyoming for the first time, looking for his roots and all that? It just doesn't make sense."

"Well, it's time we find out," Lindy said, very determined and still very dry eyed.

Gentle Lindy, the firstborn cousin, named for great-great-grandpa Whit Walker's Swedish-born wife, Lindgren. And with the determined set in her jaw and steady gaze, she now looked a little like the portrait of Grandmother Lindgren that hung in the parlor. She was the one who insisted they bring a large library and a *piano* to Wyoming. She taught her children how to play the piano and love good literature while helping her husband carve this place out of the wilderness. It was said of Lindgren Walker that she was gentle of heart and strong of character—a hardy rose, her husband called her.

As we rode back home over the sagebrush-covered prairie, we talked—and planned. It was time to act, Lindy said, and together we decided what we had to do. Like a spider trying to catch a fly, we had to weave a few webs of our own.

It was nine A.M. two days later when Alisa and I arrived in front of the Mother Earth office to set our first trap. Alisa let Lindy's Honda, which we had borrowed for the morning, do a slow roll past the building and up the street half a block.

Charlie the Crow had been very friendly when Alisa called and offered to do volunteer work for the cause. With Jed working out on the reservation, we decided it was safe for her to apply for the job and see what she could find out by looking through their files. We hoped it wouldn't take more than a few days to get a look at the database and nose around the office a little.

"I want to help you in your fight to save the earth from the polluters and exploiters—especially the ranchers around here," Alisa had told him from the fax phone in our investigation center while the rest of us huddled around listening.

Charlie the Crow had taken the bait and invited her in for an interview. A newcomer to Thermopolis, he had no way of knowing Alisa Engnell was really Alisa Walker Engnell. And as long as Jed didn't show up, he wouldn't know.

"This seems far enough away," she said when we'd gone about half a block past the Mother Earth office. "Wait here for me. It's better no one sees you right out front. What if Jed drives by?"

We both laughed nervously at that horrifying thought. The street was mostly residential with modest white frame houses and neat little yards. We had come to a stop in front of a little home business.

Antique Tables Made Daily, the sign read.

The shop was little more than a ramshackle garage. Spare table legs and bits of lumber and old paint cans were strewn around the gravel entrance.

"Doesn't look like there's much money in instant antiques," Alisa pointed out the obvious.

"Love the approach, though," I said. "Ya gotta admit it's creative."

Alisa was wearing a flowered, long cotton skirt and white short-sleeved blouse. Her hair was pulled back into a fancy braid, and she wore Birkenstocks on her tanned feet.

She looked in the rearview mirror for the umpteenth time and put some Vaseline on her lips.

"Do I appear to you to have a strong environmental conscience?" she asked.

"You appear to me to be crazy, but that's beside the point. And you definitely look the part," I said.

So with her oversized cloth bag, which contained a mini Sony tape recorder to test taping through the bag, she headed for her interview.

I got out of the car and watched Alisa walk down the street in her environmentally correct clothes. Hoping our plan would hold up, I opened the door into the world of instant aging to kill some time.

The old garage still had a dirt floor, and it was littered with wood chips and smelled of paint and kerosene. A man with a long, bushy gray beard was spreading thick gobs of green paint on a pine table, then wiping it off with an old bath towel. He never even looked up.

I browsed. Running my hand over some of the unfinished products, I discovered the plain wooden tables were actually very nice. However, the "antiqued" tables standing against the wall didn't exactly look old, only ugly.

The minutes dragged on and on, and still no sign of Alisa at the car. What was she doing in there so long? Or did it only seem long? I didn't have a watch on and was losing track of time.

Cool it, Con, I thought, trying to control my nerves. How would I explain it to Grandpa and Gran, who knew nothing of our little plan, if something happened to Alisa in that crazy man's office? What if he had Caller ID and had traced her call to the Walker Ranch? *Why didn't we think of that?* I pounded my fist on the pine table in frustration, furious that we had sent Alisa in there alone without thinking of all the potential dangers.

"You break it, you buy it," a gruff voice said over my shoulder.

"Break easily, do they?" I asked, looking into the face of the only antique in the place. The old man's eyes were hidden behind thick, dirty lenses speckled with paint.

"Ha! That's a good one," he laughed, much to my surprise. "Actually, they don't. I might not be too honest in my marketing, but I'm a good carpenter."

If I didn't leave soon, I would feel compelled to buy, so I gradually edged toward the door and ducked out just as Alisa appeared at the back door of the Mother Earth office. Only, she wasn't alone.

"Oh no," I gasped. Jed was beside her, holding on to her arm and leaning down close to her face. His back was to me, his bulging muscles evident through the T-shirt he was wearing. Alisa looked flushed. Listening. Saying nothing.

He kept on and on at her. I could hear his tense, hushed voice but couldn't make out the words.

I started toward them. Then figuring I would make it worse,

I stepped behind the car, staying low, not sure what to do.

The minutes seemed like hours. "Come on, Alisa," I whispered. "Get away from there."

Finally Jed stepped back through the door into the office, and Alisa headed for the car.

"Stay down," she said, getting the key in the ignition and starting the car faster than I could ask what happened. "Get in the backseat and out of sight. I don't want Jed to see you."

I ducked my head until we were up Main Street out of sight of the Mother Earth office, then crawled over the seat and listened in fascination as she described what happened.

Our second stop for the day was the airport. She drove as fast as she talked. But we were sitting at the counter stools of the Airport Café waiting for our waitress to show up before I got the whole story.

A glass wall looked out onto the airport's only runway. With only one flight arriving every twenty-four hours, it wasn't the world's busiest airport.

"I can't believe it," I said over and over again. "So Charlie the Crow fell for your eco-credentials and Jed didn't turn you in. That's amazing."

"The Crow fell for it hook, line, and sinker," she said, looking radiant. "But, Con, that place *is* spooky. There was a sign on his desk that said, 'Real Women Don't Have Babies—They Mother the Earth.' What does that have to do with the environment?"

"*I* already knew they're crazy. But what happened? Did he ask to see your references?"

"Yes, and I have to tell you he was impressed."

Jess, doing her part to help while stuck in Oregon, had written a glowing reference for Alisa's years of volunteer work in a nonexistent company. Using her graphic design skills, she created stationery for an environmental company called "Care for the Air," then faxed it over last night.

"Mr. Crow particularly liked the logo," Alisa laughed. "The poor little baby wolf choking on polluted air really got to him."

"And the phone number," I asked. "What if he calls to check?"

"Oh, not to worry. Jess is standing by ready to answer the phone: 'Take care, it's your air. How may I help you?' " Alisa giggled at the thought.

The waitress came and dropped laminated pieces of blue paper in front of us. It was the menu.

"Go on," I said, more interested in the story than food for a change.

"Well, I was sitting there talking to Mr. Crow. He tries to look Native American, but his blue eyes and pale complexion give it away. Anyone can wear the clothes and braid the hair, but he is definitely a paleface."

I laughed at her pathetic joke.

"So we were having a friendly chat about how bad ranchers are, and Jed walked in. My heart stopped. I must have gone very pale. Jed saw my panic and sensed somehow not to say anything. It was like instant communication, Con."

"Oh, gag, Alisa," I said. "He just looked into your face and knew your thoughts—that's what you're saying?"

"That's what I'm saying."

Our conversation was attracting the attention of the only other person—a man—sitting at the far end of the counter drinking coffee as if he had nowhere to go in a hurry. Which he probably didn't if he was waiting for the next plane, due in about fifteen hours.

"We better quiet down, Con. Remember that this is a small town. Everybody knows everybody," she warned with a lowered voice and proceeded to describe what happened next.

"He didn't see me at first. It was like he was there to pick something up or drop something off—not like he was coming to work. And he wasn't alone. There were two older men with him. They stood by the door waiting for Jed. Mr. Crow didn't treat Jed like some summer volunteer, either, but with respect. He jumped right up to greet him when he came in."

She smiled that Jed-is-cute smile with a dreamy, faraway look.

"What happened next?" I nearly yelled.

"Nothing happened," she said. "I held my breath and tried to keep on talking about my knowledge of computer skills and how I'd be glad to help out with their database work, hoping Jed wouldn't speak to me. And he didn't."

She was talking quickly now as she remembered the tense moment.

"Okay, so I thought I'd made it, that Jed wasn't going to say anything after all. Mr. Crow agreed to have me volunteer a few hours every day, shook my hand, and showed me to the door. Only then Jed intercepted me and offered to 'show the new volunteer around the office.' He took my elbow and gently but firmly guided me toward the back door."

Alisa stopped her rapid-fire pace long enough to gulp some ice water from the green plastic glass with *Thermopolis Airport Café* written on it.

"Yeah? Then what? Was he angry?"

"More like cold and hurt. He asked me what I thought I was doing mouthing stuff about ranchers exploiting the earth when my grandfather was Whit Walker, one of the biggest exploiters around."

I nearly fell off the counter stool. "*He said that?* How dare he call Grandpa an exploiter. What does he know about ranching? Do you think he went back in and told his boss he's not the only phony around?"

"That's what I asked him—only not quite like that."

"And?"

"And he didn't really answer. But I told him the truth—part of it, anyway—that I really do care about the environment and am interested in environmental organizations. He said he wanted to know what I was up to but promised not to give away my true identity to Mr. Crow until we'd talked. He said he'd call."

"And you believe him—that he won't say anything?"

"I don't know, Con. But he's not like you think. He seems to me to be . . . well, like he's caught in the middle of something. One thing I do know—he is *not* a phony like Charlie the Crow. Jed believes in what he's doing. He has found his heritage, and he is proud to be a part of the Shoshoni tribe, despite its problems. I like him, Con—and not because he's tall, dark, and handsome." She grinned. "I like him because he is genuine—maybe genuinely wrong about some things. But genuine and very interesting."

I was skeptical, but before I had a chance to respond, the reason for our trip to the Airport Café finally got herself over to wait on us.

"What'll it be, kids?" the waitress asked in a slow Western twang. We were here looking for answers, not for food, but since they were serving . . .

"A BLT for me," Alisa said, "on whole wheat toast, plenty of lettuce, and hold the mayo, please."

"Make mine the same, only white bread untoasted, plenty of mayo, and hold the lettuce."

The poor lady looked confused for a moment and asked me to repeat my order.

"Must be the accent," she said, apologizing for not getting it the first time.

"I don't believe it," I groaned when she went off to shout our order to the cook through a window cut in the wall. "She thinks *I* have an accent."

"Con, you're such a moron. We don't want to confuse the waitress, we want information from her. Let me do the talking from now on."

The waitress was a tiny, dried-up little woman with no lips. When her mouth was closed, it looked like a long thin line drawn under her very pointed nose. But she was friendly and helpful, perfectly happy to talk to us as she bustled about wiping off the old Formica counter and making a fresh pot of coffee.

She certainly did remember that day when "gorgeous Robin Blackford" flew in in his fancy plane, and she was more than happy to talk about it.

"He didn't exactly *eat* here," the waitress said, obviously still disappointed. "But he did walk through a couple of times."

"Did you see him go up in a light blue Cessna the next day?" Alisa asked, leading the waitress-witness, it seemed to me.

"Mercy no," she replied. "He had his own Learjet, ya know. Isn't he something? My, my, my! As handsome in person as he is on the screen, and to think he's interested in our little town.

I'm thrilled, personally," she said, tucking her pencil behind her ear and staring dreamily off into space.

"Did you know he's coming back for the big town celebration in August?" she went on. "The mayor is so proud you'd think he personally was responsible for Blackford choosing Thermopolis."

Alisa and I looked at each other. No, we didn't know that.

"Funny you would ask about a little plane like that, though." She got back to our question. "Because I seem to remember there was one around that weekend. . . . And it might have been blue, come to think of it."

"Can you remember who might have used it? Maybe someone from the reservation?" I jumped in excitedly.

Alisa kicked me under the table, reminding me she was supposed to be asking the questions.

We had finished our sandwiches, so I ordered a chocolate milk shake to keep the waitress talking. She leaned down into a bucket of ice cream behind the counter, struggling to fill the old-fashioned silver beaker with the hard ice cream.

"You know, young man, I do believe you're right," she said, pausing between scoops. "I seem to remember two Indian men in here who got some coffee. They took off in a little plane. Weren't gone too long if I remember right, but I couldn't say for sure. Why don't you call the Bureau of Indian Affairs—they might know if anyone from their office rented a plane that weekend. If it's all that important to you."

If she only knew how important. But calling the reservation wasn't exactly the best approach. We waited while she attached the cup of milk and ice cream to the old green electric shake mixer and stood there turning them until the milk and ice cream became one heavenly substance.

"Do you remember if there was a young man about our age with them?" Alisa asked. "Tall and muscular with short dark hair—like a marine. Very handsome."

She kicked me again before I could say anything.

But the lady only had eyes for Robin Blackford, and she

couldn't remember anymore. So with more questions than answers, we headed for home.

❖

The hum of the fax greeted me as I opened the door to my room. I crawled under the table to find one sheet already on the floor, with the thing still clattering away on page two. It was a cover sheet from Apollo Instruments Inc., Mr. Goldberg's office. *Hurray*, I thought, *a letter from Hannah*. In my excitement I bumped my head on the table coming up, but I eagerly read the next page faster than the fax could print it.

Dear Con:

I am writing you from Dad's office. I like Washington, but Dad is pretty busy so I go to museums alone. I would rather go with you, of course, but only marginally. The Air and Space Museum is my favorite. Oops, Dad is ready to take me to dinner. I shall try to fax this to you. I have tried several times to call, but no one answers the phone. Where are all of you? Oh well. By the way, I will send you a letter someday with the pictures I took of Robin Blackford at the DOI—that's the Department of the Interior for you uninformed Wyoming types.

Gotta go. Hope you are staying out of trouble.

Hannah

Transmission complete, the flimsy paper curled off the machine, and I caught it in my hand. It was nice of Hannah, but the last thing in the world I needed was a picture of Robin Blackford at some government agency in Washington, D.C.

I would have preferred a picture of her any day.

SAGEBRUSHREBELS@AOL.COM

THE NEXT EVENING, JULY 8, GRANDPA CAME DOWN TO DINner.

Maybe it was the heart medicine. Maybe it was having his family around. But Grandpa was slowly improving. His blood pressure was back to normal, and with Gran helping him keep up the physical therapy, he was walking now with a cane.

"What on earth is this?" Grandpa asked, pausing on his slow walk to the kitchen table. I had put my own Far Side–type cartoon on the refrigerator. It was a picture of a pregnant cow lying in a maternity ward talking to a midwife cow with features similar to Alisa's who was holding a gun and a bucket. The balloon caption from the pregnant cow said: *"Haven't you forgotten the scissors?"*

He looked a little confused, so I explained.

"This is Ms. 'I Knows 'Bout Birthin' Baby Calves' Alisa," I said to her horror and told the whole story.

Grandpa laughed so hard he had to sit down.

"Tell us about your job down at KKOA television, Lindy," Grandpa asked while enjoying fresh vegetables from the garden and a slice of homemade bread.

"Well, the news of the day is the upcoming celebration for the 125th anniversary of the founding of Thermopolis. The theme is A New Day for the Old West. I am interviewing some new people in the region for background—to see what is bringing or will bring more people to live here."

"What's A New Day for the Old West supposed to mean?" Grandpa asked.

"They mean," Lindy explained in her television-reporter voice, "that ranching is out. Tourists are in. The general feeling being pushed by Mayor Richards is that Thermopolis needs to emphasize its Native American history and our natural wonders like the Hot Springs in order to attract more tourist dollars. Most of all, the mayor insists that the cow lobby has run this town for too long, and now it's time for a new day of biological integrity for our community."

"Does Mayor Richards always talk gibberish?" Claire wanted to know.

"He grew up in California, dear," Gran explained.

"Has he asked the Native Americans whether or not they *want* to become a tourist attraction?" Grandpa asked. "Chief Running Wolf is not some drugstore Indian. He is a wise man, and I can't see him falling for this kind of hogwash."

Grandpa had real respect in his voice as he spoke of the old chief. I was getting more confused about his relationship to Chief Running Wolf—he didn't make it sound as if they were enemies.

"Well, Charlie the Crow of Mother Earth acts like he speaks for the tribes when planning the celebration with the mayor," Lindy said. "He and Mayor Richards are all over town talking this up—getting the merchants excited about more tourist dollars."

"Why don't you get a little background from the old-timers, as well," Claire suggested to her older sister. "Like Grandpa."

"He could tell about his grandfather putting together a vigilance committee," Gran agreed. "And how they ran Butch Cassidy and his gang right out of these parts. It's a wonderful story, and it's true!"

Lindy looked uncomfortable but explained, "Some bits of history are more popular than others at the moment, Gran. Heroics of old cattlemen are . . . well . . . not as attractive as Native American history or the environment—at least to the mayor."

"Well, it happened nonetheless," Gran snapped, putting

more mashed potatoes on the table in front of me.

"So what are people going to *do* at this celebration?" Abby inquired.

"There will be a big barbecue followed by a parade—with tribal leaders, the Casper Troopers . . ."

"Headed by our very own Kate," Grandpa pointed out with pride.

"Yes! And there will be historical reenactments," Lindy explained.

"Maybe they'll do a reenactment of the stagecoach crash on Devil's Slide. Raymond Rice and Charlie the Crow could take part in it," I suggested—mostly kidding.

After dinner I helped Grandpa to the old wicker deck chair on the back lawn. I laid over his knees a handwoven Indian blanket that Big Bear had given him years ago.

Abby carried out his coffee on a wooden tray. She had picked white daisies and placed them in a little vase next to a piece of pie Claire and Alisa had made earlier in the day. Grandpa held the book of poetry Mom had sent him.

He picked up a steaming cup of black coffee. The hot wind that had blown all day was replaced now by a cool evening breeze with the scent of freshly cut alfalfa from the bottomfield. Together we watched the sun setting behind the buttes and listened to the water rushing over rocks in Buffalo Creek, which was running low now that the snowpack in the Wind River Mountains had melted away in the hot July sun.

As we sat on the lawn waiting for Grandpa to finish his pie, the noise and conversation of the dinner table was still running through my head. I watched my grandfather's once very tanned face, now gray from lack of sunshine. The leathery skin had shrunk in his cheeks. I hated his weakness. I missed the old him.

Grandpa was taking his time eating; knife in his right hand, fork in his left, he carefully cut each bite of the strawberry-rhubarb pie, then pushed it onto the fork with his knife as if even eating was a chore. He laid down the utensils after each bite and picked up the book of Yeats to read while he slowly and deliberately chewed—lost in his favorite poet while the troubles of the ranch swirled around him. I wished he would stop reading and start acting.

We still had our evening talks each night. Or rather, I talked and he listened. I figured it was a waste of time, since he didn't seem to have any answers and the vague advice he gave me about continuing to watch things for him didn't help a whole lot, either. Raymond Rice and the BLM were still closing in, about to take away the grazing rights our family had held for years, and Grandpa was reading poetry, leaving Gran to fight the BLM alone!

"How are the orphan calves? Abby tells me Shades is growing like a weed," Grandpa interrupted my unkind thoughts. He smiled at the thought of his youngest granddaughter and her way with animals. "She'll make a good rancher someday," he added.

"*Abby?* She's a girl."

"So's your grandmother, in case you hadn't noticed. And she's a fine rancher," he replied.

Finally Grandpa laid the old book lovingly in his lap, folded his hands, and looked deep into my eyes.

"What were you and Alisa doing in town so long yesterday?"

I gulped and quickly tried to think what to tell him and how to leave the rest out without lying. In the end I left in the bit about questioning the waitress at the Airport Café and left out the visit and news of Alisa's part-time job at Mother Earth.

"The waitress at the Airport Café thinks she remembers seeing some men from the reservation take up a blue Cessna that day," I explained. "It could have been the small plane Alisa and I saw flying low over Birdseye Pasture. Someone could have lowered the poisoned salt block on a rope, then dropped it by the water tank. There were white salt blocks in the Mother Earth pickup Jed was driving that same day—Jed, who was *coincidentally* with the most important man from the Wind River Reservation. Isn't that too much coincidence for you? It ties Mother Earth and the tribes together, with Jed in the middle, all on the day of the attack."

"Maybe it ties them together, Con. Or maybe it's all coincidence. Let's say you are right that there is a connection between the two—it still leaves us with a big missing link. Motive. Even if Mother Earth hates cattle ranchers, why would they target just me? You've been to the sale barn—there's no word about any other ranchers suffering similar attacks on their herds. You're seeing some pieces of the puzzle all right, some important ones. But not the whole picture, I'm afraid. I don't like the idea of what happened to the cows up at Birdseye any better than you do. And I expect in time we'll be able to prove who did the actual poisoning. Right now I need to know why. When we know why, it will show us who."

"Yeah, right! I don't see how we're going to prove who poisoned the cows," I snorted angrily. "The law doesn't even want my evidence—which I thought was so important. Let's face it, no one is going to listen to a kid. If *you* went into the sheriff's office, I bet Sheriff Hays would get his lazy duff off the chair and check out that *supposedly* legitimate environmental organization. But I guess we'll have to wait for Alisa . . ." My voice trailed off before I told him more than I was supposed to about our plans at Mother Earth.

Grandpa's eyes narrowed intently and bored right into me. I expected him to ask me *what* we were waiting for Alisa to do.

"Listen, Con," he said instead, "forget Mother Earth for the moment and any connection to the reservation. The attack on the cattle isn't enough by itself. And losing the grazing leases wouldn't be enough alone, either. Cut fences, gates left open . . . it's the weight of all these things together. Some of them might be unconnected. But all of them? I don't think so. So are they random acts of an irritated neighbor? An old enemy on the reservation? One government bureaucrat? Or crazy environmental terrorists?"

"Is Chief Running Wolf your enemy, Grandpa?"

It took him a while before he answered, and I held my breath, waiting for the explanation I had been dying to hear.

"Sadly, I have to admit that he considers himself so. And he may believe he has reason to wish me ill. But I do not think . . .

no, I *know* he is not the one behind all of this."

"What did you ever do to him?"

"Maybe someday I'll tell you, Con." He left it at that.

I could tell from his tone of voice there wasn't any point in arguing.

"So far we are only seeing the puppets. I want to know who is pulling the strings. And I sure can't tell from where I'm sitting. That's why you've been such a help to me, son. Watching things and telling me about them. You have been my eyes and ears, just like I asked."

"But I haven't figured out *anything*," I protested miserably. "And that stupid sheriff won't even *listen* to me." I stared miserably at the Red Wall, which was turning even deeper red in the sunset.

I stood up in utter frustration with Grandpa, with myself, feeling helpless.

Pacing back and forth, my hands knotted into fists in my jacket pockets, I brooded. August was only weeks away, and nothing had changed. *Everything is going down the tubes*, I thought. *And Grandpa is off in la-la land reading poetry and thinking our silly little talks each evening are somehow saving the ranch.*

And then to my surprise Grandpa leaned back his head and laughed—that low, throaty chuckle I hadn't heard all summer. It was a joyful sound usually associated with something his grandkids had done, but it didn't seem especially appropriate at this moment and added to my irritation with him.

"Con, you are so much like your mother," he explained. "Impetuous, impatient, rushing ahead all the time . . . just like her." He was still chuckling. "Watching you pacing about there makes me miss her something terrible."

He wiped tears away from his smiling eyes and saw, perhaps, the frustration in mine.

"Sorry, son, not laughing *at* you, you understand."

My grandfather motioned me to sit back down. "You have seen a great deal more than you think, Con. Your descriptions and perceptions have told me more than you know. You did see the white salt block in the Mother Earth truck. And your description of the scene at the water tank and memory of where you saw the baby-sitter cow helped Ben find the calves. They would have died a very painful death without your memory and his quick action. And there have been other things. I'm too tired to relate it all, but you have helped more than you know. Now time is running out, and there is much still to do. I need you more than ever."

I calmed down and listened closely, wanting what he had said about me to be true.

"Remember," he went on, "when you were small and your grandmother would draw animal pictures for you? A bunch of dots on a page. Not like the easy dot-to-dot things in books that had numbers. No, her pictures were the kind of thing you actually had to use your brain on. That's what you have to do now. Look for a pattern, find the head on this animal, and connect the pieces from the top down."

"I remember," I groaned. "The trick had been to find where to *start*, otherwise the picture never made sense."

"Precisely! Now you've got it, Con." He looked as pleased as if we had solved the problem and saved the ranch. "What we need," he went on quite seriously, "is a spy in the BLM and that so-called environmentalist outfit. But I know none of you would be so foolish as to attempt such a thing."

I kept my head down so I wouldn't have to lie even with my eyes or let him see my smile.

Long after Grandpa had gone to bed, I sat there still, listening to the creek bubble its way along over the rocky bottom. I watched the last touches of light disappear from our wall of rock, turning it from a thing of beauty into a dark, forbidding barrier to the rest of the world.

"Never ceases to amaze me, either," Gran said, joining me on the grass. "To think God has allowed us to live in this good and wondrous place all these years."

"It's not always easy, though, is it?" I swatted a large mosquito on my hand, splashing my own blood in a messy smear.

"Easy?" she huffed. "Who said anything about easy? I said

good. There's a big difference, ya know. Life here is a constant battle—too hot, too cold, too dry, too much snow, too windy." Her voice made it clear she was not complaining, only stating a fact.

"Your grandfather's grandfather, the first Whitfield Walker, and Lindgren, his wife, built this house. They designed it to endure anything Wyoming weather could throw at it. It has, and we will endure this storm, too, Con."

I wondered if ideas wouldn't prove more dangerous than the rough Wyoming elements. Times were changing, and maybe Alisa was right. They were behind the times. Maybe there were historical forces beyond our control.

"Some people say times have changed and that people like you and Grandpa need to put your own needs aside and let the land return to its natural state," I said. "They have these posters down at the Mother Earth office. . . ."

I couldn't actually see steam coming out of her ears, but I figured it was building up.

"Con, don't put too much stock in that psycho-babble-bumper-sticker philosophy. The Walkers put down strong foundations for the physical structures of this place, and their philosophical ones were pretty solid, too. 'The highest heavens belong to the Lord, but the earth he has given to man.' I believe that psalm, Con. And we have spent our lives taking very good care of this land. But we worship the Creator, not the creation."

As I listened to her, I laid back on the grass and looked up into the highest heavens, all lit up with stars.

"Ooh," we both gasped as a shooting star fell across the sky and left sparkles of dying light in its wake.

"To be good stewards of such a gift is a big responsibility," Gran said. "God created human beings in His own image and commanded them to fill the earth. To benefit from it, enjoy it, and care for it but not to worship it."

She gently took my hand, then continued. "Don't you worry, Con. We've been in tight spots before. Those allegations about environmental abuse are nonsense. If the Walkers hadn't taken good care of the land, hadn't been protecting the environment all these years, we wouldn't still be here generations later. We'll still find a way to prove they aren't true."

By August? I wondered.

She patted my hand and walked back into the house without any trace of her limp.

When I finally went in, I found Alisa, Gran, Lindy, Claire, and Abby sitting at the round oak table in the kitchen. Lindy was holding a pencil and paper, acting as the scribe.

"You're not all drawing dot-to-dot pictures, are you?" I asked, joining them at the table, resting my boots on the old claw table leg.

"Not really," Lindy explained. "More like a fact sheet and timeline. What do you think?"

I took the sheet of paper. She had doodled across the top and down the sides of the paper our Flying W brand, making the *W* look even more like a bird in flight.

- Mother Earth: New to Thermopolis. A radical "environmentalist" organization with ties to Chief Running Wolf and other reservation leaders. White salt block seen in their truck on the day the cattle were poisoned. Motivation—destroy ranchers in order to restore the earth.
- Fred and Lilly Marvin: Neighbors who stand to gain most from Walkers' losing grazing rights. Motivation—acquire valuable BLM grazing rights. Plenty of access and opportunity to cut fences, kill cattle, retrieve poisoned salt block, etc.
- BLM/Raymond Rice: Harassing the ranch with bogus charges of environmental violations. Motivation—none. No obvious personal gain.

Lindy had underlined that last bit in black ink.

"There have been other things, smaller things," Gran said. "Drought, death, disease . . . normal pestilence—we thought."

"The question is," Claire said, "how much pestilence is normal?"

"I think we can leave the drought and the cattle market last year in that category," Gran responded. "It's hard to blame that on anyone. The rest, I don't know."

Lindy added to the page:

- Drought last year: Natural causes. Unrelated.

"Grandpa's right," I said, chewing on the end of a pencil I had picked up. "What we're missing is the missing link."

Everyone looked at me expectantly, as if I had a clue to what the connection might be. For an answer, I snapped the pencil. It flipped across the table to Alisa, whose quick reflexes allowed her to catch it.

"Let's hope you're that quick at other things," I told her, which everyone but Gran knew meant she better quickly get in the database at Mother Earth and find us a connection.

"Check our email before you go to bed tonight, Con, and see if our Jess has any helpful information for us," Lindy suggested. "She's surfing all over looking for information on Mother Earth, Charlie the Crow, or anything at all that might relate."

"I'm sure I don't know what all that computer stuff is in aid of," Gran complained as she headed up the winding staircase to bed. "We have gotten along jolly well all these years without a television, and I'm not sure I want our open space filled up with cyber-clutter—or whatever you call it. We do have phones, which is more than enough modern technology around here. If you want to talk to your cousin, pick up the thing and use it."

A wise woman, our grandmother, we all agreed. But quite behind the times. How could she have known *our* high tech was about to come to the aid of *her* Old West?

I promised to check for email from Jess and give her an update.

Logging on took a few minutes, and I rubbed my tired eyes, wondering what the point of this was when I had to get up at six the next morning to feed the cattle in the corral and ride a fence line for Big Bear to see where the bulls were getting out. My clock radio read 12:10 A.M.

Please wait, the screen informed me.

I wadded up a piece of paper and lobbed it in the general direction of my cowboy boots.

"Three points," I said as it dropped cleanly in. I made a pile of paper balls, then went back for a lay-up.

"And he hits again," I cheered myself on until my boot was full of tightly formed paper balls. I picked up the misses and dunked them.

"Sagebrush Rebels, thirty; Mother Earth, nothing," I cheered my basketball victory over the imagined opponent. Then I forced my eyes back to the computer screen.

Information rolled by, and I sleepily punched the Next key until I got into our mailbox: *sagebrushrebels@aol.com.* "You've got mail," the electronic voice announced. It was from Jess.

> *Hello, cousins. Why don't you guys ever check your mailbox? Here I am stuck in Oregon, and no one is listening to me! So . . . I spent hours last night surfing the Net 'cause I have nothing better to do until I get to join you. I came up with the* most *interesting little bit of information under Jobs and Employment/Federal Government, etc. I saw a place to post resumes for jobs with the BLM. I had to hack a little, but I got in and read some of the ones already posted. NOW GET THIS—Mr. Raymond Rice has applied for a job at guess where? The Bureau of Land Management in Washington, D.C.! Do you think he is tired of harassing ranchers and wants out of Wyoming? Or maybe he sees harassing ranchers as a means of promotion to a Washington job. Anyway, thought you might be interested. Please write. Can't wait to see you on August 15.*
>
> > *Jess*

So Mr. Rice wants to go to Washington. So what? The sooner the better, was all I could think. My tired brain stared at the blue screen, wishing she had found something helpful instead of boring information about the career of Raymond Rice. What we needed was something useful to turn up before it was too late.

I logged off and fell asleep before I hit the bed.

ABBY'S ACT

ACTUALLY, SOMETHING VERY INTERESTING DID TURN UP THE next afternoon, not on the Net, but in our living room.

"Where is everybody?" I called out, coming through the back hall from the west side of the house. Unable to see the driveway from there, I was unaware we had a guest. So I stumbled on to everyone gathered around Mr. Robin Blackford in our very own living room. And I couldn't believe my eyes. Lindy, off at work, was going to be mad she missed this.

Sweaty and thirsty from working in the corral, I had come in looking for a large glass of lemonade and a shower to wash off several layers of cattle-generated dirt. Blackford noticed my appearance in the doorway, looking very briefly my way without so much as a smile or nod. He rubbed his nose like some foul-smelling thing had just crawled in. Maybe he hadn't ever smelled good old-fashioned manure before.

"This is how ranches smell, Mr. Blackford," I said under my breath, bummed at the way he had looked at me, as if I were some sort of hired hand intruding in the main house.

Oozing Hollywood charm to Gran and the girls, he leaned dramatically on the mantel of the old stone fireplace. Any other time I would have been excited to see my favorite actor again. But I knew why he was here, and it scared me.

"Mrs. Walker, I don't think you understand," Blackford said. "I authorized my agent, several weeks ago, to offer you a *lot* of money for your ranch. More than it's worth, actually. And you never even countered with a higher price." He was smiling warmly at Gran, but there was an underlying tension even his best acting skills couldn't mask. "Remember, Mrs. Walker, price is *always* negotiable."

"The price of *this* ranch isn't negotiable, Mr. Blackford, because it isn't for sale," she said self-confidently, totally unimpressed by her guest.

Alisa and Claire were staring openmouthed at the handsome actor. He smiled their way and noticed behind them on the wall a framed needlepoint Kate had made when she was a little girl. He ran his finger over the words as he read it out loud: " 'Grandchildren are the crown of old men; and the glory of children are their fathers. Proverbs 17.' How sweet," he said, turning back to the matter at hand.

"But everything has a price, Mrs. Walker," he went on. "And besides, the winters out here in this empty place must be hard for you and your sick husband. With the kind of money I'm offering you, you will be able to buy yourself a beautiful home in . . . a warmer climate. Arizona, maybe."

He looked expectantly at Gran, still waiting for her to leap on his generous offer. No one said a thing. The girls went on staring. Gran's silence and composure seemed to unnerve him; Blackford tried harder.

"A lot of people . . . ah . . . advanced in years find life much easier when they live together with other old people in a retirement community . . . without the noise of children or the effort of taking care of their own place."

I watched my grandmother's face for a reaction to that. But she let him go on.

The layer of grit was itching under my shirt collar, and I shifted my weight uncomfortably in the still, warm room. I longed to go take a dip in the river—but I didn't want to miss the drama.

I fingered my pocketknife nervously, sliding it back and forth between my fingers. If he thought his money and Hollywood charm would impress Gran, he was in for a terrible surprise. She had never even heard of him when his agent had first called with an offer. And if he thought he could talk her into selling the ranch and going off to live in some retirement community, he was in for an even bigger surprise. Gran's steady gaze may have looked safe to him, but I had watched her stare down a rattlesnake caught in the cross hairs of a twenty-two in much the same way. The girls might be captured by his charm, but Gran definitely was not. As unaware as the snake had been, Mr. Blackford went on, using his round, silver-rimmed sunglasses like a prop, making sweeping gestures with them as he talked.

"I am only making such a generous offer," he went on, his voice dripping charm, "because I want you and your husband to be well taken care of. And I have heard your ranch *has* suffered some . . . financial setbacks recently. . . ." His voice trailed off while he let that bit hang in the air, then sink in for a moment, before going on.

That's interesting, I thought. *How would he have heard that?*

"But despite that sad fact, I am prepared to pay much *more* than the ranch is worth in today's market because you have worked so hard on this place and you deserve the money—even if the ranch has lost some of its value in recent years."

Some almost invisible change in Gran's expression or her body language made him sense he'd made a tactical error, and Blackford quickly changed his approach.

"What lovely grandchildren," he said, looking only at the girls. "I'm certain you would like to be able to help these beautiful young ladies with their dreams. New cars, travel, college . . . whatever they want."

Alisa's and Claire's faces glowed in his praise. I was waiting for him to mention me, too, but before he had a chance to do so, Big Bear called through the front door for me to hustle out and give him a hand with a sick bull.

"Get a grip, girls," I muttered, mad that they got to stay and have fun while I went off to do the dirty work.

"Hi, Con," Abby called to me as I headed for the corral. As usual she was outside, standing on a wooden fence next to the old rusted branding chute, her feet planted firmly on the bottom board. She was looking at the orphan calves, pencil and paper in hand.

"Hey, Abby," I said, joining her. "Another poem?"

"Uh-huh. Want to read it?"

She handed the wrinkled piece of paper to me and put her skinny little arm through the boards to scratch Shades on the nose while I read it. Abby was always scribbling poetry on something. Her poem was titled "Crackle."

Black and gold,
A short, sharp beak,
caved-in eyes no more to seek.
On the rusted metal
the body lies,
the scent of blood attracting flies.
Soon to be bones,
small and mute,
the dead bird lies on the old branding chute.

"Wow. That's cool, Abby. A little morbid maybe, but very cool. Why aren't you in the house with the others?" I handed back her poem and looked at her inspiration. The dead bird had nearly rotted away in the sun. "You're out here writing poetry about dead birds and missing your chance to see 'the hunk.' "

She shrugged her thin shoulders for reply. Not only the youngest of the group but also the most independent of the cousins, Abby was usually off in her own little world, which more often than not included animals.

"Where's your snake?"

"He got away."

"I'm sorry," I said, smiling at my funny little cousin. She had found a garter snake last week and had been trying to teach it to wrap around her arm so she could wear it like an Egyptian princess would.

"Hang around a few minutes, will you, Con? I have to get a syringe and some antibiotic," Big Bear called to me, heading for the tack shop, where the vet supplies were kept.

I shrugged, not too pleased to be missing the action inside, but something about Blackford's attitude had made me uncomfortable. And I didn't like the fact that he wasn't taking no for an answer.

I left Abby and wandered over to take a closer look at Blackford's Range Rover, which was parked between the house and the corral.

It was a brand-new dark green job, which made our old pickup parked next to it look pretty tacky.

Drooling, I looked over the all-terrain luxury machine made by Land Rover. He had all the extras: combo brush bars with winch mounting, CB for off-road emergencies, CD player—the works. He probably had a cell phone with him in the house, too.

I stuck my head in the open window and breathed in the new-car smell, running my hand along the top of the smooth leather. I noticed a slick gold folder on the front seat. A futuristic design on the cover proclaimed, *Lin and Lin Architectural Firm*, with a subtitle, *Homes for the Stars*.

Naturally curious, I picked it up for a closer look.

It didn't seem like much at first. Just a lot of blueprints I couldn't make out. I was about to put it back when I discovered a watercolor drawing of a modern house built into a red stone wall. Its beauty took my breath away. It was genius. The house was mostly glass with wood the same color as the rock around it, and it seemed to literally grow out of the side of the cliff, descending in several levels down to a landscaped terrace with a path leading down to a rocky stream.

"No way!" I exclaimed, raising my eyes off the drawing to the exact red rock wall and river in front of me. I could actually see how the house in the drawing had been designed to fit perfectly into the rock wall. Our wall. And down by the river, looking up at the beautiful red granite, was a woman.

Blackford had not come alone.

He's pretty confident, isn't he? I thought, my anger growing. *He's already designing his house on our land. And she—whoever she is—is probably now down there planning where to put her furniture.*

My chest felt tight. That smug, lying movie star was inside

trying to con my grandmother. I considered going back in there and confronting Blackford with the folder. But caution, something rare for me, made me slow down. It probably wasn't against the law, I figured, to have a house designed on land you didn't own.

I continued to look through the rest of the folder. There were several topographical maps with the borders of the Walker Ranch outlined in red. And some additional drawings on part of it. Like Old Stagecoach Road, which was marked in with darkened lines. There were other things written in the margins and over the stage ruins. I couldn't make out everything, but things were becoming more clear.

My favorite movie star, the guy I had been looking up to as completely cool, wanted our ranch, and it had nothing to do with ecology or preserving the West for future generations, like he had said. He wanted to tear down our old house, build a beautiful new one, and live here. I wished Alisa or one of the girls were here to help me decide what to do, but they were still inside sitting moony eyed at the feet of the man who wanted what we were trying to save.

Except for Abby.

"Abby," I called quietly. "Come here. Quick."

The lady down by the river had turned around and was walking slowly back toward the house.

Thinking quickly, I held out the folder. "I don't have time to explain this, but you have to take this folder up to my room and use the fax to make copies of every page. It might help us catch the guys who poisoned Shades' mom, and it might help us save the ranch."

I didn't have a clue how, of course, but instinct told me we needed a copy of this stuff. Good ol' Abby. She didn't even blink at my outrageous statement or ask any silly questions. Just one good one.

"How?"

"There are three buttons on the fax. Red, gray, and green. You do know which one the fax is, don't you?"

Her expression was one of disgust as she looked at me with

bright eyes through her long bangs, and it reminded me of how Gran looks at me when I come up with some totally crazy idea.

"I'm not stupid, Con. I've finished fourth grade."

"Right," I went on, suitably chastised. "The gray button is for copying. Put the sheet in like this"—I showed her how to turn the paper face down—"and press the button. Do them all, and hurry."

"Shouldn't you do it, Con?" she asked, a little nervous at her task after all.

I pointed to the woman walking slowly toward us. "I can't. I have to somehow keep that lady away from the Rover until you make the copies and put the folder back. Put it right here on the seat, this side up."

She was listening to my every word.

"Now run, Abby. And be careful. Hey, this is your most important part ever!" I said, reminding her of her continual complaint that she always got the unimportant roles in our summer plays.

"And you better be good at this part, or we're both in big trouble," I added.

Cheered by the importance of it all, she sprinted across the yard and turned at the front door to give me a conspiratorial little wave, then opened the door and walked in.

"Good girl," I muttered to myself as she disappeared inside. All her practice acting in our summer dramas was paying off. I hoped the same was true for me, as I had my own acting job to do.

My stomach was churning at the thought. Wondering why I had started this and how on earth I was going to keep that woman from returning to the car before Abby got back, I set off.

Fortunately, the woman had paused to look up at a red-tailed hawk riding the afternoon updrafts, stretching his magnificent wings to catch the lift. She continued to look up—her back to me. The sound of the rushing water in Buffalo Creek drowned out my steps as I crossed the little wooden bridge and came up unnoticed behind her.

I cleared my throat so I wouldn't squeak nervously and said, "Hello. Enjoying the view?"

Her startled reaction told me she had expected everyone to be inside listening to her famous companion sweet-talk us out of the ranch.

Certain my face showed as much shock as hers did, but for a very different reason, I tried to gain control before I spoke again. I was, however, speechless, because in all of my life I had never before seen anyone so beautiful. Unable to speak, my mouth probably hanging open, I continued to stare—extremely glad the girls weren't there to see me.

I stared at her smooth, olive-colored skin and coal black shiny hair that floated freely around her face in the breeze. Her pale green eyes were formed perfectly to the oval shape of her face, and her enticing smile revealed straight white teeth to match everything else.

"Excuse me." Her mouth was moving now, but I was having trouble concentrating on her words, which sounded something like . . . "Do you live here, young man?"

Get a grip, Con. "Sort of," I replied lamely, still struck dumb by her beauty.

"Sort of? What does that mean?" She put the book she had been writing or drawing in behind her back and frowned like I was the intruder.

Fumbling for a response, I replied with a somewhat more steady voice, "It means yes, I mean . . . in the summer, anyway. Beautiful, isn't it?" I gestured up at the view she had been admiring.

"Funny, you don't sound like you live here," she said. "More European than Western, I would say."

Probably uncertain whether I had a right to question her presence, she started to walk purposefully back toward the house—and the Range Rover.

I kicked myself into action.

"Are you Mrs. Blackford?" I asked, following after her, desperately trying to think of something to slow her down as I looked in vain for any sign of Abby by the Range Rover.

She ignored the question and kept walking.

"Wouldn't that be a nice spot to build a house?" I asked innocently, then proceeded to describe the one in the folder. "In those lower rocks, at the foot of the Red Wall itself, I mean. With lots of glass."

That stopped her. She turned around and looked intently, first at me, then up at the Wall once more. I couldn't read the look behind the ravishing green eyes. "I wouldn't know about that," she said coldly. "What makes you ask?"

"Architecture has always interested me," I said innocently and not terribly truthfully.

She didn't look convinced, so I went on.

"I think a house built into its environment, something like the Frank Lloyd Wright Fallingwater house, would be very cool there on the Red Wall, don't you think?" Pleased that I had her attention and again amazed how things you learn at school do occasionally come in handy, I began to breathe more easily as she turned and looked back at the very spot where the drawing had placed the house. None too soon, either, as I could see Abby in the distance, dashing out of the front door. Before I heaved a sigh of relief, however, she tripped and the papers went flying. Abby came to a full stop, stooping down to retrieve the scattered sheets.

I stifled a fit of laughter, trying to keep my face calm and our visitor occupied long enough for Abby's nimble fingers to retrieve the papers and deposit them safely back in the Rover. At the split second that happened, I mumbled a good-bye and left the beautiful woman there with *her* mouth open.

Big Bear was still in the tack shop, so I ran back in the house to see what was keeping Blackford occupied. I arrived in time to hear Grandma deliver the *coup de grace* to the stunned movie star. His face was contorted in anger, and the actor's mask had slipped to reveal a spoiled man being denied something he wanted. It was most enlightening.

"You've made your offer," Gran said, standing up and bringing the conversation to an end. "Now, if you don't mind, we have a ranch to run. The answer is still no. And it's not likely to change."

I looked at the girls, who appeared to have come to their senses. Claire had moved over protectively by Gran.

"I don't expect you to understand, Mr. Blackford. But this 'empty place' as you call it is far from empty. It is full of God's creatures. And it is our home. You own many houses, I imagine, but I doubt if you know the meaning of a home. My husband's family built this house. They lived and died working this land, taking good care of it. Taking good care of the land is not some passing fad for us. It's what God commands. It also happens to be a necessity in our business.

"And escaping the winters!" Clearly unable to describe such lunacy, Gran paused before going on. "I sit here in this room when the snow is deep, watching wild animals come down from the hills, feeding the hardy birds who—like us—stay for the winter. I wait for the meadowlarks to sing in spring. My husband and I love the quiet of the frozen, hibernating ranch. Every summer my grandchildren come back and play under that cottonwood tree out there." She stood up and pointed at the majestic old tree.

" 'In custom and ceremony are innocence and beauty born,' " she said, quoting the Yeats poem I had heard from Grandpa my first day back at the ranch. "This place is filled with years of custom and ceremony that make our lives rich. That's why we stay here, Mr. Blackford. And we stay here because we believe our responsibility to our children goes on to their children."

Gran turned back from gazing at her tree and looked daggers at the man who had dared suggest she sell all the memories and pleasures of her home. "And despite offers like yours, and yes, some financial trouble now and then, that old tree will still be here for generations of Walker children to play under."

Blackford had grown more uncomfortable and angry while she spoke. Dropping the charm, he sneered at her. "Pretty speech, Mrs. Walker. But I think you may regret rejecting my offer. The next time I make it, it will not be so generous. And

you may not be so . . . smug when you're broke . . . or alone
out here. These kids won't thank you then. You and your old-
fashioned ideas will not interest your grandkids when you've
squandered their inheritance."

Claire stepped forward at that, opened the door for the fum-
ing man, and said, "You don't get it, do you? We already have
our inheritance. Find another pretty spot, Mr. Robin Blackford.
This one's not for sale."

"What do you kids do for excitement out here?" he asked
with one last condescending parting shot. "Sit around and
watch the buttes change color?"

"How'd he know?" We laughed as he stormed off to his
beautiful lady friend now waiting in his expensive Rover.

"He took rejection well, don't you think?" I said flippantly,
trying to hide the real disappointment I felt about someone I
had actually once looked up to.

Abby joined us on the sunny front porch, and a cheer went
up as the now dusty Range Rover tore out of the yard. A large
horned owl was sitting on the peaked roof of the barn. He
turned his head and watched, without comment, the trail of
dust that followed the speeding vehicle.

10

LINDY GETS HER GUN

As July came to a close, Wyoming was getting drier every day. The colorful wild flowers Alisa and I had picked were only a distant memory now with the prairie grass gone from green to golden brown. And the excitement of watching Gran stand up to Robin Blackford had cooled in the sweltering hot days that followed one after another with no answers in sight and his offer to buy the ranch still hanging over us like afternoon thunderheads.

Alisa had been working at Mother Earth for three weeks, and so far Jed had kept his promise not to reveal her true identity. Entering names in the database and running errands for the rest of the office staff had proved not only boring but unproductive. Alisa had not been able to discover anything to tie Mother Earth to cattle salt, poison, or the Walker Ranch in general. Nothing. Zero. Zip.

I had made countless visits to the sale barn in those three weeks, too, and each time I came home with nothing.

The folder from Blackford's Range Rover, which I had risked so much to have Abby copy, hadn't helped us, either—except confirm Robin Blackford as a liar. One with a good architect. The house he had had designed by Lin and Lin Architects *was* beautiful. I didn't blame him for wanting to live in it on our ranch. Only I wondered why he had lied to the people of Thermopolis. I had played his words at the airport over and over in my mind. *"I have no particular ranch in mind."* He had also stated that his purpose in buying a ranch was to save a piece of the West from the destructive cattlemen and open it up for public use. Public use, my aunt fanny. The blueprints in the folder showed all cattle guard crossings, which Grandpa put up to *give* people access to the historic road, changed to gates. Gates could only mean Robin Blackford meant to keep people out, not let them in.

"It's horrible," Lindy assured me when I explained that to her one night as I pored over the plans. "It's horrible, but it isn't criminal. If Blackford buys this ranch, he can put gates wherever he wants to."

Lindy was becoming a popular newscaster at KKOA, spending a lot of time at the station in Thermopolis. But so far her investigative reporting had not turned up any corruption in high places and nothing helpful to our own investigation.

Claire sat at the computer each day endlessly writing to Jess and chasing dead ends. With two weeks to our deadline, the Sagebrush Rebels had no place to go for ideas.

Claire drew a big black circle on the kitchen calendar around August 15 and called it Black Saturday. We marked the days off as Black Saturday approached. Time was running out.

The *Sagebrush Rebellion Investigative Center* sign had curled at the edges, pulled away from the tacks, and fallen on my floor—joining the rest of the mess.

"God will provide," Gran said after family devotions every morning. But her walk had slowed, her limp was back, and she had taken to buying bread in town rather than making it herself.

Claire always replied, "If only God will provide until He provides."

The whole family was speaking in proverbs now. Not a good sign.

It was July 30, and with gloom all around, I figured Abby needed some fun. All of the cousins had learned to drive going to get the mail. It was her turn.

"Come on, Abby," I said after we finished pitching hay to the orphans. "Let's go get the mail. You can drive."

It was a mile down our lane to the county road where the

mail was delivered about noon every day into a big wooden mailbox with the Flying W burned in the side.

"Okay!" She ran to the truck, not needing a second invitation.

"First, Abby, first gear," I said as she put the pickup in third, popped the clutch, and nearly sent me through the windshield.

Several fits and starts later, we approached the crossroads of private and county roads. The mailbox stood in front of a lone elm tree. "Isn't that Alisa?" Abby said as we came to a jerking halt a few feet from the crossroads.

I had been so intent on helping Abby drive, I hadn't looked up—one didn't expect traffic at the mailbox.

Our maroon Lincoln was parked by the side of the road. Next to it, facing the other way, was a battered old pickup. Jed and Alisa were standing between their vehicles talking.

"She's home early," I said, feeling betrayed. "And look who she's talking to."

It was too late to back up and avoid them—they had seen us.

Alisa blushed.

Jed started toward us. He was no longer driving a Mother Earth pickup or wearing the T-shirt with their logo. I noticed he had let his hair grow. And two months in the sun had darkened his already naturally dark skin. Jed had seemed like any other extremely fit college kid the day I met him on the plane. Now he looked every inch a Native American. And liking it.

Well, one of us has succeeded in what we came to do, I thought bitterly. Jed had found his roots. I was about to lose mine.

"Hello, Con," Jed said without the hint of a smile. He rested his big arm over his head on top of the cab and leaned down through the open window to talk to me.

"Nice to see you again," he said.

"Is it? I wouldn't have thought so."

"Con," Alisa said, joining us, "give him a chance."

"Chance to do what? Poison a few more of the Walker cattle?"

"Con, he's bigger than you." Abby poked me nervously.

Alisa glared at me.

Jed surprised me.

"I don't blame you for being angry, Con. You think your way of life is being threatened. And Alisa tells me you think I have something to do with it. Well, that day on the plane when we met, I really didn't understand all that garbage you were spouting about your grandfather's ranch and your heritage there. Your pride looked like arrogance to me, and it made me mad. I couldn't imagine caring so much about anything, especially a piece of land."

A gust of wind came up, making tiny dust eddies as it swirled on the hard-packed road.

Jed leaned farther into the truck window.

"Well," he went on, "that was before I saw our land, my land—the Wind River Reservation. All those things people around here say about the Indians' drunkenness and the poverty . . . well, it's all true—there are lots of problems. But it is only part of the truth, and now I understand your pride because I have it, too. Native pride." Here his voice dropped lower, slower still. "I would fight to keep it."

"Well, you may have to," I threw out without thinking, wishing I wasn't trapped in the truck with him leaning in the window inches from my face. "But right now you are on Walker land, not the Wind River Reservation."

Alisa took a step closer. "Con—"

"No, Alisa," Jed said, looking from one to the other of us. "Con is right. I don't belong here and shouldn't have come. I drove by hoping to see you again . . . wanting to see the Walker Ranch, too, I think. It was a mistake."

He started to walk away then but stopped and turned back. Alisa reached out to touch his arm. Tears filled her eyes.

"Your heritage once got in the way of mine, Con. Well, maybe now the roles will be reversed."

Despite the words, his voice didn't sound threatening—more sad than anything. Before I could decide what to say, he turned to Alisa.

"I'm sorry," he said, removing her hand from his arm. "I won't call you again."

And he was gone. Got back in his truck and drove away.

"How could you be friends with the enemy?" I finally asked after a stunned silence while she dried her eyes.

" 'The enemy of your enemy is my friend,' " she responded with one of her proverbs. "What does that make Jed, who does seem to be a friend to our enemy and also a friend of mine?"

"I'm confused," Abby whispered, obviously not wanting to her hurt her cousins' feelings.

"So is Alisa!" I replied, wondering if she had noticed Jed's non-denial of poisoning our cows when I accused him. Or if she cared.

"I think Jed will turn out to be the enemy of our enemy and in the end will be our friend. Please, Con, trust me on this."

"I would rather trust my life to Abby's driving ability," I said, furious with her for letting her heart get in the way of her head. "Let's get what we came for and go home, Abby."

I knew Abby felt caught between two people she loved, and she could see the hurt on both our faces. But she started the pickup and made a smoother drive home

Gran was not pleased to see the mail. There was a letter from the Department of the Interior, Bureau of Land Management. It bore the official seal of the U.S. Government.

"What is it, Gran?" Abby asked, worry lines crinkling her eyes as she watched her grandmother open the letter with trembling hands. We all listened as she read it aloud.

" 'Your appeal to have charges of environmental violations dismissed has been denied. A final decision on the merit of the violations charge will be handed down on August 15, as previously noted. Mr. Raymond Rice, our senior representative in the Thermopolis regional office, has been authorized to make a final judgment and render it on the stated date. Should the leasing rights granted to you under the Taylor Grazing Act of 1935 be revoked, you will have thirty days from August 15 to remove all livestock from such lands as are covered by these lease agreements between the United States and Whitfield W. Walker.' ''

Gran dropped to a kitchen chair and gazed into space.

"Our fate seems to be in the hands of that yo-yo Raymond Rice," I said in despair. "And August 15 is only two weeks away."

Nigel and Mom and all the other aunts and uncles were expected to arrive just days after the deadline. It was beginning to look like Nigel's first visit to the ranch was going to be his last.

"Our fate," Gran said bravely, "is where it has always been, in the hands of God. Now, don't you all have some chores to do?"

Abby and I left to give her some space.

We went to my room to throw darts at Robin Blackford.

Actually, it was a large color poster of Robin Blackford with Thermopolis in the background. It was an advertisement for the upcoming 125th Anniversary Celebration of the first settlements in the community. Charlie the Crow had sent Alisa around town asking merchants to tack up the posters in their shops. She brought one home for our office wall. My dart game had improved noticeably.

We hadn't heard from the movie star since Gran told him to take his "generous offer" somewhere else. But we had more than a hunch he hadn't given up.

Abby pulled a tiny lizard out of her shirt pocket and asked me if I wanted to hold it.

"Kind of you, but no thanks," I said, throwing another dart at Mr. Blackford instead.

"There is the new owner of Walker Ranch, Abby. You should write a poem about him."

"That's not funny, Con," she said, stroking the nervous reptilian head.

"Sorry, Abby, I'm only kidding."

The town was excited about having a movie star wanting to buy a local ranch, according to Lindy. She would be interviewing the mayor about the celebration for that evening's news broadcast.

When we joined Gran, Alisa, and Claire in the living room, the girls were still setting up the recently purchased portable television on the bookshelf. A displaced pile of books was stacked on the floor.

"Leave the books there," Gran directed them. "This *thing* is not staying in my house—I only agreed to it so we could watch Lindy tonight."

The screen faded from red to yellow in wavy lines; the hills between Thermopolis and the ranch made for bad reception.

Local news anchor Kathy Sherwood was introducing Lindy.

"Lindgren Larson is live in the studio this evening with Thermopolis Mayor John Richards in our continuing *Citizen Series Interviews* as we lead up to August's '125 Years of History' celebration."

Despite Claire's best efforts to tune the set, Kathy Sherwood's face was still pulsing from red to yellow and back again.

"That's good enough," Claire decided, leaning back against the couch to watch her sister.

Lindy was sitting at a round table in the KKOA studio with the equally rotund and beaming mayor.

"Thermopolis will become as famous as Jackson Hole," he told Lindy in response to her first question about the future of the town.

"Jackson Hole, Wyoming, has Harrison Ford, and we will soon have Robin Blackford. Just think, little lady," he said in sweet, drippy tones, winking at her, "maybe someday the president of the United States will come on a vacation to our little town and stay out at the old Walker Ranch with Blackford and other famous people who are sure to follow him. Now, what would you think of that?"

"Malarkey!" Gran exploded. "He's talking like we're already gone."

Mayor Richards leaned back in his chair, adjusting the lapel microphone on his Western shirt, which barely snapped together over his bulging belly, and waited to see if he had impressed his young interviewer. Lindy was playing it very cool. She showed no emotion about his outlandish statement.

She had done her research on the mayor. He was not a native to Wyoming. In fact, sick of all the noise and overpopulation in California, he had moved to town several years ago, started a travel agency, and set right out to *attract more people* and noise to the quiet, remote community. He didn't seem to notice that would turn Thermopolis into the kind of place he had left.

"I didn't realize the Walker Ranch had actually been *sold* to Mr. Blackford," Lindy said, her voice steady.

He shrugged.

"Are you saying, then, that it *has* been sold to Mr. Blackford?" she pressed him.

"As good as," the mayor finally replied, tilting his face down, revealing several more chins, and winking like he was sharing important inside information with the young reporter. "And I can assure you, his presence will be good for this community, too. More famous people will want to move here. Growth and tourists dollars, that's what this is all about."

"Won't do him any harm, either," Alisa added.

"Shh," Gran said to us. "Listen."

"What happens to the small family farms and ranches when that kind of big money comes in—like they did in Jackson Hole and in scenic areas of Montana? Doesn't it raise land prices, drive up taxes, and force out people who have raised cattle on the land for generations? Not to mention the little stores on Main Street—they will be replaced by national discount stores on the edge of town. Is that the kind of growth you are hoping to bring?"

"Go, Lindy!" I shouted. "Way to bring out your big guns." I couldn't believe this was my mushy-hearted cousin carefully, skillfully taking Mayor Richards apart. And it looked to me like he was beginning to realize it.

"Now, don't get me wrong, little lady," he said, dropping the wink. "Many ranching families in the area are good people—been here for years, of course—but the West is changing. We need to take better care of the environment, you know, and cattle grazing is downright bad for the land. Ranchers don't *have* to sell their land, of course—no one's forcing them. I'm sure the Walkers are right happy with the money they'll make selling their ranch. They can stop working so hard and move about anywhere they want to, I reckon. Florida . . . or Arizona, maybe . . . where the winters aren't so bad for old people like them."

Groans went up all around the room, but Gran motioned us to be quiet and listen.

Lindy let that go, and using her best professional voice, she asked him to explain to her how the land could be used in a more productive fashion than running cattle on it.

"Productive?" His agitated face swelled and got bright red. Either that or the reception was messing with his features—it was hard to tell with him.

"I'm surprised at a question like that from a person of your generation," he sputtered. "I thought the schools were teaching you young people that we have to think differently now about the land, that we have to stop exploiting nature for materialistic purposes. You know, like Rousseau once said—the earth belongs to all of us or none of us . . . or something like that. . . ." He paused and looked a little confused but charged forward more confidently: "Everybody should be able to hike and fish and enjoy all that space. Mr. Blackford is buying the land so it can be saved from exploitation and opened up for everyone to enjoy. He is thinking about his children and all our children in future generations. Greed destroys the soul, you know, so the land must be shared."

The camera swung to Lindy's face. We could see she was struggling now to keep her cool.

"Get him, Lindy!" Abby shouted, leaping to her feet on the old piano bench. "Don't let him get away with that. Who's he calling greedy, anyway?"

"Quiet, Abby," Gran gently scolded her. "We'll miss it. And be careful with the piano bench, please. It's older than Thermopolis."

"I don't think Mr. Blackford is married or even has any children, Mr. Mayor," Lindy pursued. "But more to the point, what exactly do cattle do to the environment that destroys it?"

The wilting mayor had not expected hardball questions from such a young, pretty face. He was starting to look decidedly less comfortable and smug. His eyes disappeared into his fleshy face, and the leering look was long gone.

"They . . . eat the grass?"

"They eat the grass? That's it? The environmental damage of grazing cattle is the loss of a renewable resource?" Lindy was going in for the kill.

The mayor was getting tired of this conversation, which obviously wasn't going the way he intended, and he was looking trapped.

"Yes, they eat the grass," he said defensively. "But I don't think you would understand the philosophical and environmental impact of that, so let's just leave it to the grown-ups, okay?"

Mayor Richards stood up, took off his microphone, and slammed it on the table. The camera cut away from him to Lindy saying a polite thank-you to her special guest and encouraging viewers to stay tuned for a ten o'clock news wrap-up.

Clapping and shouting broke out in the old Walker Ranch house. Lindy the Tenderhearted had shown no mercy for the pompous man. I remembered her dry eyes the day Abby found the dead calf. She had that same look tonight interviewing the mayor. This was a new, determined Lindgren Larson. Her great-great-grandmother seemed to smile down from the faded portrait.

"Let's eat," I said. "I'm always looking for a reason to celebrate over food."

Everyone traipsed with me into the kitchen to see what we could find.

"Let's wait for Lindy," Gran suggested, happier than I had seen her in weeks. "We'll make it a party for her. You know, she could be a lawyer like her dad, that girl. . . . Of course, it's the Walker genes we saw tonight."

"So what should we make to eat?" I asked, bringing us back to the important stuff. Everyone began opening cupboard doors, looking in the pantry and refrigerator.

We decided on nachos and ice-cream sundaes.

"And what do you think the philosophical implications of cattle eating grass might be," Claire mimicked Lindy's voice using a long wooden spoon stuck in my face as the microphone.

"Well, little lady." I winked at her. "It has to do with what that French philosopher feller said. If I can't own this land, you ain't going to own it, either."

"He's nuts," Abby summed up. "Do we have to wait for Lindy to get home to eat this stuff?" She picked up a chip to dip in the salsa.

Claire tapped her finger gently, knocking the chip out of her hand.

"Cut up strawberries for the ice cream, Abby. It'll keep you busy."

Tragedy leaped down from her perch on Gran's chair to eat the chip, complaining all the while. "Poor old thing, getting fat won't help. You should lay off the chips!" Alisa said, stroking the crabby cat.

Alisa and I had a strained truce. She thought I was wrong about Jed, and I knew she was. I hadn't told her so, but I was sorry her feelings for him were caught in the middle.

I watched what was going on around me and pretended to help, picking up things and moving them around on the table. But something was bothering me about the way the mayor had talked, and I couldn't put my finger on it. Something more than the fact that it sounded pretty dumb. I had heard similar stuff before . . . the same kind of thing about greed and even quoting the same French philosopher, Rousseau.

"The airport!" I exclaimed, dropping the bowl of sprinkles I happened to be holding.

"Hey, watch it with the goodies, Con."

Everyone stared at me like I'd gone crazier than usual.

"You know what the mayor was saying just now—about greed and future generations and all that stuff, quoting Rousseau," I explained excitedly. "Well, that's the same way Robin Blackford was talking to the reporters at the airport—only with a lot more class and intelligence. That's odd, don't you think?"

"You're right, Con. I remember that, too," Alisa said, sitting down on one of the stools around the island countertop where we were working.

Everyone stopped what they were doing. There was a tension in the air like something important was about to happen.

"I think Con's right," Claire said. "And that's odd, too."

She ducked the strawberry I flicked at her.

"Mayor Richards couldn't think his way out of a paper bag, and the chance of him reading any French philosopher is kinda slim, don't ya think?" I went on, encouraged by their response. "Blackford must be influencing the mayor—convincing him he is going to buy the ranch to help tourism in Thermopolis. The mayor wants to be mayor of something other than a hick cow town, and he sees the movie star as a way to put the town on the map. But"—I was so excited I was rambling—"the topographical maps we copied show Blackford intends to *shut off*, not open up, the ranch to visitors."

"So what are you saying, Con?" Claire asked.

"There is something not quite right about his offer. He lied at the airport about not knowing which ranch he wanted to buy, when he was already having a house designed on this one. And he had already made an offer to buy it. And he isn't telling the truth now. Hang on. I want to show you something."

I left them staring at me and ran up the stairs to my room, our investigation center, and got the plans Abby had copied. When I returned, Alisa and Gran helped me move chips, fruit, salsa, and Cokes to make room on the counter, and everyone gathered around to look at the contents of the Lin and Lin Architecture folder as I spread them out.

"Look at each place the road goes through a fenced area of the big pasture. Now," I pointed with the knife Abby had been using to slice the strawberries, "each cattle guard has been changed to a gate according to this key at the bottom. That means Blackford intends to cut off access, not open it up."

"Even the stagecoach ruins," Gran said sadly. "School kids have been coming out here for years exploring their local history."

"Not exactly what 'Mr. Friend of the Earth' is telling the mayor and townspeople, is it? I rest my case."

"Blackford is everywhere," Alisa agreed. "Or his ideas. We need Jess to do some research on our movie star. Girlfriends, wives, Lin and Lin Architecture . . . everything. There's probably a Robin Blackford chat room on the Net."

"Good idea. Have Jess check it out," Gran said and then added quickly, "I'm not saying that computers are good—in general—but Jess is so clever on those things that it's worth a try."

We all smiled at our no-tech grandmother.

"Sure, Gran," I said. "Next thing we know you'll be wanting a laptop."

With August 15, Black Saturday, only two weeks away, we were grasping at straws, but at least it was something. Everyone started eating and talking all at once about the possibilities and coming up with questions for Jess to check out on the Net.

Lindy arrived home half an hour later to find empty bowls of chips and melting ice cream—and four very embarrassed but comfortably stuffed cousins. In our excitement we had consumed Lindy's party food without her.

A BIRTHDAY POWWOW

TIME MIGHT NOT HAVE BEEN ON OUR SIDE, BUT THINGS WERE beginning to heat up for the Walker cousins—in more ways than the summer weather.

"That girl has got to slow down," Gran said, watching Alisa return home from Thermopolis on the last day of July, tearing up the lane and screeching to a stop nearly *on* the front porch, where Gran and Grandpa were enjoying some fresh air. Time seemed to be renewing his strength; he walked each day with a cane, and now we had our evening talks on the back lawn where he could see the Red Wall and listen to the river.

Alisa leaped out of the car, her long blond hair falling in all directions out of a haphazard knot on her head, and buzzed past them to the door.

"What is the hurry, child?" Gran called after her.

"Nothing. Sorry, gotta run. Hi, Grandpa, how're you doing?" She let the door slam shut behind her and took the stairs to my room two at a time.

Standing by the open window upstairs, I had watched her mad dash down the drive and heard her run past our grandparents on the porch.

Alisa didn't move that fast without good reason. I was excited before she opened her mouth.

Her face was flushed, and she was gasping for air. Lindy and Claire helped her to the edge of the bed. I handed her a bottle of ice-cold water I had been drinking and waited impatiently.

"A very big fly flew into our web today," she finally managed. And once she started talking, she picked up steam, waving her arms, talking with her whole body until we had trouble keeping up.

"I was on the computer today and stumbled upon a file labeled 'Enemies.' It looked promising, but before I could get in, Mr. Crow stuck his head in the door. I pushed Escape and the screen changed—I don't think he saw where I was, but it scared me so much I gathered up my stuff and nearly ran for the car. Only I forgot my purse with my car keys, so I crept back in, past Crow's door—which was shut—and picked up my purse. I was tiptoeing back past his door when I heard something terrible. I froze. Literally. I mean, I couldn't move. It was awful. . . ."

She stopped to take another drink.

"Go on!" we more or less shouted in unison.

"Okay, okay. I have had the scare of my life here."

But she went on describing what she'd heard.

"Remember, I couldn't see who he was talking to. Couldn't hear the response of the other person, but Crow's yelling came through the door loud and clear. He said, 'You will go back to the Walker place and finish the job. And you will do it tonight. He wants it done while we are all at the powwow.' Then there was a bit I couldn't hear until Crow started yelling again, 'You can't back out now. We have an agreement with your family that they won't want broken.' "

Alisa paused for breath, then delivered the most interesting news of all.

"Then he said, 'Put the stuff in the water tank this time. That'll be the end of those fancy Angus bulls.' "

"No way!" Claire finally managed as what we heard sunk in. "Someone knows a lot about this place. And knows those bulls are worth a fortune."

"A fortune Whit Walker can't afford to lose," Lindy added.

"Hello . . ." Alisa said, drawing us back from the news to her story. "I was standing there frozen to the floor when I heard a chair scrape across the hardwood floor as if someone was getting up. I unfroze and ran. I ran to the car and drove without even stopping for lights, I think. I was scared to death and excited and oh . . ." She collapsed back on the bed, totally spent.

"Do you know what this means?" I said, ignoring her theatrics. "Jed was in that room, and he is coming back here tonight."

"I don't know *who* was in that room, Con," Alisa protested, sitting up. "How could it be Jed? It doesn't fit. He has no family here. He told you that."

"Could he have been in the office and you not know?" Lindy asked.

"Sure. My office is in the back. I didn't see who went into Crow's office. But we can find out—tonight."

Everyone started talking at once. With only a few hours to get ready and so much at stake, we struggled to come up with a plan.

Lindy was going to cover the powwow for KKOA, and because it was a special celebration of Chief Running Wolf's ninetieth birthday, she couldn't possibly get out of the assignment.

"We could call the sheriff," Claire suggested. "Have him catch the guy."

"I can see that happening," I replied sarcastically. We knew he wouldn't come.

In the end it was decided. Claire would go back with Alisa to the Mother Earth office while everyone was safely out of the way at the powwow and help her get into the "Enemies" file. Alisa had been leaving the window next to her desk open a crack, just in case. . . .

"In case" had arrived. But with the two of them needed in town, and Lindy at the powwow, that left Abby and me to catch our eco-terrorist.

"We are going to leave Abby out of this," Lindy insisted. "She's too young. Grandpa and Gran may overlook the foolish chances we're taking—especially if we succeed—but I wouldn't want to face them if something happened to Abby."

Everyone looked at me.

"That leaves you, Con."

"Not to catch him, of course," Lindy quickly added.

"Just hide in the haystack, watch, and see who comes. Then make sure the bulls don't drink the water. You will be an eyewitness. That's all we need."

"Gladly," I replied. "I'll wait for him. I've been waiting for this since June first."

"Con," Claire said, "I don't like the look in your eyes. Don't you dare do anything stupid like confront whoever comes."

They took my silence as assurance.

Six hours later, the Sagebrush Rebels were all in place. Alisa, Claire, and I had gathered in the kitchen after Lindy left and Abby went to bed. Dressed all in black like when we play flashlight tag, we set out.

"It's now or never," Claire said.

"Be careful, Con," Alisa said. Each one of us felt the excitement of the night, tinged with our fear of failure. This one wasn't a game.

◆

Using my penlight, I looked again at my watch. Eleven o'clock had come and gone. It was less than one hour away from August, and I was hiding in the haystack high over the corral. Alisa and Claire should be inside Mother Earth by now. If the window was still open.

And if no one saw them crawl through it.

An owl hooted from the barn roof. I stretched my tense muscles, wondering what we had missed and what could go wrong.

The night was quiet, except for the occasional nighthawk swooping down in search of mosquitoes, which I was thoughtfully feeding for them.

"Don't wear any insect repellent," Claire had reminded me when we were getting ready. "No point in wearing black to hide when you smell like that." So I hadn't, and the mosquitoes were driving me crazy, buzzing around chewing on my exposed hands and face.

It might be quiet for me, but not for Lindy at the powwow

miles away across the Wind River Canyon. There would be ceremonial drums beating out the ancient songs around a bonfire. Dancers with war paint covering their faces, wearing traditional costumes made from buffalo hide and eagle feathers, would be circling the fire, celebrating Chief Running Wolf's long life.

Clouds moved away from the full moon, and feeling exposed in the light, I shrunk back against the hay. Two full moons ago tonight had been very clear and made it easy for me to see all the dead cattle Jed had poisoned. Chief Running Wolf had been near death that day. Grandpa, too. Now Jed was coming back to poison more cattle. Only this time I was not going to blow it. I was ready. And waiting.

And as the waiting went on and on, my legs got stiff from the cold. I began to wonder if he'd come.

In the distance, from my high vantage point, I could see the shapes of the old tractors, hayracks, and combines retired over the years to the field behind the barn. It looked like a machinery graveyard by day, but the old farm equipment transformed in the night into dragons and giants and all sorts of imagined scary things—our playing field for flashlight tag.

"Someone's going to get hurt," Gran would always say. And someone always did. But minor scrapes and bruises were more than worth the fun. Every year we played, building our nerve and learning strategy of where to hide and when to move while dashing through the night over old rusty equipment. Only tonight wasn't a game, and someone might really get hurt. I was hoping it wouldn't be me.

Thunderclouds had covered the moon again and turned the usually starry sky shades of black. I could hear the bulls moving restlessly around the corral, as animals do before a storm. I had convinced Big Bear to move them out of the pasture into the corral tonight before he left to attend the powwow. The bulls were the most valuable stock left on the ranch and worth a small fortune. I knew Grandpa couldn't afford to lose them—someone else knew it, too.

My hiding place was in a wall of freshly cut hay. The first cutting had been put up by the corral, making a series of twelve-foot-high stacks running the length of the corral. I was hidden midway up on a ledge between two of the towering bales, where I could see anyone approaching. Some of the bulls were continuing to eat the hay I had thrown into the wooden feed bunks that line the corral fence on my right. But I kept my eyes on the water tank across the road in the pasture—where the bulls were usually kept.

An hour passed. I thought about Hannah. I hadn't heard from her in ages. Hadn't even received the picture of Robin Blackford, which she promised to send weeks ago. I wondered if she had forgotten about me.

The quiet was getting to me. Even the comforting sound of the bulls chewing their cuds had stopped. I was having trouble remaining alert as the night dragged on.

Still no sign of anyone by the water tank.

I looked at my watch again. It had been only half an hour since the last time I looked.

I continued to worry about Alisa and Claire. What if someone in a passing car saw the light from the computer screen and called the police? The two of them dressed like cat burglars crawling in a window didn't sound like such a good idea now. I hoped the funny guy next door didn't choose tonight to go into his shop and make his instant antique tables.

All this worrying was making me even colder. I decided to put on my leather jacket over the sweat shirt, amazed as always how the scorching, hot summer days in Wyoming could turn into very cold nights. The clouds continued to rumble overhead with an occasional flash of lightning followed by distant thunder. I kept the sweat shirt hood up over my blond hair for better cover. I was getting stiff from sitting still so long, and sharp dried blades of straw were poking through my sweat pants and making me itch.

Occasionally the clouds would blow past the moon, letting enough light shine on the whole area for me to see it clearly if only momentarily. I took out the Thermos of hot chocolate Lindy had made me and twisted off the lid. Steam escaped, warming my face, but the aroma was not the sweet smell of chocolate I expected, but coffee. I tasted it. Strong, bitter black coffee.

"Yuk," I spit it out. Then I realized what my clever cousins had done. *A little caffeine might help*, I decided and slowly sipped the hot liquid, glad for the warmth and the jolt.

Before I emptied the Thermos he came.

I heard the soft crackle of dried grass and weeds being crushed beneath his boots. I heard legs brushing against the sagebrush before I recognized the tall, bulky shape moving quickly but carefully through the night up to the big tank of water. My whole body tensed; I flexed my muscles, remembering his bigger bulk, hoping the heavy work on the farm had helped.

Thick cloud cover darkened the sky again for several minutes, and I lost sight of him momentarily. Startled by the intrusion, the bulls were moving around, making it impossible for me to hear Jed's movement.

I willed him to dump the stuff quickly before some tiny movement of mine gave my position away. He had to actually complete the act of sabotage, or catching him wouldn't do us any good. I waited motionlessly while clouds once again covered the moon. I couldn't see what he was doing or what he had done.

When the moon peeked out from behind the clouds, giving me some light again, Jed had disappeared. And then I heard footsteps coming toward me. The next thing I knew, he was almost under my feet, walking between the stacks toward the corral.

It's now or never. Alisa's words came back to me as I sprang over the ledge of hay, dropping on top of a large body and propelling it forward. He landed face down with me on the top. Three years older, Jed was bigger than I was and bound to be stronger despite my meager weight-lifting efforts and work on the ranch. But he was stunned for an instant and I managed to pin him down and pull one of his arms up behind his back, holding him down with my knee.

"You eco-maniac, where's the poison you're bringing us

this time?" I managed to get out between gulping gasps of cold air and hay dust.

"Let me up and I'll give it to you," Jed's voice said, his face still planted in the straw and dirt.

Jolly likely, I thought, pushing down even harder. "Sure you will—and say you're sorry, I suppose, for the other time?"

I had counted on surprise, but not on him walking so conveniently right underneath my hiding place. Excited by my good luck, I struggled to secure his arms with a thin leather strap I had tucked in my pocket. But my surprise advantage was eroding fast, and instead of answering my question, Jed succeeded in throwing me off. We struggled between the walls of hay for a few seconds, with me ending up face down, my mouth full of alfalfa.

"I mean it, Con. Stop struggling and I'll give you what I brought. I didn't use it . . . didn't intend to use it."

Like I was dumb enough to believe that. I could see a pitchfork stuck into the side of the stack in front of me. It had been thrust in at an angle and might not be too deep to pull out with one tug. With a desperate lunge, I rolled left and reached for the pitchfork with my right. The handle slid into my hands, giving me a blunt weapon that I swung up toward his chest, blocking his arms and knocking him off—careful to keep the dangerous prongs out of his face and out of his reach.

Only he was much stronger, his arms longer. As he grabbed the horizontal handle, I tripped over something hard and fell backward, hitting my head on the sharp edge of the feed bunk. The cat screeched. The bulls bucked and bawled, running across the corral, and it seemed as if Jed was saying "I'm sorry" as everything went completely, utterly black. . . .

◆

Rain was splashing gently on my face when I finally got around to opening my eyes. I was surrounded by faces, including Jed's with black war paint covering all but his eyes, which were outlined in a lightning design. I struggled unsuccessfully to get away from him. Car headlights shone from somewhere behind me, highlighting concern on the faces of my cousins.

"He's coming around. It's okay." Lindy was holding my head, and tears streamed down her cheeks. "He's okay," she gasped again through her sobs. The worried faces of Alisa and Claire came into focus, too.

"Look out—he's here." I struggled to sit up, trying to warn them about Jed, wondering why they couldn't see him. But a stabbing pain across the back of my head prevented me from sitting up or making much sense.

"Ouch," I moaned, feeling the back of my head and finding it wet with blood.

"I caught him," I tried again.

"Doesn't look like it to me," the ever practical Claire pointed out not too kindly, as Jed held the flashlight so they could inspect my cut.

"Sorry, man, I didn't mean to hurt you." Jed's eyes looked eerie staring out of his war paint.

Totally confused, I laid my head back down again. "It's all right, Lindy, you can stop crying. . . . Lindy, I'm okay." Fighting the pain, I tried to figure out how Claire, Alisa, and Lindy had all gotten there so quickly and what Jed was doing *helping* them inspect my wound.

To make things worse, the rain was beginning to really come down.

"Let's move him up to the porch," Alisa suggested, holding a bunch of tissues to my bleeding head. "Can you walk over to the car, Con?"

I found that I could—only on slightly unsteady legs—and they helped me in. Lindy cut the lights and coasted quietly down to the porch, where they helped me into the swing. Claire went off to find Tylenol, peroxide, a bandage, and a nice warm blanket for me.

Jed stood in the background looking like a brooding evil presence. Finally the girls stopped fussing over me and agreed that the gash on the back of my head was not too deep and could wait until morning since they had more or less cleaned the wound and stopped the bleeding.

The large covered veranda was dry, and we could listen to the rain and talk without disturbing our grandparents. Everyone pulled a chair up close to me where I was reclining in the porch swing like some kind of invalid. This was not how I had planned this night to end. Lindy handed out cups of hot chocolate she'd made while Claire and Alisa had played Florence Nightingale on my head.

"Now, would someone please explain to me what happened after I passed out and what *he* is still doing here?" I demanded, wiping the last bits of blood and peroxide off my neck.

Jed joined the circle, keeping a respectable distance from me. There was some swelling above his left eye, and several scratches had messed up the design painted on his face. He sat down with some discomfort, also. *Good*, I thought. *I owe you that and more for Shades' mom and all the other dead cattle.*

"I don't blame you, by the way," he said as if he could read my mind. "I told you that the other day. I don't blame you at all for being mad. And I didn't come tonight to carry out my orders. I was going to leave the poison with a note explaining the whole thing."

"So why come at night and sneak up to the tank? And how do we know you didn't dump some of that stuff in the water, then have a quick change of heart when I jumped you?"

"I came at night—tonight—because I wanted Charlie the Crow to think I *was* going to carry out my instructions. Otherwise he would have sent someone else. I walked past the tank on my way in. I didn't expect anyone to be watching, and I stood there thinking about what I had done before and felt sick at what I was supposed to do again. I intended to find a place to leave the note without waking up any of you. I had seen Lindy at the powwow, and I planned to get away from here before she returned."

"Yeah, right!" I muttered, unconvinced.

"Oh, Con, stop being such a jerk and listen for a minute." Alisa then explained what had happened to her and Claire. "We got into the office all right, but that was our last success. We came up with nothing."

Shaking her head, Claire explained, "The Enemies file was only more of the same 'ranchers are bad, loggers are bad, wolves are good' nonsense. Nothing new. And nothing about the Walker Ranch."

"We met up with Lindy in town at the Broken Spoke Café," Alisa picked up the story again. "And she told us Jed was at the celebration earlier in the evening, but she noticed he had disappeared around midnight. I was still convinced he wasn't going to be the one carrying out Crow's orders." Alisa smiled at Jed as she said that. His face was hard to read through the paint. "So you can imagine my shock when we drove up and found him kneeling over your unconscious body."

"*Our* shock," Lindy added. Everyone started talking at once, explaining what happened next. And the gist of it was they all leaped out of the car ready to rescue me, only to find Jed asking for their help and assuring them of his good intentions.

"And you believed him—just like that?" I was surprised at the gullibility of girls.

"Instinct, Con. Girls are good at it," they assured me.

"Oh, please," I groaned. Before I could say more, the screen door opened slowly and a very sleepy Abby emerged in shorts and a T-shirt, wanting to know what was going on. When she saw our clothes, she asked why she hadn't been invited to play flashlight tag.

It broke our tension, and we quickly assured her, despite our clothes, that we had not been playing tag without her.

"Good thing hearing loss accompanies old age," Claire said as I made room for Abby under the blanket. "Otherwise Grandpa and Gran would be joining us, too."

"Here, Con," Jed stood up and handed me a parcel. It was a small brown bag with a handwritten note stapled to the bag—addressed to Alisa. Inside was a plastic bag and a small bottle.

I read the note out loud:

" 'Enclosed you will find an empty bottle purchased by Mother Earth, Inc. It once contained sodium fluoroacetate (1080), which was poured over a salt block and dropped by a low-flying plane in the Walker pasture at Birdseye Butte. If you have any of that salt block left, you can prove it is the same poison that killed your cattle. Under orders from Mr. Charlie the Crow, I delivered the poisoned block of salt to the airport and saw it loaded in the plane. I don't know the name of the pilot, but I think I have seen him before on the reservation. I was asked to use this stuff again tonight. For reasons I would like to explain to you, I decided I couldn't go through with it. I *am* sorry for everything. Jed.' "

"You do still have the sliver of salt, don't you, Con?" Alisa asked.

"Yes," I said, stunned at finally hearing the truth I had suspected all along. The truth about Jed, the plane, the whole thing. I couldn't wait to go back to that smug sheriff now. And I realized Jed couldn't have written this note after I attacked him, so I listened to the rest of what he had to say with new interest and a tiny bit of growing trust.

"It all started last year when I was invited to join an environmental club at school in Salt Lake City," Jed explained. "Through them I met a representative of Mother Earth, and he seemed especially interested in me because of my Native American heritage. Well, I didn't think much more about it until mid-May, when this guy Charlie the Crow called up and offered me a summer job in their office in Thermopolis. It seemed an amazing coincidence to me and my parents that it was near the Wind River Reservation—since I am part Shoshoni." Jed was carefully picking his way through this part of the story and, it seemed to me, not telling the whole truth.

"I read and believed all that stuff about cattle damaging the creek beds, overgrazing the range, destroying the environment for others with 'pure' motives who only want to enjoy the natural surroundings. And—" he looked at me, willing me to understand before he went on—"Charlie the Crow assured me I could help them restore a proper balance for land use between the big, rich ranchers and the tribes. I wanted to believe that about the ranchers being the enemy—"

"The enemy of your enemy—that made Charlie the Crow your friend," Lindy said sympathetically. "It's not so hard to understand why you would feel that way."

"Maybe, but it doesn't justify what he did," I said bitterly.

"You were wrong about Jed, Con. Get over it," Alisa snapped. "He didn't come tonight to hurt us."

"Thanks for standing up for me, Alisa, but Con is right. My new native pride doesn't justify what I did before. I have been very wrong—done wrong—and I am sorry."

Lindy patted him gently on the back and wiped away a few more tears.

I breathed in the sweet smell of settled dust and wet sage-brush, listening to the sound of the rain pinging on the porch roof. It was a slow, gentle, soaking rain. "The best kind," Grandpa would've said.

Jed had helped try to ruin Grandpa, and I for one wasn't feeling as forgiving as Lindy—who we all knew was kind to a fault. Anyone who could cry over roadkill couldn't be trusted with her emotions. But I had to admit, Jed had showed real guts in defying orders and coming here to tell us what he had done.

Abby, who had been paying very close attention to every-thing, including the bloody bandage on my head, said with sus-picion, "Does saying you're sorry make killing Shades' mom and knocking Con over all right?"

Out of the mouths of babes. I waited eagerly for Jed's re-sponse.

"No, Abby. It doesn't make it all right. Saying I'm sorry can't bring back your beloved cows. It was wrong, and I will have to pay for what I did—with the law. But I would like to help you first, if you'll let me."

"How?"

It took him a while, but when I heard his plan, it sounded good. "It didn't take me too long to realize Mother Earth was not what I expected. They sounded more like pagans than en-vironmentalists. It's a religion with them. Crazy, radical stuff. Anyway, I was glad when I got to spend most of my time on the reservation. The poverty and problems shocked me, and I wanted to go on blaming the farmers and ranchers. And Yel-lowdog told me to keep working for Mother Earth—that it would help people on the reservation. So I did what they asked. But increasingly I knew Charlie the Crow didn't really care about my people. The whole thing is phony. Someone higher up, someone other than Mr. Crow or any of the tribal elders is giving orders, and I don't think it's out of love for the earth."

"Do you know who that someone is?" I asked hopefully.

"No, I don't," he admitted. "But if you will wait a little before you say anything to the sheriff or take that bottle of poison to him, I may be able to help you. We know Charlie the Crow was directing me. Together, I think we can figure out who is directing *him*."

Still connecting the dots, I thought, rubbing my hand back and forth across the bandage that covered my cut. We were running out of time and still looking for the head of this beast.

12

THE OLD WRINKLED ONE

THE HOUSE WAS SMALLER THAN I'D EXPECTED FOR SOMEONE so important. Chief Running Wolf's one-story frame house was freshly painted stark white with bright red and yellow geometric designs drawn around each window. There was a new metal barn in the distance and several log sheds and other outbuildings surrounding the house. Pickups and people were everywhere.

A dozen horses were kicking up dust in a circular training corral beside the driveway, where Benjamin Big Bear brought our pickup to a halt. A short kid with a long ponytail was swinging the loose end of a rope at the neck of a leggy brown-and-white paint colt who was managing to escape the lasso without much trouble. The boy's friends were sitting on the top rail, enjoying his failure and cheering on the colt.

"Hey, Big Bear," one of the boys called out. Ben returned the greeting with a wave and leaned on the front fender of the hot pickup.

"I'll wait here," he told Grandpa.

Grandpa didn't reply but started to walk with my help up the short path to the front door. The boys by the corral stopped what they were doing to watch us go by. They waved to Jed and looked at Grandpa and me with curiosity. And hostility.

I was feeling more than a little curiosity myself. One week had passed since Jed joined our side. When I had stumbled down for breakfast at six this morning, I found him there with

Grandpa, drinking coffee together like old, long-lost friends. Grandpa looked stronger than he had all summer. Stronger and happier.

"Morning, son, you're late," he had said with his old smile.

"You two know each other?" I had asked, shocked to see Jed in our kitchen.

"In a manner of speaking," Grandpa replied.

"How's your head, Con?" Jed asked.

Before I could answer, Grandpa went on. "Jed here brought an invitation for us to meet with Chief Running Wolf on the reservation this morning."

"Chief Running Wolf? I thought he didn't like you."

Grandpa ignored that and stood up, moving toward the door.

"Forget breakfast; this is more important than food."

Few things were more important than food. But with a longing look at the bacon, scrambled eggs, and French toast Gran was about to serve me, I had followed them out the door.

I learned very little else as Big Bear drove us across the Walker Ranch, around the end of the Wind River Canyon, and deeper into the reservation than I had ever been before. Jed said little. Grandpa had seemed lost in thought and answered everything with "Wait and see."

Yellowdog opened the door. I had seen him before, at the airport and at the hospital. He was a tall, distinguished man with unsmiling, hard eyes and a flat, round face, his black hair pulled back in a ponytail.

"Hello, Youngbird" was all he said. Wondering who on earth he was talking to, I followed as he led us into a large sitting room where the old chief stared at us from an ornately carved straight-back chair. It looked too large for his shriveled frame.

There were several more comfortable-looking chairs arranged around the room, all facing his. A woven rug with shades of turquoise woven in the pattern covered the pine floor in the center of the room. Native American art mixed with twentieth-century comfort.

"The Old Wrinkled One," as the children of the tribe called

him, raised his hand in a welcoming gesture. But not a very friendly one. Except for the long white braids bound with beaded turquoise ties, he was dressed like any rancher.

He motioned Grandpa into the chair nearest him. Two old enemies in the same room. Grandpa appeared calm, eager for this meeting and very respectful of the leader. *What could Grandpa have done to make the chief his enemy?* I wondered for the millionth time this summer.

The walls of the room were covered with pictures, some of them badly framed old black-and-white photographs. And there was a grand oil painting of the peace treaty signing with his ancestor, Chief Washakie, and Ulysses S. Grant. It filled the wall behind his chair and gave the room its only grandeur. That and the view.

There was a large window overlooking the vast sagebrush-covered prairie and rocky ledge that dropped sharply down to the Wind River Canyon, the divide between these two men's land.

Yellowdog stood protectively behind the chief.

"I wish to tell you a story," Chief Running Wolf began as soon as Jed and I were seated. I had to lean forward and listen closely, as his voice had lost any force it might have had and came out not much above a whisper.

"When Chief Washakie, my ancestor, was given a silver saddle by your President Grant, he was asked to make a speech. Instead he said, 'Do a kindness to a white man, he feels it in his head, and his tongue speaks. Do a kindness to an Indian, he feels it in his heart; the heart has no tongue.' "

He stopped then, as if gathering strength to go on.

A fly buzzed in the background. No one moved. No one else spoke. I felt like I was the only one there without a clue. Jed must have known what was going on, but he hadn't bothered to tell me. He looked expectant—not confused.

"I have waited too long for my heart to find its tongue," the old man finally spoke again. "The distance between your ranch and our land, your family and ours, has been higher than the walls of the Wind River Canyon that divide us. I have treated you like my enemy. I know now, that was a mistake."

I glanced at Yellowdog. He didn't look happy at Chief Running Wolf's apology to Grandpa. I met his cold eyes and looked quickly away. Whatever the chief had had against my grandfather seemed to still be bothering him. Or it was general dislike of all non-Indians.

"Whit Walker," the chief was addressing Grandpa in that quiet, raspy voice, "you stood together with the Shoshoni people during a very hard time, and I have never thanked you for that. In fact, I have hated you for it."

My grandfather lowered his eyes, out of pain or pride I wasn't sure, and I was more confused than ever.

A great tiredness—or sadness—seemed to overcome Chief Running Wolf, and he went on even more quietly.

"Peace treaties—which our people accepted long ago because we had no choice—took away our dignity when they took away our land. We lost our will to live, to work. Eventually we became victims not only of that great injustice but also of our own weakness. Thirty years ago my only son became friends with a non-Indian. He wanted me to let go of the past, accept change, learn new ways—including cooperation with neighboring ranchers. My son saw the hopelessness of our people living without working, drinking up each monthly government check. He knew we had to change. But I was stubborn and would not listen. We fought, and I sent him away from the reservation . . . considered him dead. Then late in life he married a white woman and took her Christian religion. She gave him a son in his old age. To me he was a traitor to his people. Most of all I hated the non-Indian friend who had led my son away from our ways."

Chief Running Wolf pointed a shaky finger at a picture on the wall. He said something in Shoshoni to Yellowdog, who hesitated before pulling the dusty frame from the wall and thrusting it at me. Startled, I nearly dropped it, and looked at Grandpa for direction. His face gave away nothing.

"Read it, please," the old chief said.

It was a picture of an ordinary sign posted outside the local swimming pool. An ordinary sign with extraordinary words printed in bold black letters. I brushed off the dust, gulped uncomfortably, and looked again to Grandpa for help. He nodded for me to start.

" 'No dogs or Indians allowed . . .' " I read those hateful words softly, and they landed like explosions into the quietness of that room.

"Go on . . . read the rest," Jed spoke up for the first time.

" 'No dogs or Indians allowed in the city park, swimming pool, rest rooms, or changing facilities of the municipality of Thermopolis. Signed, Mayor Charles Murray.' "

Penciled in at the bottom was the date: June 1959.

No one said anything for several seconds. I looked at Grandpa.

"Did you know about this? How could you . . . how could you have lived here when there were laws like this?" I blurted out without thinking. "This is terrible—"

Chief Running Wolf stopped me before I could go on. "It is easy to poke fire with another man's hand."

I hoped I wasn't supposed to respond to that, since I didn't have a clue what he meant. So for once I wisely kept my mouth shut.

"I . . . I have waited too long to speak . . . but you speak too soon," the chief went on. "Before you judge what your grandfather should have done, listen to what he *did* do. Your grandfather was that friend of my son. Together they led the effort that ended the discrimination you see in that picture. Your grandfather made many non-Indians angry with him for siding with us, including many people from his religion. But together with my son he managed to change laws—if not hearts."

Embarrassed at my outburst, I looked at Grandpa. I should have known.

"Many non-Indians still treat us like dogs, and I have watched our poverty increase and the hope of our young people die. Twelve young people killed themselves last year rather than face the kind of life they see around them. I should have listened to my son, and I should have thanked you, Whit Walker, for helping us. The worse things became for my people, the more I missed my son and hated you for my loss."

Chief Running Wolf's tired old voice sounded like it was nearing the end of its strength, his eyes nearly closed, papery-thin lips quivering with emotion.

Jed moved protectively to the chief's side. Squatting down beside the chair, he laid a hand on the old man's arm.

"That's where Charlie the Crow and Mother Earth come into it," Jed said, "pretending to care about the tribe. Promising Chief Running Wolf to help his people if he cooperated with them."

"What did they promise you?" I asked.

Grandpa frowned at me and motioned me to be quiet and listen.

"Mr. Crow promised to use his 'connection' with someone in the Bureau of Land Management office to return more water rights to the reservation and more land for grazing. Would I mind, Mr. Crow asked me, if the big Walker Ranch was destroyed in the process?"

"That no-good Raymond Rice and the BLM are in this, too!" I exclaimed.

"Hush, Con," Grandpa said. "You will show proper respect." Embarrassed, I hushed and waited while the chief went on.

"I had waited years for revenge against the Walkers and would have agreed right then to do what he asked. But the foolish man who pretends to be like us by taking a Native American name didn't know that, so he offered me something else to ensure I would cooperate—he offered me the son of my son."

"No way," I muttered, understanding Jed at last.

I seemed to be the only one surprised at this revelation. Jed must have told Grandpa this morning before I got up. That explained why Grandpa had been acting like he had just met a long-lost friend; in a way he had.

Jed was Chief Running Wolf's grandson. No wonder he had been at the old man's bedside. Some roots. I looked from grandfather to grandson. Chief Running Wolf's eyes might be clouded with age, but he was seeing clearly now.

"Then Youngbird—that is Jed's Indian name," he explained. "He came to me last week, the day after the powwow, and said it was over. That he would no longer take part in destroying the Walkers—because of a friendship with them, especially one young lady. It was like history repeating itself. I was losing my grandson to the same enemy. Then . . . well . . . you tell them what you said to me, Youngbird."

Jed looked sheepish. "Well, I told my grandfather that sometimes it's hard to tell who the enemy really is."

"I am sorry," Chief Running Wolf said, "for many things."

In another room a telephone rang. The sound seemed out of place in the home of this ancient man.

When someone answered it, Grandpa finally spoke: "I accept that apology, Chief Running Wolf. I, too, am sorry for the pain I have caused you, the trouble with your son. Our history is complicated. Our roots—yours and mine—go deep in this land, and for good or ill they have grown together now. I am not proud of the past. Even my beautiful land, which I am now in danger of losing, once belonged to your people. The river we share was once yours. But we who live off of this land and share a love for it and a desire to preserve it have more in common, despite our past, than the newcomers who would like to divide us now and conquer this place for themselves."

Both old men were comfortable with silence, and it went on some time in that warm, still room after Grandpa's speech.

It was as though they both thought about the words that had not been spoken for so many years and were now out in the open. This meeting had not been easy for Chief Running Wolf, and he finally ended the unusual encounter by standing weakly to his feet. Jed jumped to his side and took his arm to steady him.

"I think you are right," the old man declared. "Today is a new beginning for us. Thank you, young man, for befriending my grandson."

I smiled sheepishly, thinking of all my unkind thoughts about Jed.

"Youngbird has told me about you." There was the first hint of a smile as he looked at me. The folds of skin around his eyes crinkled, softening the harsh face. "You still have much to learn from your grandfather. Whit Walker *is* a friend of the Sho-shoni people, and someday we will all celebrate together when Youngbird returns . . . with his father."

Surprised by his words, I was speechless again and looked at Grandpa for explanation. But it was Chief Running Wolf who spoke, and when he did the smile had disappeared.

"I wish to see my son before I die."

A sadness descended with those words, for we all knew there wasn't much time left for that wish to come true. I noticed that at sometime, unseen by me, the brooding tribal elder Yellow-dog had slipped out of the room. I wondered where he'd gone in such a hurry.

A WIDOW BY CHOICE

A LARGE WINDOW FAN DRONED ON, TRYING TO MOVE STALE hot air across the old Thermopolis auction barn. The auctioneer spit out his patter quicker than the ring man could flick his whip at the wild-eyed longhorn cow in the ring. Men on each side of the holding pen stood behind a cast-iron protective shield as the angry cow charged back and forth. Cow traders sitting safely in the semicircle of bleachers lining the room bid in mysterious microgestures known only to them and the auctioneer—done to avoid detection by fellow buyers.

The nonstop, take-no-breath staccato auctioning went on until finally all bidders but one were out and the auctioneer slowed down and slid into real words:

"Sold at sixty-two dollars a hundred weight. Move her out, boys." He turned to the side, wiped his mouth with his sleeve, and took a quick sip of water.

"And what do we have here," the auctioneer went on as a docile-looking Guernsey milk cow ambled into the ring like it was her very own milking stanchion. She didn't even bat an eye as the ring men moved out from behind their barriers and cracked their whips at her in an effort to keep the cow moving, allowing everyone to get a good look.

"Aaaalll right—and whatcha gonna give for this old dear? She'll come on in when it's milking time and volunteer to give her milk, she's so gentle. So . . . who'll bid a quarter and a half and a half." And he was off and running.

I looked around the ring. Buyers and spectators sat, looking as miserable as I felt in the sweltering heat. Flies buzzed annoyingly around my head. I took a long drink of my ice-cold lemonade, made downstairs in the sale barn café from fresh-squeezed lemons, and wondered why on earth I was sitting there looking for something only Grandpa understood but for some crazy reason thought *I* might see. He had insisted that I come—again.

Cowboy hats of every variety were sprinkled among a few bare heads. The serious buyers, cow traders, were easy to spot. Their hats were Stetson, and their boots the most expensive. Each one had a fist full of long white cards for tracking their purchases. Some of them carried pocket calculators, which they took out occasionally to figure their best guess of potential profit or loss on the cattle they were attempting to buy. Usually they had only a split second to make a decision on thousands of dollars. Cow traders, according to Grandpa, could be fine folks, but you definitely wanted to be wide awake when doing business with them.

Farmers, ranchers, and a few wives and kids were there, too. I recognized lots of men from my many years of going to the sale barn with Grandpa.

A small group of Native American ranchers were sitting together down near the ring across from me. Yellowdog was with them, not looking much happier than when I had seen him three days ago.

That day still seemed unreal to me. Jed, grandson of Chief Running Wolf. And the son of grandpa's friend. It's funny how some things work out. Only it didn't solve our problem with the BLM, and neither Jed nor Chief Running Wolf knew the name of Mr. Crow's contact at the BLM. So I was still trying to connect the dots.

I looked across the sale ring at Yellowdog and the Native American men with him who were successful ranchers, like Grandpa's partner, Big Bear. Hard-working, proud men who would have been treated like dogs in this city not that many years ago. Somehow I didn't think Yellowdog had forgotten or forgiven, or appreciated it the other day when Chief Running Wolf apologized to Grandpa. And I wondered if his loyalty to the old leader was strong enough to accept that, or if he had gone to talk to Charlie the Crow and told him what he'd heard. Yellowdog scared me. He had good reason to hate, and his unsmiling face across the ring from me did not give me a warm fuzzy feeling.

Up several rows and behind Yellowdog, our neighbor Fred Marvin sat with his stained straw hat tipped down over his face and his dirty boots propped up on the railing. He appeared to be sleeping. I decided Gran was right—he didn't look like much of a threat to anyone but himself.

August 10 flashed across the digital board. Under it the head count, weight, price, and buyer number changed after each sale. Bored, I looked at my watch. It was three o'clock. I had watched hundreds of animals move through the ring, sweated buckets, and swatted flies till I was sick of the place. I decided to give the whole thing another half hour before packing it in and calling Alisa for a ride home, when a very big black Angus bull came charging into the ring. He was snorting mad and, with his head down, charged the ring man, who barely managed to leap behind the iron shield. The bull slipped on the cement floor under the sawdust and slid into the shield. He shook his head and charged again.

Somebody whistled, kids cheered the bull, the announcer laughed at the nervous ring men, and I lost my concentration.

While my eyes had been on the bull, someone had joined Fred Marvin. Marvin sat up, straightened his hat, and was listening as if his life depended on it.

Now, who could that be? I wondered. *Even tourists don't dress that bad.* The man wore a silk shirt, gold necklace, and tiny wire-rimmed sunglasses. An alien couldn't have stood out any more in that crowd of cowboys. He looked like the guy who had shoved me down the steps of the plane when I first arrived in Thermopolis. In fact, when I thought about it, I felt sure it was the same guy.

A slight tingle ran down my spine. I took my cowboy hat

off and wiped away the sweat. *"Watch for anything unusual,"* Grandpa had kept saying. That guy was about as unusual as you could get. He hadn't come to buy cattle, and unless I missed my guess, he wasn't part of the Marvins' social circle, either. So what was he doing at the Thermopolis sale barn talking intently with our not-so-friendly neighbor Fred Marvin?

Determined not to miss anything important, I swallowed hard and started making my way in that direction. But before I could even get close, the silk shirt got up and practically ran out through the side door, followed moments later by Marvin.

Moving quickly now, I dashed down the center steps, out past the office and café, and through the front door. I ran around the old two-story building to the side exit. Scrambling past pickups, big eighteen-wheeler bull haulers backed up to loading chutes, and horses tied up to a rail by the door, I arrived only to find a few stray dogs and a bunch of kids playing by the door. No mysterious stranger. No Fred Marvin.

"Drat," I said, patting a big bay horse on the rump and nearly getting myself kicked in the bargain. "Where could they have gone?"

Well, they won't be hard to spot if they're still here, I decided, heading back inside to search the sale barn. Still trying to blend in like Grandpa had told me, I moved quietly, pulling my own cowboy hat low over my eyes.

It must not have worked too well, because several guys called out.

"Hey, say hello to Whit, will ya? Hope he's feeling better."

"You bet," I replied each time. So much for the secret-weapon stuff. Everybody seemed to know me.

I looked in the café. Not there. Not along the business counter, where buyers were settling up the day's deals, either. I looked on both sides of the ring, where the crowd was now thinning out. Yellowdog had disappeared. A group of cow traders were playing cards in a small room at the top of the sale ring. *The sale must be nearly over.* I went to call Alisa, still convinced I should find Fred Marvin and see what, if anything, was going on.

"Alisa, listen," I said quietly into the dirty black mouthpiece of the pay phone. "The sale's about over, but I need to hang around a little bit. There may be something interesting going on—at least, I want to look around a little more. Come when you're ready, and I'll meet you out front."

She groaned.

"Look, I'm sorry," I said. "I would be happy to drive myself if the state of Wyoming would just recognize what a good driver I am and give me a license. In the meantime, I need a ride."

Alisa agreed, none too happy with the arrangement. "And by the way, Con, you got a letter from Hannah in the mail today. It's a small manila envelope. Looks interesting . . . should I read it to you?" she teased.

"Bring it," I replied. "Unopened."

Another sweep of the sale barn and corrals outside failed to turn up anything. Defeated, I walked back into the ring to sit and wait, like a kid, for my ride.

Still looking for Fred Marvin and his visitor, I nearly missed Raymond Rice. It was the few plastered-down hairs pulled over his little bald head that alerted me. With nothing else to do, I followed him, wondering why he had arrived as the sale was ending. He went out of the ring area and into the crowed lobby, straight into the sale barn office—leaving the door open. I moseyed past—real casual like—to see who else was meeting with Mike Boyle, the sale barn manager. I had sat in that office plenty of times listening to Grandpa discuss business with his friend Mike Boyle. But the sale barn manager was *not* at his desk.

I made a second pass and stopped right outside the door, pretending to look at an old sign hanging on the wall. A noisy, angry discussion was going on inside.

The large wooden desk was in my line of view. Papers were strewn all over with a cordless phone tossed on the top. From my angle, I couldn't see the face of who was sitting in the leather rocking chair behind the desk, but I could see a hand. I recognized the gold jewelry. I had found my man. And he was holding up a folder bearing *our* Flying W brand in big, bold black strokes.

I gasped, stunned. Fred Marvin was there, along with Raymond Rice, Charlie the Crow, and Yellowdog. I couldn't believe it. Talk about connecting the dots—they all seemed to be having a meeting.

"Oh man, oh man, oh man, what am I going to do?" I muttered under my breath nervously, desperately trying to figure out a way to hear what was going on without actually sticking my head in and asking if I could join the group.

People were already beginning to stare at me, and I knew I should move on. But I *had* to hear what was going on.

Edging away from the door a couple of steps, I leaned my back against the wall—which was actually a flimsy door that gave way—and I fell in backward, landing hard in a little storage room.

Hoping no one saw my less-than-graceful fall, I brushed myself off and stumbled to my feet. As my eyes adjusted to the dimness, I saw tack equipment, mops, and buckets around me. A little light was coming through a large crack in the wall.

Moving carefully over the buckets and saddles, I put my face to the wall and peered through the cracks.

"Yessss," I whispered. I was looking into the smoke-filled sale barn office.

Not wanting to attract any attention, I leaned across the narrow space in that musty room and closed the door to the hallway so I wouldn't be seen from the outside. Then I scrunched uneasily beside an old saddle thrown on the floor and tried to avoid the metal buckets stacked against the wall. They would make a real racket if I knocked them over. Bracing myself against bridles and halters hanging on protruding nails, I tried not to think about sneezing. The group of men in that room definitely would not like to know I was listening to their conversation.

Things were a bit blurred at first as I pressed my face against the crack and peered in.

My heart was racing so fast I thought I wouldn't be able to hear their voices, but gradually things came into focus.

Rice was sitting down, and so was Fred Marvin—talking to the fancy dude behind the desk. He had laid the folder down on the messy desk and was leaning across it, staring at the men angrily.

"Listen," his voice seethed with anger. "We have business to do before the manager of this dump comes back."

It was the same sneering voice of the man who had pushed me out of the plane. The same man I saw welcome Jed to the Mother Earth office.

Small world, I thought. Small and becoming clearer every minute.

Two other chairs were pulled up near the desk—Charlie the Crow sat in one, with his back to me, Yellowdog in the other.

Practically hyperventilating, I tried to remain perfectly still. *I'm connecting the dots, Grandpa, right up to the head.* But in order to do that, I had to keep from falling over, sneezing from all the dust, or knocking over a mop bucket.

"Let's make this as quick as possible, men," the Californian said in short, clipped tones. "This place stinks like cattle, and I have a plane to catch."

"It was your idea to meet here, Mr. Dillard," Raymond Rice said defensively.

"I certainly don't make a habit of attending *cattle* auctions, either," the Mother Earth executive threw in, making cattle sound like a bad word.

Dillard . . . Not a name that we had come across yet. I strained to listen, not wanting to miss a word.

"I want to take some good news back to California today, boys . . . for a change." Dillard's voice was condescending and sneering, pitched a little high.

"Our mutual friend is getting tired of all your mistakes and delays."

This was it. This was really it. Sweat was still dripping off my forehead and tickling my nose. My legs were cramped and I didn't dare move, but nothing was going to make me miss this. Nothing.

I reached up carefully to scratch the itch on my nose, and that's when I felt the sticky pull of a spider's web. Jerking my hand back quickly, I looked up through the streams of sunlight hoping against hope for an empty web. At first I couldn't see anything except an uneven mesh with a funnel-shaped retreat at one end attached to the low ceiling of the closet. Unable to move away without making a racket and giving my position away, I carefully plucked a strain of the web near my head again. I didn't like the feel of it.

Sticky and tough, it made a faint rattling sound.

"Oh no," I whispered to myself, now in real panic as I saw the shiny black body scamper out of her retreat to see what had landed in her trap. There was a bright red hourglass on the perfectly round, shiny belly of a big, hairy spider. I was in the web of a black widow spider.

"As dangerous as a rattlesnake when you bother them," Alisa had warned Abby.

Frozen in panic, I hoped desperately the spider wouldn't consider my visit a bother. How could I concentrate with the deadly black spider hanging right over my head? If I didn't move I'd be safe. So I forced my eyes off the spider and back through the crack. The meeting was heating up. Yellowdog was speaking.

"The tribe is no longer participating in this scheme. I came only to tell you that face-to-face. Now you know and I am going." He rose to his feet and headed for the door.

"What do you mean, no longer a part of the plan? It's too late to change your mind," Dillard yelled, shaking his sunglasses at the back of Yellowdog. "Explain what you mean by—"

"I mean—" Yellowdog turned and paused long enough to answer, calmly, coldly—"that Chief Running Wolf no longer wants to be used as a pawn by Raymond Rice, Charlie Crow, or your boss. We have been lied to. Something that has happened before in our history. We don't like to be lied to. The deal is off."

"You can't do that now." Raymond Rice jumped to his feet to confront Yellowdog by the door. "We—the BLM—had a deal with Chief Running Wolf. I demand to speak to *him*. You are dealing with a government agency, you know."

"Chief Running Wolf has spoken," Yellowdog growled, slamming the door shut behind him.

Boy, anger must be his only emotion, I thought, realizing I had never seen him smile.

His exit shook the flimsy wall of my hiding place. I glanced up again and saw the spider had moved closer to me.

My muscles were starting to go into spasms; I had to move . . . couldn't move. "Please go away, spider," I whispered hopefully. "Have all the baby spiders you want. I won't hurt your egg sac. I promise." For an answer she moved closer down a thread toward me.

I couldn't stand the tension. *I've got to go,* I thought, trying to decide whether or not to burst in and confront all of them or sneak away with what I'd heard so far. The problem with that was I hadn't heard enough. I closed my eyes and could see Gran sitting on her porch watching her birds, and Abby standing on the branding chute gate writing poetry. I could hear Grandpa's voice asking me to help him, to be his eyes and ears. I still didn't know the name of the boss Dillard referred to, and I didn't figure he would just tell me if I waltzed in and asked.

Determined to hold on a little longer, I leaned my head against the wall again, my eye peering at the back of Raymond Rice, who was nervously running his hand over his few remaining hairs, trying to get them to lie down and cover his bald spot.

"Stupid Indian," he spluttered. "I told you we couldn't trust them. But don't worry, Mr. Dillard. I can take care of it. Besides, we don't really need them anymore. They did their part, and now we have the town leaders on our side. That twit of a mayor thinks everything Blackford says is gospel. Forget the Indians. Let's take care of more important business."

Blackford. I nearly fell over. The name came pounding through the wall of my hiding place. Robin Blackford was Dillard's boss. Robin Blackford was more than greedy and hypocritical. He was pulling all the strings. The head of the beast.

I shouldn't have been surprised, after all his offers to buy the ranch and those plans for a house in the Red Wall. But if I hadn't been so busy thinking how cool he was, how rich and macho and famous, I might have used my head and seen the obvious sooner. I hadn't wanted to admit to myself that my favorite movie star was capable of such cold-hearted greed. It occurred to me that Grandpa probably already knew Blackford was involved but had needed me to help him prove it.

Blackford had the money, the clout, the motive. And Dillard was his man.

Dumb, Con. You have been so dumb.

Stunned, I listened as Fred Marvin jumped in, demanding what he had been promised.

Dillard, perched now on the edge of the desk, leaned forward and shook the Flying W folder at him.

"Get what's coming to you? You have done very little, Mr. Marvin, except annoy the Walkers by cutting a few fences and pick up the salt block after it had done its work. You will profit, all right, once this little thing is settled. In the meantime, shut up and wait your turn." He pounded the desk with the folder. "But you, Rice, you were in charge, and you are behind schedule. Can't you even make a few charges of environmental abuse stick against the old man? Robin and Linnea are most unhappy with your progress."

"We have given them a deadline of August 15, and I am on schedule," Rice whined. "I have to be careful, you know— make this thing look legal. It hasn't been easy. You wouldn't believe those people. Especially Mrs. Walker. She scares me."

The other men laughed at his unwise admission.

"You can't even intimidate a couple of old people," Dillard sneered. "Blackford wants them to accept his offer. Now!"

"Soon," Rice tried to stop the flow of charges against him. "A decision will be handed down in five days. Then they will have to sell. You'll see—"

Dillard wasn't impressed and interrupted: "They better. Charlie, you can drop the phony Indian name with me. Where is this environmental terrorism you promised for last week? The final straw, I believe you called it—poisoning some expensive bulls. What happened to that?"

"It wasn't my fault," Charlie whined.

"Of course it was your fault. You were in charge. Now shut up and listen. It would be wise of you to remember where you got the money to build your cushy little Mother Earth office and set up your comfortable base of operations, Charlie. Linnea's house has to be built in the Red Wall by next spring in order for it to be considered for the architectural prize. Robin is, as you can imagine, very eager for his fiancée to win this great honor. He wants the world to see and acknowledge her architectural genius, which can't happen if they can't build the house, now, can it?"

He sat down and lowered his voice a little.

"I mean, people, please, we are talking about a couple of old people. Sick and old. What on earth will it take for you guys to get this job done? And don't forget, if anything goes wrong, you take the blame. There is no way any of you can prove a connection to Robin Blackford. And he would of course deny meeting any of you or having any part in this."

Furious, everyone leaped to their feet, talking at once.

It was at that moment that Mike Boyle turned up.

"Sorry, fellas, but I need my office."

Suddenly the room went still, no one sure what to do next. Then, just as abruptly, everyone made for the door.

I figured it was a good time to make my escape. But as I moved, my eight-legged companion did too—down her web toward me. Too late, I realized my shoulder had been touching a tiny light brown ball. An egg sac. I jerked away but felt the sting of the spider's fangs sinking into my arm. I smashed at her wildly, knocking down most of the closet as I did so. Sinking to my knees in pain, I put my hand over my mouth to keep from yelling but couldn't stop myself from slumping to the floor and knocking the flimsy closet door open. Clutching my shoulder, I felt my arm going numb and the cheeseburger I had for lunch start to come up as I rolled out of the closet and onto the gray cement of the sale barn floor.

A CONVOCATION OF COUSINS

"ARE YOU OKAY, CON?" THE FRIENDLY BUT WORRIED FACE of Mike Boyle came slowly into focus. Other faces crowded around, looking down at me.

"What happened?" Boyle went on. "An ambulance is on the way, just hold on."

"A black widow spider," I mumbled through the pain, trying to see if Rice or any of the others was in the sea of people staring at me.

"Oh no," the longtime friend of Grandpa gasped, much more worried. "Somebody go call the Walker Ranch and tell Whit his grandson is in serious trouble."

"Shh," I tried to stop him from announcing the Walker name, but it came out a moan. Voices were swirling around me.

"Fell out of this closet, did he?"

That last voice rang an alarm bell in my brain. I tried to see who was speaking, tried to think through the fog of pain, but I didn't get very far.

"Could he have been hiding in there listening to business in your office?" the same voice inquired with a deadly edge I understood but everyone crowding around me found funny.

"Not hardly," Mike said, and the cow traders standing nearby joined him in laughing at such a silly idea.

"This boy is Whit Walker's grandson. He's been around here every summer for years. He certainly wouldn't have any reason to listen in on my business," Boyle explained. "Besides, it's pretty boring business—eh, boys?" The cowboys around him laughed at the thought of Whit Walker's grandson wanting to listen in on their discussions about the price of cows.

I groaned. And they all thought it was only from pain. The voice suggesting my true purpose in the closet faded away in the crowd.

Next thing I knew, Alisa was crawling into the ambulance with me. Real tears ran down her cheeks.

"Con, what's happened to you? Oh dear . . . Con, you look terrible. Just terrible. Mike Boyle said something about a black widow spider. I'm sorry I didn't come sooner. . . ." She was sobbing.

"It's not that bad. . . ." I tried to reassure her, hoping I was right. "Everything is going to be okay now."

"I know," she said, thinking I was talking about my health.

"No," I tried again weakly. "Everything is going to be all right. I figured it out. . . . I know the answer. . . ."

"He's not making much sense, is he?" a medic said while hooking me to various tubes and drips. "Probably hallucinating from the poison, but he'll be back to normal in no time. A young man his size—won't kill him, you know."

She looked a little reassured. "Good." She squeezed my hand and gave me a wry smile. "He doesn't make much sense most of the time anyway."

◆

Twenty-four hours later, Alisa and I were heading for the ranch together, returning from the Hot Springs Hospital, where she had picked me up. My quick reflex, the doctor figured, killed the spider before it managed to deposit all its venom. It couldn't do too much damage to my "big, strong body," as the doctor called it, anyway.

I liked his description, but I felt as weak as Tragedy the cat and about as crabby. Despite plenty of antiserum, my arm was still numb and my digestive system was in a state of rebellion, which was too bad because I felt ravenous.

It had been two and a half months since Alisa picked me up

at the airport and we first drove this road to the ranch together. Lots of water under the bridge since then.

"Con, I'm so sorry," Alisa said, observing my misery and driving much more carefully than usual. "The doctors and Gran made us stay away from the hospital so you could rest. But I have been dying to ask you what you were mumbling about in the ambulance. Gran hasn't told us anything."

"I haven't told Gran anything yet, either. And don't be sorry about the bite. It was worth it," I said. I had been waiting a whole day to tell someone the good news.

"What on earth do you mean? You got something besides a spider bite out of that closet? And by the way, you're not about to be sick in here, are you? You look very green."

I nodded yes to the first question, not too sure about the second.

"What were you doing anyway? Mike Boyle was very upset that you were hurt. He was a little confused, however, about finding you falling out of his tack closet."

Before I told Alisa the good news, I had to know the answer to a very troubling question. It kept me awake last night—that and the pain in my arm.

"Alisa, this is very important. Think carefully. Yesterday when you got to the sale barn and people were crowded around me, did you see Charlie Crow or Raymond Rice . . . or someone in a silk shirt and lots of gold jewelry before they carried me into the ambulance?"

"Con, are you hallucinating again? Charlie Crow? He's the last person who would be at the cattle auction, or Rice for that matter. No, Con, you must have been mistaken."

"Think hard, Alisa. It's very important. How about the guy who pushed me down the stairs at the airport when I first got here? He had on a silk shirt and lots of gold jewelry."

"There was lots of confusion, people standing around staring at you on the floor, women fainting at the horrible sight, that kind of thing," she kidded. "But no, I would have seen *him* in that crowd. Besides, Con, why would he be there?"

I was relieved to hear that, if not totally reassured. I savored, for a moment longer, my great news.

"What I was doing in the closet was connecting the dots." I smiled, remembering Grandpa's instruction and my frustration with him. But as usual, he'd been right.

"*I have found the head,* and now all the pieces fit." I let out a weak little yelp of joy. "I know the answer!"

Alisa slammed on the brakes, nearly knocking me off the seat, and pulled the truck off the road. She killed the engine and turned to face me.

"I think I better be sitting down for this. You're serious, aren't you?!"

Dust from her screeching halt caught up with us and rolled in the open windows. A hawk flew overhead. I watched him soar, like my spirits. Everything was going to be okay again.

"Yes, I am very serious," I said. "In fact, deadly serious, as it turns out. And you *are* already sitting."

So I told her everything I'd heard, as clearly as I could remember it, thankful for my good memory. She leaned toward me, her arm resting on her knee, hand under her chin to close her mouth, which kept flying open in astonishment. And finally, like me, she let out a shout for joy.

"Con, you did it!" She gave my arm a playful jab.

"Ow! That's my bad arm." I winced. Actually, a little more pain didn't faze me. I was too excited.

"Oops, sorry. Con, you mean you stayed there and listened even after you saw the black widow? That's terrible! Were you scared to death?"

"Well, I didn't actually think the spider would bite me if I was careful. I kept remembering everything you had said about how they only bite if their egg sac is threatened. And I tried not to remember the part about a bite victim's lungs filling with fluid, starving him of oxygen . . . frothing at the mouth . . ."

Alisa laughed at my exaggeration of her fairly mild warning to Abby to stay away from the poisonous spider. But the terror of watching that spider's deadly rush toward me had been real, and I didn't much like to remember it.

When we got back to the ranch, Lindy, Claire, and Abby

joined Alisa and me. And to my surprise, the last two cousins—Jess and Kate—had both arrived and welcomed me with careful hugs and gentle assistance as I walked inside.

Kate looked as gorgeous as usual, smiling at me through her green, almond-shaped eyes. Her short, honey blond hair flew around her face in the breeze. She explained that the Troopers had a few days off before the Thermopolis parade and that she would meet up with them on Saturday.

"Hey, are you okay?" Claire asked, peering at me up close, as if I were some sort of specimen.

"Yeah, fine," I replied, liking all the attention more than I would admit. "You were pretty worried, huh?"

"Even you, Con, are part of the ecosystem and must be cared for," Claire said with a straight face.

They all laughed. Simple girls.

"Well, well," Grandpa said, coming slowly into the room and observing our happy reunion. "A convocation of cousins!" His wrinkled face was glowing with pleasure at the sight of all seven of his grandchildren in the same room, but he looked at me with concern.

"You've had us worried, Con. But the doctor assured us you'll be fine in a few days. No lasting damage. Weak and unable to eat much, but you can handle that, right?"

"Except for the not eating," I said. Even the mention of food seemed to bring on more waves of nausea, so Gran brought me a glass of special herbal tea with a bent straw so I could drink the cold liquid while reclining.

All this attention was nice. *Too bad I can't take advantage of it by asking for chocolate cake.*

"Quiet, everyone. Listen up," Alisa commanded. "Con has the most unbelievable news."

Abby was at the piano playing "Ode to Joy"—which seemed about right.

Perfectly tuned despite its age, the old piano had been hauled on wagons pulled by mules all the way from the rail line in Casper one year after the first Walker family settled in this valley. It had stood on the same spot ever since.

Lindy, Claire, Kate, and Jess were sitting on pillows on the floor, gossiping and giggling and catching up. Alisa, who knew my news, couldn't sit still and kept flitting around the room telling everyone to listen up.

"Quiet, Abby," Lindy said. "Let's hear Con's news." Abby hopped down from the piano stool and snuggled on the floor with her three sisters and cousin Kate.

With all eyes on me, I told my tale again. I was feeling weak but hadn't lost my timing, and I drew the story out, building the drama, carefully avoiding mentioning Blackford. I downplayed the details about the spider for Grandpa and Gran's sake, only it didn't work.

Grandpa said sternly, "Con, you know *nothing* is as important to us as your health—certainly not this ranch. I can't believe you saw the spider and went on listening."

He looked very upset and went on blaming himself. "I never should have sent you there."

I knew he meant it, but I also felt sure he was proud of me, too.

"So *who* is the man pulling all the strings?" Lindy finally exploded.

"Are you sure it isn't Raymond Rice? I have never trusted that man," Gran added.

"No, he's only a lackey . . . but he thinks very highly of you, also. No, you will never guess who the real power is—"

"CON! Tell us!" Claire yelled, frustrated by my dramatics.

"Okay." I was out of energy anyway.

I looked at all the eager faces around me, loving every minute of it. Grandpa looked pleased, more than expectant.

"You know, don't you?" I asked Grandpa.

"Probably," he replied. "Guessed more than know. But guesses aren't worth a hill of beans. So proceed. Tell us what you heard."

"Robin Blackford," I said triumphantly. "That smug, hypocritical, overrated, two-bit actor—"

Before I could finish my description of him, Lindy and Claire jumped to their feet in protest.

"It can't be," Claire said. "Not Robin Blackford. He's famous. He wouldn't do stuff like that. I mean, he might be pompous, greedy, and spoiled—but he's surely not a criminal. How could he, anyway? He wasn't even here when most of the things happened."

"He didn't *do* the things, dummy," I said affectionately. "He paid for it. Pretty smart, too. He used everyone else's own motives—strong motives in some cases. The Marvins were always jealous of the more successful Walker Ranch and wanted the BLM leases, so they did petty stuff like cut fences, pick up the salt block after the cows died, and so on. And the tribes had their own reasons, which we already knew about from Chief Running Wolf. Mother Earth *is* a radical terrorist group doing what it does best—and for a great deal of money."

"And Raymond Rice?" Gran asked.

"I don't know for sure. I'm still a little vague on his motive," I admitted.

Jess jumped to her feet excitedly. "I know. It makes perfect sense. Con, didn't you read the email I sent about Rice applying for a big hot-shot job in Washington, D.C., at the Department of the Interior? You and Alisa saw Blackford arrive at the airport with . . ." She waited for us to fill in the blank.

"Important Washington, D.C., officials from the Department of the Interior."

"That's motive, all right," Claire said. "But it doesn't quite prove Blackford used his influence in Washington, D.C., to promote Rice. Do you think he could?"

"Done all the time, I imagine," Gran added.

"I don't know. But who cares *why*," I said frustrated. "I heard them. They all worked for Robin Blackford—Dillard said so many times. Used his name. Now we know it all. It's a done deal. We tell the sheriff, and now he'll have to do his job."

Something was worrying Grandpa. "What's wrong?" I asked him. "We've won."

"What I'm worrying about, Con, is your health. I never thought anyone would harm you personally, but now I'm not so sure. Did any of the men—Crow, Rice, Dillard, or Marvin—

see you tumble out of that closet? If they did, this is not so much over as just beginning, and it has suddenly become very dangerous for you, Con.''

Alisa assured Grandpa as she had me that she hadn't seen any of those men when she arrived. I wasn't so sure, but I wasn't about to tell him how Mike had announced my name to everyone in the crowd as I lay on the cement floor. Or the vaguely familiar voice that so correctly guessed what I had been doing in the closet.

"I don't want to discourage you further, Con," Gran said with weariness and worry creeping into her voice, also. "But we haven't won if we can't prove the connection with Blackford. You said Mr. Dillard threatened them that if things went wrong, Blackford would just deny his involvement. And if they can't tie Robin Blackford to any of this, we sure can't, either. And furthermore, accusing a rich, powerful man with nothing but—I'm sorry, but its true, Con—a kid's word against his is not going to stop him or any of them. Robin Blackford could hire more lawyers than we have cattle left.''

This couldn't be happening. It wasn't possible. I had risked all this misery, found out what we had all been struggling to discover, and now it wasn't going to save the ranch after all. I slumped down on the couch, the pain in my arm increasing with my depression.

"Hey, what is this?" Jess said. "Are you all giving up now? I can't believe these are my cousins before me. From what you have told me, you *can* prove Mother Earth poisoned the cattle. Right? We have Jed's word, we have the poison, and we have the piece of salt that will tie them together.'' Her short hair flipped from side to side as she tried in her usual exuberant way to make her point.

"No offense, Jess, but you and Kate have no idea what we've been going through," Claire said, annoyed with her cousin.

"Wait, she's right about Mother Earth," Lindy added. "We can prove their part, and that would at least get them kicked out of Thermopolis. But it doesn't do diddly squat to tie in Rice *or* Blackford. We can't even prove they *know* each other."

The cloud I thought I had personally dispelled at great risk to my life descended back down on our "convocation of cousins." And the question still remained—would this summer be our last cousin gathering at the ranch? And while I didn't want to dwell on Grandpa's point about my safety, I thought there was a better than average chance at least that Charlie the Crow had been the one to ask what I was doing in the closet. He had also heard Mike Boyle tell the whole crowd I was Whit Walker's grandson.

Abby came over and gave me a big hug. "I don't know about all that stuff. But you were very brave and fooled them, Con. You found them out, and I know you won't let them get away with it."

With that she went off in search of Tragedy, who had been missing for several days. I took the strongest pain-killer the doctor allowed and headed for my room, carrying the manila envelope from Hannah, which I still hadn't read. I wanted to suffer in privacy. My head ached, my shoulder hurt, my stomach was churning from the smells of dinner baking in the oven. And I was wondering what those men might do to keep me from "connecting the dots" for the law.

I was too tired to check our email or even open my letter from Hannah when I managed to drag myself up to bed. There were no faxes on the floor. I lay down on the bed, clothes and boots still on, and fell asleep, Hannah's envelope resting on my chest.

It was pitch dark outside when the pain in my arm woke me up. I squinted to see the red numbers on my digital clock, which showed I had been asleep only a few hours. It was eleven o'clock. Time for another pain pill.

It was then that I tore open the letter, glad for something to occupy my mind until the medication kicked in. A picture fell out of the envelope first.

I stared at it for several seconds. My yell brought the girls down from the attic.

The picture came out quite good, actually. Not that Hannah

was a great photographer, but she had captured the important stuff. There was Robin Blackford with his arm draped around the shoulders of Mr. Raymond Rice. The two men were smiling at each other under the seal of the United States Government with the words *Department of the Interior*.

"What we have here is motive," I said, proud that *my* friend Hannah had supplied us with it. "Mr. Important Movie Star Blackford, who spends his time impressing government officials of his concern for the environment, uses his influence to help his friend get a cushy job in Washington—if Rice in turn runs Whit Walker out of business so Blackford can buy our ranch. It's perfect."

"It's perfect," Alisa said. "But can we prove it?"

"We have to." Jess was getting excited again. "Otherwise, even if Mother Earth is run off, Blackford can find some other greedy person to keep harassing our grandparents until they move. Grandpa and Gran are too old to keep fighting. We have to stop Blackford." It was easy for her to talk—she hadn't been here all summer. But we were all feeling excited, hopeful again.

"Then we will stop him," Lindy said. She got a pencil and legal pad off my desk and started making notes. "Let's get to work. Con, tell me everything again. Everything you heard and saw at the sale barn."

We tacked the picture up on the wall for inspiration.

Jess logged on to the computer and found the Robin Blackford message board to see if any fan out there in cyberland had come up with answers to her questions. Claire, Alisa, and Kate set off for the kitchen in the most important assignment: to get food.

A yummy, buttery smell preceded their return. Kate entered armed with a large brown bag of buttered, salted popcorn. Claire and Alisa had enough Coke to get us through the rest of the night if it took that long.

"Sorry about this, Con," Alisa said, handing me another glass of medicinal tea, which was all my poisoned stomach would accept. My loving cousins began to devour the popcorn without me.

Abby must have smelled the popcorn and came in late, joining me on the bed. She was clutching a big, fluffy pillow from the bed upstairs. "Have you seen Tragedy?" she asked, looking around my room, where the crabby cat usually hung out. "I still can't find her, Con. I'm getting worried."

With more important things on our minds, no one bothered to answer her. Jess was getting something on the Net and was jumping up and down excitedly as she read it.

"Can you believe this?" she said. "There are people out there who actually spend hours discussing the personal lives of people they don't know."

"I'm glad they do," practical Alisa responded. "Read us the good stuff."

"Okay. No, Robin Blackford is not married, but he is engaged to a Linnea Lin—"

"That's right. They said she designed the house he wants to build here," I interrupted excitedly. "Dillard said, 'Robin and Linnea are most unhappy.'. . . Remember her, Abby? She's the one I talked to while you ran in to copy the pages in the folder. All the while, I might add, Alisa and Claire were inside drooling over Blackford."

Claire lobbed a pillow at me, which I deflected with my good arm.

"I wonder if she's an actress, too. I've never heard of her. Was she beautiful, Con?" Jess continued to hack away at the keyboard, looking for more stuff on Blackford and Linnea.

I squirmed a little and lied a lot. "Not really. I . . . ah . . . I didn't really notice. . . . Yeah, maybe she was okay."

Jess kept the mouse moving, looking through a bunch of unimportant information about Blackford's movies, fan club stuff, his lobbying efforts on behalf of the environment, anything. Claire was hanging over her shoulder giving advice.

"Here we go," Claire shouted. "Here we go. Linnea Lin is not an actress but an architect!"

Jess twirled around from the computer and continued to wave her hands excitedly above her head. "You heard right, Con. Linnea designed the house, and she is pushing her future husband to get it built for her so she can enter and win the prestigious Frank Lloyd Wright competition. Yesssss! That's why Blackford wants this particular ranch and none other." Jess shared Alisa's nonstop way of talking.

Everyone was talking at once now. Suggestions were flying.

"Wow. Brilliant and beautiful," I said without thinking.

"I thought you said you didn't notice," Claire remarked.

I threw the pillow back at her.

"What's so funny?" I asked Lindy, who had pulled out our copies from the folder and was giggling hysterically.

"Robin Blackford," she said, trying to stop laughing. "We all thought he was the big wheel directing everyone else, but it turns out he's just following orders, too—his girlfriend's orders. If he doesn't get the ranch, he probably won't get the girl."

I didn't think it was that funny, but the girls all seemed to, and they collapsed in laughter.

"I think I'll ask him about that in my interview," Lindy said, wiping away the tears from laughing so hard.

At least her famous tear ducts were still working.

"What interview?" I asked, more than a little surprised.

"Didn't anyone tell you?" Alisa said. "Yesterday while you were hanging out in the hospital, the station manager at KKOA told Lindy she liked her interview with the mayor so much she could interview Robin Blackford live at the big parade Saturday."

"No way." I was stunned by the implications of this opportunity. Everyone else realized it, too. All eyes turned on Lindy.

Gran was right, and we all knew it. We had no way of beating Blackford in court, and the people in town had been fooled into thinking his presence would draw tourists dollars to the area. So our only hope was for Lindy to trap him on the air and discredit him in front of the good people of Thermopolis.

If only she could pull it off. We stared at our oldest cousin, pinning all our hopes on her.

"Just don't cry," Claire said, breaking the tension. "You'll ruin everything."

"I get it," Abby said. "Lindy is our black widow. She will look beautiful and then surprise the male with a nasty sting. I'll write a poem about it."

As usual Abby got the point, but I groaned at the analogy.

"I think the poem might be a little premature, Abby," I told her, patting her on the head. "And only you, little cousin, could think of a fat black spider as beautiful."

It was getting late and we were all tired, but this would take a group effort. Drawn even closer together by the summer of trouble, we set to work to plan the sting. Years of planning our summer plays had prepared us for our most important theatrical production ever.

Kate, as a member of the Casper Troopers, had a schedule of the parade events upstairs in her bag. She ran to get it.

Jess continued her search on the Net for more information on the Frank Lloyd Wright award. Claire and Abby were in charge of making copies of the house plans.

And tomorrow Alisa and Jed would take the poison, his story, and my piece of salt to the sheriff. This time the lawman couldn't possibly refuse to investigate Mother Earth.

It was nearly two o'clock in the morning when the girls came to the bottom of the popcorn bag and the end of our plans. My arm was hurting again, and I suggested they all remove themselves so I could sleep.

"Alisa," I said, very bummed because I was too sick to go with her tomorrow and miss the pleasure of wiping the smug smile off the sheriff's face with this evidence. "Take the salt now so you won't wake me in the morning. It's there in the mug—inside a little envelope I made out of a note from Hannah. Be careful. It's all we've got. And don't read the note. It's private."

Everyone began gathering up the litter. I closed my eyes while Alisa looked for the mug on my messy desk.

"Con!" Alisa screamed in a whisper. "It's missing."

She was holding the envelope, still neatly folded together, looking at the bits of dirt and sand—all that was left.

"What do you mean *missing*?" I exclaimed, horrified.

"As in *not there*," someone helpfully pointed out.

"Check the floor," I said, panic choking me. "Maybe the cat knocked over the mug and it fell on the floor."

Everyone trooped back in and together nearly covered the floor they were searching. Under the bed, under the desk, on the desk, everywhere. I kept staring into the empty envelope. I couldn't believe that after all I'd been through getting that stupid piece of evidence, now that we needed it, it was lost. Lost in my room and probably swept up in the dust bunnies that grew naturally in my room. If Mom had been there, she would have pointed out that things often got lost in my room. Everyone else was kind enough not to say so as they dragged themselves back upstairs for a few hours' sleep.

"Don't worry, Con. It'll work out," Kate reminded me as she closed the door, leaving me alone.

Miserable in mind and body, I drifted off to sleep again.

◆

It was midmorning Thursday before the fax phone finally woke me up. It was Hannah. I filled her in on my recent excitement and thanked her for the picture of Blackford, telling her its significance.

"Glad to help," she said, more interested in my close encounter with the black widow and my fight with Jed. "You really waited on the haystack and jumped him in the dark?" she asked, suitably impressed.

"Yeah, piece of cake," I said modestly. "By the way, my grandpa may be sick, but his mind's still all right. He figured most of this out."

"But you brought him the information."

"Nice of you to say so, Hannah. But most of the time I didn't have a clue what the things I was telling him meant. And I have a little bad news myself. The poisoned sliver of salt is missing. . . ." I waited for her reaction.

"You're surprised you lost it, Con? Why? Does your room there look anything like your room at home?"

"Very funny. It's not my fault. Some tidy person, probably a girl, swept the room and threw it out. So that means we won't be able to prove the poison Jed gave us is what poisoned our cows. And those creeps at Mother Earth will deny his story. So we're back to square one—almost."

"That's too bad, because I have watched my dad do dozens of demonstrations on the SpectaTrak and with just a tiny sample."

I groaned. "Don't tell me."

"It's true. With only a minuscule particle—"

"Hannah, you aren't listening. I don't have it anymore. None. Zip. *Keine*. Only the sand I scooped it up in."

The line went real quiet.

"Con, did it rain the day the cows were poisoned?"

"Rain . . . I don't think so. What difference does it make?"

"It's important," she said impatiently. "Think carefully. Did it rain at all that day?"

I concentrated and tried to recall everything that happened that day.

"Well?"

"I'm thinking, I'm thinking."

I knew the sky had been clear when Alisa and I were out that morning. Then I spent the rest of the day shut up in the windowless corridors of the hospital. The night had been crystal clear. I could never forget the bright moonlight as I rode and the sight of those dead cows in that eerie light. Yet . . . something made me pause a second more before answering her. I touched my finger to my tongue and remembered tasting fresh water that night—on my fingertip out of the little pool in the mushroom rocks as I rested Yeats.

"Yes," I said. "There must have been an afternoon cloudburst. But it couldn't have rained much. Why?"

"Because even a little rain would have washed some of the poison off the salt into the soil around it. It means there should be traces of the poison in those few grains of sand—which you still have carefully wrapped in my note, I hope." She sounded positively floating with excitement. "And the SpectaTrak is so sensitive it can measure parts *per trillion* and show with conclusive chemical analysis that the poison was there. . . . Con, are you with me here?"

I was unable to speak, in a state of shock hoping she was right. I wondered aloud how on earth she knew all that technical stuff.

"Because I have been following Dad around all summer watching him demonstrate this thing," she explained before I could even ask. "It is a super-sensitive portable laboratory. In fact, it's a new version of what NASA sent to Mars in the Viking probe."

My head was spinning. "That's all great, Hannah. But we don't have the time."

Hannah put down the phone and ran to talk to her dad.

"Dad says to say hello and that he still owes you one. So FedEx the dirt overnight to us. It will take him a few hours to run the tests, and we'll FedEx it back to you. Should get to you by Saturday morning—guaranteed before ten-thirty. Is that okay?"

I was speechless. Almost. "Better than okay. Thanks, Hannah. And thank your dad."

The parade and interview were scheduled to begin at noon on Saturday. Forty-eight hours. That was cutting it close, but it might work. It had to work.

15

THE UNWINDING

WHEN BLACK SATURDAY FINALLY ARRIVED, WE WERE READY for it. And despite its nickname, August 15 began with promise.

Abby found Tragedy. Snuggled in loose hay high in the barn loft, she was purring away, happy at last after giving birth to three beautiful little kittens. Buttermilk gave a gallon of warm, creamy milk, some of which Abby took up to the new mother.

Jed stopped by to get Alisa in a Wind River Reservation pickup truck. She would be riding with him today in the parade. There were two paint horses stomping impatiently in the back of the truck.

"Way to go, man," Jed said, giving me a high five. "Alisa told me all about your little bit of eavesdropping. I told Yellow-dog, and he said you heard right. By the way, he was so impressed with your nerve that he decided you must be part Native American and invited you to ride with us today, too."

"Yellowdog scares me," I said.

"No way," Jed laughed. "He's not as scary as he looks. I even saw him smile once."

It would have been great to ride with Jed and Alisa in the 125th Anniversary parade celebration today. Grandpa said he would have let me ride Yeats, but I was still too weak to hold on, and falling off in front of hundreds of people didn't sound so great.

"Tell Yellowdog thanks for the offer," I said sadly. "I would have been honored to ride with him."

Jed looked very different to me now that I knew who he was. He looked much older than when I first saw him on the plane. He still looked at Alisa the same way he had when he first saw her on the tarmac waiting for me. It seemed like a long time ago.

"Alisa and I will ride together as a symbol of a new friendship between Native Americans and ranchers," he said proudly. "The friendship that was started years ago by my father and Alisa's grandfather can be the role model for the future."

"So the two of you riding in the parade today is purely symbolic, is that it?" I asked. "I mean, the fact she looks good on a horse has nothing to do with it, right? And there are other granddaughters of Whit Walker who can ride a horse."

Lindy nodded. "I'd be glad to join you," she teased.

Alisa snapped her riding quirt at us in mock threat.

It was a beautiful morning, but we were all a little edgy knowing what was riding on today.

"Knock 'em dead, Lindy," Jed said. "We'll be cheering for you."

"Don't fall off and embarrass the cowboy side," I called out to Alisa encouragingly as she got in the truck and waved to us as they drove away.

Kate looked very cool in her Casper Troopers uniform. She assured me, however, that it was actually very hot marching in it, and that it was a long way from Main Street to the reviewing stand set up in front of the Hot Springs terrace.

"We all have to do our part," Gran said to Kate. "And your grandfather is very proud of you heading up the Troopers today. He wishes he could be there to see you."

"At least it will be covered on television so Con and Grandpa won't miss it all," Abby said kindly.

The reviewing stand would hold the town dignitaries and the special guest, Mr. Robin Blackford. Among the dignitaries were Mayor Richards, Raymond Rice as head of the BLM, and Charlie the Crow representing the new emphasis on environmental concerns. And Lindy, KKOA's host for the parade, would join the unsuspecting men. She was dressed in a white cotton blouse and navy blue skirt, with her curly hair pulled neatly up on her head and a leather briefcase in her hand.

"Bye, Con." She hugged me. "I don't think it's fair that you can't come, too, after all you did." She patted the briefcase and smiled. "Thanks to you, I'm armed and ready."

Lindy looked great, but so much like her soft, gentle self that I wondered if she was up to the task. Gran, Jess, Lindy, Claire, and Abby set off for town together—each with a job to do. The fate of the ranch hung in the balance.

And I was stuck home watching the action on television. *Stupid spider*, I thought. *How could such a small amount of venom do so much damage to my system?*

At 11:00 A.M. sharp, Grandpa and I settled our weak limbs down in front of the little television, which Gran had let us keep, to watch the parade. For once, the reception was good. Thermopolis looked great as the televised pre-parade coverage showed the festive route it would take. There were special booths, banners, and even some old covered wagons parked on Main Street. Many ranching families were riding together in the parade, some dressed in turn-of-the-century costumes. They were mingling with folks from the reservation in their ceremonial clothes. The cameramen did a good job showing crowd shots. Grandpa kept pointing out people he knew.

My stomach was finally able to hold down some plain food, and the girls had left us a tray of crackers, watermelon, peaches, and a pie for Grandpa. My nerves, however, were on a heightened state of alert, and I couldn't sit still, let alone eat.

"There she is," I said as the camera picked up Kate at the head of the Troopers. She tossed her baton high in the air as she marched, twirling around, and still—amazingly—caught it every time.

Alisa didn't fall off her horse, either, and I had to admit she looked great riding proudly between Jed—now called Youngbird—and the tribal elder Yellowdog, who was representing the elderly Chief Running Wolf.

"Nice pony," Grandpa said. But I figured he was looking at his granddaughter, not the horse. I wondered if the old chief was watching on television, too, and how he felt seeing his grandson riding with a Walker granddaughter. I very much hoped he was as proud as Grandpa.

"I wish Jed's father were here to see that" was all Grandpa said.

The Native American riders were colorful in their costumes of feathers and buffalo furs, sitting proudly on the bare backs of sleek paint ponies.

The 4-H float came next, followed by 4-H kids and their animals, a parade of sheep, pigs, and fat, well-groomed calves. The first-prize Angus steer was led by its proud owner, a girl about Abby's age.

Lindy was giving the television viewers insight into each marching group, with Robin Blackford adding his Hollywood charm. Even I was almost fooled by what seemed to be genuine appreciation on his part for the community spirit and diversity shown in the parade. He beamed at Lindy each time the camera lit on them.

"Like the spider to the fly," I said.

"What's that?" Grandpa asked, unaware of what his grand-kids were planning for this day.

"You'll see," I said.

The "Kids for the King" First Baptist Church Vacation Bible School marched behind the 4-H troop, followed by the Lutheran and Catholic groups.

A Mother Earth float was near the end. It was their logo come to life—a large green earth made of tissue paper and wrapped in a banner: *No Compromise in Defense of Mother Earth!*

Robin Blackford complimented Charlie Crow as it went by.

Susan Hawkins, this year's Rodeo Queen, brought up the rear of the parade, riding a prancing, spotted Appaloosa horse. She flashed a broad, sweet smile at Robin Blackford, waving her gloved hand in his direction. The camera caught Lindy, sitting next to him, wiping away a sentimental tear at who-knows-what.

Following the parade, Lindy was to interview the dignitaries on the future of Thermopolis. This was our moment. I hoped she was ready.

Grandpa beamed as the camera came to rest on Lindy and her guests. He had loved the parade. These were his friends and neighbors and grandchildren. His life.

For how long? I wondered. I felt like I was going to throw up again. This was worse than sitting in the closet waiting for the spider to run down her web and bite me. There was Lindy about to take on the most charming man in Hollywood—all by herself. What if the FedEx delivery had missed the one morning flight out of Denver into Thermopolis? Claire and Abby were standing by at the airport to receive it and rush it to Lindy. But what if it didn't come or was late? What if Lindy blew it? *Why couldn't I be there?* I thought miserably. There was so much that could go wrong.

"Stop worrying," Grandpa said, sensing my nervousness. "Remember Lindy's interview with the mayor."

"Robin Blackford is not as dim as your mayor," I replied.

"I say, Con, isn't that Abby? What's she doing up there?"

I looked closer at the small screen. Sure enough, Abby was moving up behind Lindy. She slipped her sister a red-and-blue FedEx envelope.

"Boy, that *was* cutting it close," I groaned, thinking Lindy wouldn't be able to use the information now without time to read the technical jargon on the SpectaTrak report.

Blackford looked calm and gave Lindy a smile meant to melt her heart as the camera zoomed in on their faces for the interview.

A city cleanup crew was moving past the grandstand, taking down the yellow tape that had blocked off the viewing stand for the parade. As they did so, the crowd surged forward, eager to see Robin Blackford. He gave a short speech about what a great place Thermopolis was and about its bright future. The crowd cheered. Then Blackford sat down and turned with a smile to Lindy.

"Thank you, Mr. Blackford," she said, "for being with us

here in Thermopolis today as we celebrate 125 years of our history."

Her voice was sweet, her smile as bright as his.

"You have visited here before, I believe. Could you tell our viewers what first brought you to our little community?"

"It's beauty, of course. And young people like you," he replied smoothly.

"I'm afraid you'll have to explain that." Lindy looked genuinely surprised by his answer.

"Young people like you represent our last, best hope for this country and the earth. You may know I spend a great deal of my time, and my own money"—he managed to sound humble even as he bragged—"to lobby our government in Washington, D.C., on behalf of the environment, a cause I believe in deeply."

"You lobby Congress and the Department of the Interior—that kind of lobbying?"

He smiled condescendingly at the simple local girl.

"Right, that kind of lobbying. I came here because Thermopolis is so beautiful, and I want to help preserve some of the surrounding wilderness for future generations."

A small cheer went up from the crowd. Mostly from a group of girls who had pushed to the front to be as close as possible to the movie star.

"So which ranch you buy doesn't matter so much, then, since preservation is your object. Is that correct?"

He never missed a beat.

"Absolutely. I have made an offer on a fine ranch nearby. But any other place would do as well."

Lindy's smile remained sweet and not too bright. Even I was fooled, and I knew better. I also knew he had walked into her first trap and was moving on to number two.

My tension was unbearable.

"Sit still, Con," Grandpa said. "I don't want to miss this."

"Do you know the other distinguished guests here today? Mr. Raymond Rice of the Bureau of Land Management."

The camera moved to the pudgy, beaming face of the BLM official, his few hairs plastered down across his little bald head.

"No," Robin Blackford smiled politely and answered with certainty. "I have never had the privilege of meeting Mr. Rice before today—right here on this platform."

"Got him again!" I shouted, jumping up. "Way to go, Lindy."

Grandpa looked confused.

"Con, is there something you haven't told me?"

But I couldn't answer; Lindy was moving too fast.

"And Mr. Charlie Crow, the executive director of a local environmental organization, Mother Earth."

"Yes." They smiled and shook hands warmly for the camera. "Mr. Crow and I go way back. Mother Earth is a great organization, and it's good to see it welcomed in Thermopolis. It shows how progressive you all are out here."

"So you share the same basic ideas as Mr. Crow's organization, then . . . seeking biological renewal, a back-to-the-land idea that seeks to protect wildlife habitat, encourage biodynamic farming, biological purity, and the end of materialism and consumerism, which destroy the land."

Surprised by Lindy's knowledge of his favorite topic, Blackford looked at her with real interest now and turned up the charm another notch. Charlie Crow was basking in the warmth of her words, too. Only the mayor looked confused. Fortunately for us, Lindy had not been at the ranch the day Robin Blackford visited. He thought he was talking to just another pretty face.

Like the fly who thought the web was a safe place to hang out.

The crowd was growing, and cowboy hats were sprinkled through the group of farming and ranching families in town for the celebration. The girls in front were going wild so near their idol.

"Exactly," Blackford said, praising Lindy. "You captured my philosophy perfectly, young lady—and that of my good friends at Mother Earth."

"Actually," Lindy said modestly, "I was quoting Ernst Haeckel, one of the fathers of Nazi philosophy. He taught that there is no fundamental difference between people and other creatures. This, of course, made it easier when the Nazi regime started killing people. Rudolf Hess, Hitler's right-hand man, followed Haeckel's ideas when he designed the Nazi 'Back to the Land Act.' Heinrich Himmler even established organic farms to grow herbs for the SS officers outside concentration camps. I was actually quoting the philosophy followed by Third Reich men."

I choked on my watermelon, spitting out a mouthful of seeds onto the nice white cloth on our tray. Even Grandpa couldn't contain himself.

"Wow," he said. "Smart girl, my Lindy."

Blackford was stunned, but before he could respond Lindy quickly changed back to the sweetness and light routine as if she hadn't a clue what she'd just done. She changed the subject to a discussion of the day's celebration, commenting on the role the Native Americans had played and pointing out some local ranchers in the crowd. Blackford's face began to recover from his shock at having his views compared with those of the Nazis. But before he could totally relax again, she held up a bumper sticker for the camera.

"I picked this up at the Mother Earth office the other day," she said. "I wonder if you would comment on whether or not you agree with this particular philosophy."

For the benefit of the gathered crowd, Lindy read, " 'The Only Good Cow Is a Dead Cow.' " A few gasps and murmurs could be heard from the farmers and ranchers. Charlie Crow was on his feet in protest.

Lindy ignored him and reached down to remove a paper bag from her briefcase.

"Not only does the radical environmental group Mother Earth print such ideas in their material, but they take it a step further." Lindy was going in for the kill. "Here I have a bottle of sodium fluoroacetate (1080) and an invoice to Mother Earth signed by Mr. Charlie Crow to prove it was purchased by them."

"That's rat poison," Charlie said, smug as anything. "We've had a rat problem."

"We have, too," Lindy mumbled. And then quite clearly she explained, "Actually, this *is* rat poison. It has a clear warning on the label. Keep away from all domestic animals including *cattle*. It is odorless, tasteless, and kills instantly."

"Young lady," Blackford lectured her, "you are way out of line if you are accusing this fine organization of purposely using this poison on cattle. That is a very serious charge—one without proof. And quite frankly, I am shocked."

Blackford looked more shattered than shocked.

Very methodically, showing no emotion, Lindy handed him the SpectaTrak analysis out of the FedEx envelope and held up a second copy for the camera—which zoomed in on what looked like a sea of numbers and graphs.

"This is a chemical analysis done by a laboratory in Washington, D.C., of evidence removed from the Walker Ranch site where over one hundred head of cattle died from ordinary cattle salt laced with this substance. As you can see, it shows very clear traces of the same rat poison fluoroacetate purchased by Mother Earth."

She spoke with a confidence I figured she couldn't feel, since Abby had handed her the information from Hannah only a few moments earlier. She was looking at the chemical analysis for the first time, also.

"This is slander," Mr. Crow screamed at her, then grabbed her copy of the SpectraTrak report and fled off the VIP stand.

Brief pandemonium followed with the camera following him. I caught a glimpse of Jed and Alisa and Jess behind Sheriff Hays and a beefy deputy who stood in the way of the fleeing, furious man.

"Con, what. . . ?" Grandpa mumbled, unable to believe his eyes.

"Shh. Lindy is back."

Robin Blackford's famous blue eyes were narrowed to thin slits, his smile forced. Jumping sides quickly, he said, "Unbelievable. And you think you know somebody."

"Yes," Lindy agreed with him. "Amazing how he fooled everyone, wasn't it? But let's get back to you . . . and today's celebration. People here are very interested in your wonderful plans for our community." Despite the shambles she had created, Lindy still looked composed and quite innocent, and she renewed Blackford's comfort level with a couple of soft balls.

"So you personally do not have a problem with cattle ranching?" Her smile radiated sweetness.

"No . . . of course not," he hesitated and looked out over the crowd, remembering how most of them made their living. "Of course I don't. I prefer other uses for the land I buy, but I believe any local rancher who becomes my neighbor will be happy to have me live nearby."

His fans up front started cheering wildly, "Welcome, Robin. Welcome, Robin."

The camera finally moved away from the screaming teenagers in the front, and as it returned the view to Lindy, I saw her taking out a copy of the house plans from our folder with the Flying W on the front.

"Where. . . ? How. . . ?" he gasped. "How did you get those?"

I almost felt sorry for him. Grandpa looked about as confused as Blackford.

"This"—Lindy held up the drawing for the camera, which once again zoomed in tight—"is an artist's rendering of a magnificent house designed to be built at one of Wyoming's most magnificent spots. All of our viewers will recognize the famous Red Wall, a landmark of the Walker Ranch. This beautiful house, a masterpiece, I think you will all agree, is already being acclaimed in architectural circles. It is designed to be built into that particular red rock canyon and has already been entered in the Frank Lloyd Wright House of the Year competition."

General cheering broke out once again from the crowd. Lindy handed out extra copies to the others on the platform. There was praise all around.

"Isn't that something," she said to the now confused man. "Think of the attention Thermopolis will get when this design by your fiancée, Linnea Lin, wins this prestigious competition."

The flattery *seemed* real. He smiled at her weakly, looking to see which way the wind was blowing.

"And the house must be built this year in order to win—as I understand it. So tell all of our viewers and the good people gathered here today . . . let us be the first to know you aren't interested in just any ranch in the Thermopolis area, are you?"

Lindy leaned close to the star and gave him a conspiratorial smile. "Tell us. Have you already purchased the historic Walker Ranch, where this beautiful house will be built?"

"No . . . well . . . yes, sort of . . ." he stammered.

"Go ahead, tell us when work will begin on this . . . this masterpiece."

The crowd was definitely into it now. Some of the girls looked disappointed at the news of a fiancée, but the merchants could see visions of tourist dollars pouring into Thermopolis.

Grandpa was leaning forward, holding his breath, waiting to hear the answer.

"I don't know how you could have possibly gotten hold of that drawing," Blackford stammered. "This is a private, strictly confidential drawing. How did you—"

"Good reporters never reveal their sources, sir," Lindy said smoothly. "But don't keep us waiting. I know you *must* now own the Walker Ranch, otherwise Ms. Lin couldn't enter her house for the Frank Lloyd Wright award. What better time to announce your purchase than right here at this celebration?"

"He knows," Grandpa said. "He knows she has him trapped, but what can he say with everyone watching?"

"That *was* the idea," I responded proudly. "He has just been stung by the Sagebrush Rebels!"

"Yes, I am in final negotiations with the Walkers," Blackford responded. "Linnea and I will be married and move here before the snow falls."

"Really," Lindy said. "That is marvelous. Well, our time is about up, but before we conclude, I want to introduce our viewers to Mr. Raymond Rice of the Bureau of Land Management."

The government official moved gratefully into the chair vacated by Charlie Crow.

"Did you two say you knew each other? I've forgotten." Lindy looked a little confused.

"No." Blackford's answer was crisp—and cold. He was sick of Lindy and the interview by now. "We have never met before today."

Reaching one more time into her briefcase, Lindy drew out a picture, which she flashed before each man long enough for impact, not quite long enough for reaction. She then motioned the camera in close—for the viewers.

Both men froze. Their lies were exposed.

"Who are you?" Blackford hissed under his breath. But the fine technical equipment of KKOA picked it up loud and clear.

There on the screen for all to see was Hannah's clear photography, the picture of Robin Blackford and Raymond Rice standing like old buddies together under the seal of the United States Government, Department of the Interior. Home of the BLM.

The camera moved off the picture to Lindy, who was helpfully handing them each a copy.

"Would either one of you like to comment on this? No? Well, let me suggest that you intended to buy the Walker Ranch all along, Mr. Blackford, so that Ms. Lin could build her architectural masterpiece. I further suggest that when the Walkers refused to sell their home, you used the radical environmental group Mother Earth to sabotage their ranch—poisoning their cattle. And that Raymond Rice, unknown to his superiors at the BLM, used a falsified report to accuse the Walkers of environmental violations in an effort to bring financial ruin and force them to sell to you. In return you, Mr. Blackford, used your lobbying efforts in Washington to secure a promotion for Mr. Rice."

"You can't prove any of this," Rice said weakly.

"Shut up," Blackford blasted his whimpering companion.

"Well," Lindy went on, "I have a copy of a job listed at the Department of the Interior, which has been filled by Mr. Raymond Rice." Lindy permitted herself a smile.

Both men were on their feet shouting at this point. Only Blackford had a microphone.

"I'm not going to sit here and be insulted in front of a bunch of country bumpkins by a sneaky little . . . I shall sue this rotten little television station out of existence—" At that point he remembered to rip off his lapel microphone, so we missed the rest of his compliment about Lindy.

Crazy with frustration, he grabbed the leather briefcase by Lindy's chair and threw it out over the crowd. Unfortunately for him, it was too late. All the hand grenades had already exploded. Right in his face.

"He seems to be taking it well, don't you think?" I said to Grandpa, who continued to look about as stunned as Rice and Blackford.

"Sneaky little what?" Lindy said in a chirpy voice, her microphone still on.

Chaos erupted in all directions. It was hard for us to see exactly what was happening, but the camera followed Blackford and a bodyguard, who made a path for him off the platform.

Grandpa and I stood up on our wobbly legs, hugged each other, and cheered.

"It only goes to prove the old proverb," he said. " 'Money buys everything but sense.' Blackford had plenty of money, but Lindy had all the sense."

16

PASSPORT TO DANGER

THE ENDGAME

" 'THE GREAT STING OF THE SAGEBRUSH REBELLION' IS DEStined to become a part of Wyoming lore now," I said. "Like the vigilance committee that drove out Butch Cassidy . . . and the South Pass gold rush . . . and other less important historical events."

"You think Wyoming school kids will be required to study it?" Kate asked, laughing.

We were savoring our victory that evening after the parade, lying in the grass under the spreading branches of the old cottonwood trees where we often performed our summer play.

" 'The Sting' was our best production ever," Alisa said, proudly wearing a feather in her hair.

"And our viewing audience grew from our parents and grandparents to all of Thermopolis," Claire pointed out.

"Maybe," Gran said. "But I preferred your Shakespeare performed at the Mushroom Rocks last summer. This cast had some very nasty characters."

Only Abby had lost interest in the telling and retelling of our finest moment. She had run off to the corral and returned with Shades, pencil in hand—working on a new poem probably. Shades was sleek and fat; the dark circles around his eyes—his sunglasses—still gave him that tough-guy look. On his right flank was the Flying W brand.

"Keep that calf out of my flowers," Gran called to Abby from the swing, where she was sitting next to Grandpa.

"How did you get that lazy sheriff off his duff, Jess?" I asked. Her role had been to get him to the viewing stand to catch Charlie Crow, who we figured would flee when Lindy presented him with hard evidence of his eco-terrorist acts.

"Actually, I don't know why you found Sheriff Hays so difficult, Con. He was quite nice to me," Jess explained.

"Excuse me," I defended. "A cute girl shows up, looks helpless, and says, 'Please help me, Mr. Sheriff. A bad guy is trying to steal our ranch,' and he rushes out the door with you."

"Not true," Jess laughed. "I didn't look helpless at all. I used pure logic to convince him. You should have tried that, Con."

"Oh, please," I protested. Actually, she had not only a copy of the SpectaTrak report but a handwritten confession signed by Jed. He hardly could have ignored that.

"Anyway . . ." Claire continued the story. "The sheriff took Mr. Crow into custody for questioning—right then and there before he could escape. He seemed to think that with all our scientific evidence and Jed's testimony, Charlie the Crow might be in jail for some time."

"He's not the only one. Sheriff Hays has already alerted the L.A. police department to pick up Mr. Dillard on charges of aiding and abetting in a felony. Fred and Lilly Marvin must have seen or heard the broadcast and are either hiding out or getting their story ready to explain to Sheriff Hays."

"We don't want to press charges against our neighbors," Gran said. "Maybe they have learned their lesson."

"Most important," Grandpa said, "the BLM office in Washington, D.C., called to apologize for the actions of Mr. Rice—assuring me that no lease agreements will be withdrawn. I will have grazing land this winter."

The sun sank low in the sky, dropping behind the Wind River Range while we talked. Scattered clouds rimmed its peaks and began to turn red as the sun set. The beauty matched our mood. We all lay back on the damp grass looking up at the first star visible in the young night sky—thinking about how many other Wyoming skies we could now enjoy together.

"What about Blackford and Linnea?" Kate asked.

A falling star shot across the sky. We all oohed and ahhed.

"My guess is she won't marry him," Lindy said. "He's not that attractive when he's angry."

Abby giggled.

"And he's going to be angry for a long time," Claire added. "Hiring lawyers to get him out of this mess will cost more than it would have to build the house."

"Amazing. Mr. Blackford's motives were not about the environment or saving the West after all. My, my, my, what a surprise."

"And I bet he doesn't think Lindgren Larson has much of a future in journalism, either. He certainly didn't seem to enjoy his interview with you, anyway."

"When someone pointed out I was a Walker granddaughter, he nearly died on the spot. He went into a screaming rage cursing the whole family. It wasn't pretty."

"Spoiled people do not like to be denied," Gran said.

"Did Alisa look good riding with Youngbird or what?"

"And Kate heading up the Casper Troopers."

Our laughing and musings on the day continued unchecked by time or chores.

For once, no one wanted to cook. Even I wasn't thinking about food. We were all content there under the vast canopy of the Wyoming sky.

"Lindy, you were the best," someone said for the umpteenth time.

She shook her head modestly. "It was Con who figured everything out. He put himself in harm's way to save the ranch. And everyone helped, too. Abby copied the folder. Jess and Claire looked up all that stuff on the computer. Even Hannah helped—without her techie stuff we were sunk. I forget what Alisa and Kate did."

Alisa or Kate threw grass in Lindy's general direction.

" 'My children, big and small, are prodigies all,' " Grandpa settled it with yet another proverb. "Grandkids are 'the crown of old men.' And"—there was a tremor in his voice as he looked directly at me—"can be a very useful secret weapon, too."

"Our Sagebrush Rebels saved the ranch," Gran agreed. "But what did you expect, Whit? They're Walkers, after all."

◆

The next afternoon, all the cousins took the ranch vehicles, along with the *Welcome Home* sign, to the airport to await the arrival of Nigel and my mom from Austria, and Aunt Leigh and Uncle Richard from Oregon. They were arriving on the same day as Lindy, Claire, Kate, and Abby's parents, Aunt Sharon and Uncle Ted, who were driving over from Casper later in the afternoon.

A *four-layer* chocolate cake topped with alternating rows of strawberries and blackberries stood on the kitchen counter. Things were as they should be in the old ranch house at the foot of the Red Canyon Wall.

A week later we all went to church together.

> *"Faith of our fathers living still, in spite of dungeon, fire and sword!*
> *Oh, how our hearts beat high with joy when-e'er we hear that glorious Word:*
> *Faith of our fathers, holy faith! We will be true to thee till death."*

The old organ in the First Baptist Church of Thermopolis belted out the strains of the familiar hymn. Nigel's English accent blended with the Western ones around him. Grandpa's old, deep baritone voice and Abby's young, high one joined the rest of us Walkers filling two whole pews, our presence dominating the small congregation.

> *"Faith of our fathers! We will love both friend and foe in all our strife;*
> *and preach thee, too, as love knows how by witness true and virtuous life.*
> *Faith of our fathers, holy faith! We will be true to thee till death."*

The oak pew felt cool and comfortable against my back. My body had finally grown up enough to fit its smooth, carved form. Thick brick walls and stained-glass windows kept the sanctuary cool except on the very hottest Wyoming days. Jed and his father, who had come home for a visit, sat next to Alisa. She was sitting next to Lindy, then Kate, Abby, Claire, and Jess. Their parents, Grandpa, Gran, Nigel, Mom, and I filled another row.

My mind wandered down to the lawn by the river where we were going to have a big cookout after the morning worship service. Visions of barbecued spare ribs, roasted potatoes, homemade bread, mountains of fresh fruit, and chocolate cakes filled my head. There would be a friendly game of croquet on the lawn, followed by a horseback ride. My last chance to ride Yeats this summer. I wanted to show Nigel Devil's Slide and Birdseye Butte. The chokecherries were ripe now along Grass Creek, and Gran would be making chokecherry jam and jelly for next year. It was our last Sunday in Wyoming; all three families would return tomorrow to where we lived between summers. Back to school, to work, to other friends. But our "perpetual place," filled with custom and ceremony, cakes and cousins, would remain. I smiled on the inside.

Some maternal, mysterious sixth sense kicked in, and Mom sensed my mind wasn't on the sermon. She nudged me back to the present.

"God is a generational God," the preacher was saying. "Faith and the blessings of faithfulness are to be spread abroad *and* passed down through families—one generation to the next."

Afterward, as I walked to the car with Grandpa after the service, his large hand loosely grasping my elbow for support, things seemed clearer than they had all summer. His walk was still slow, his body weak, but my grandfather's strength was not in physical might or power but came from within and would remain "by witness true and virtuous life."

◆

Don't Miss Con's Next Adventure
in PASSPORT TO DANGER
Available May 2000!
Checkmate in the Carpathians

It's winter break, and Con and Hannah head to the Carpathian Mountains to visit the U.S. Ambassador to Romania—who happens to be Hannah's uncle. It's probably safer than Vienna anyway, now that "Dirty Harry" has escaped from prison. While in Romania, Con and Hannah do some "undercover" work for the ambassador—acting as photo-snapping tourists amid a neo-Nazi demonstration to gain any information the embassy might find useful. But the demonstration gets out of hand, and Con realizes Dirty Harry could very well be part of the throng. They flee the riot, only to find themselves cornered. Who will come to their rescue?